VAMPIRE NIGHTS

VAMPIRE NIGHTS

LA VEGA VAMPIRE SHOWSTOPPERS, BOOK ONE

by

GINNA MORAN

SUNNY PALMS PRESS

To my Beta Babes,

You're the best team an author could ever ask for. Noel, Felicia, Missy, Chelsea, Danielle, Mona, Monique, Heather, and Bailey...you are my dirty, sweet, and quick & easy ladies, and all beautiful, funny freaks. Thanks for your hard work and for letting me be your personal brand of delicious torture.

"YOU LOOK HOT tonight. The crowd is going to be anxious for a taste." Opal smacks me on my ass, getting me to move from my spot. "Maybe Master Alexander won't be such a dick after the show. It's a packed house and quite the excited crowd. I knew the new choreography would bring more people in. You've been doing great.

Keep up the sexy work. They love you."

I force my lips to smile, trying not to react to the beautiful vampire in charge of dolling me up for tonight's performance. While Opal doesn't get under my skin like some of the others, she was the one to suggest a change in the show. But I can't expect much from the one who is in charge of all of the performers and the show. She's been my caretaker for as long as I can remember and only wants what's best for the club.

"Of course they do. I haven't met a vampire who doesn't appreciate some skin. You would think the assholes have never seen boobs." Mya yanks off her pastel purple wig and drops it onto the costume counter a few feet away. She bounces her naked boobs with her hands, laughing as Opal shakes her head. "And they sure love yours, Hayley. Listen to them. They're already chanting your name. Give them a show they won't forget."

I inhale a deep breath and flick my gaze toward the wall mirror one more time. Glitter sparkles across my eyelids and lips, and I look like my posters plastered around the casino floor. I can appreciate all the work Opal put into my costume, all rhinestones and tulle. At least I like the way I look.

"You're up, my gem," Opal says. "Hustle."

Music thumps through the air, and I follow Opal as

she leads me up the stairs and to the huge platform hidden above the audience. I can't make out anything but shadows and rainbow light, but it's better this way. It makes obeying Opal that much easier when she directs me to position myself on the aerial ring she'll lower closer to the stage.

The music lowers in volume as Alexander Aris enters the stage below me. He wears a glittery, gaudy suit jacket that sparkles in the rainbow lights. Two men roll out a bed behind him at vampire speed, and I concentrate on keeping my nerves under control. The bed was the worst addition to the performance. I prefer my aerial routine over the floor routine, especially with how unexpectedly creative Alexander can be as the emcee. He's a perv on purpose, though he's never touched any of us. Opal would never allow it. But as for the vampires in the audience? They get what they can pay for to an extent. Alexander will happily let them bite me anywhere they please. It's the whole gimmick.

Glancing up, Alexander winks at me, ensuring I'm ready. I blow him a kiss and smile in response. I just want to get tonight over with.

I should be used to this, putting on an exciting show in Vampire Nights as I've been on stage since hitting eighteen. This club is the hottest main attraction in La

Vega, bringing in patrons from all over. This isn't the first choreography change, but it seems like soon I'll just be dropped on stage naked one of these days and offered to table one as a meal.

According to Alexander, no other hotel compares, which is why we must stay on top. I wouldn't know for sure, because I've never left the Aris Hotel property. For one, I'm not allowed. And two? It's not like I want to. I can see the nightlife from my room window, and I wouldn't make it a few feet without being bitten or worse. It's why I don't complain about having to perform for the hungry and rowdy vampire patrons. If this gives me protection from getting thrown on the Blood Strip, then I'll do what I have to do. It's not like blood donors can make lives for themselves anyway. I'm better off than most. I know what the room service staff deals with being alone, and unlike me, they don't have the same protection.

"Thank you, Vampire Nights and La Vega!" Alexander shouts, taking a short bow like the audience is here for him alone. I missed his short dance number he likes to do to make the crowd anxious. He knows no one is here for him, which is why he pushes boundaries. Whatever Alexander Aris wants, he gets. He's one of the leaders of La Vega as far as I know. What he says goes. He is the law. "How are you all enjoying the show? Weren't my precious

Crystal and Emerald simply magnificent? Their bodies and blood are just...mmm." Snapping his teeth, he grabs his junk and humps his hand.

Hoots and hollers fill the air and screeching wolf-whistles sting my ears. Opal whispers something into her old headset and the lights dim except for the bright spotlight on the middle of the rolling bed.

"We have something special for you all tonight, but I'm going to need a little help from one of you lucky assholes. You see, my beautiful baby doll is a bit nervous that none of you want a taste of her exquisite blood," Alexander continues, goading the crowd for a response. "So, I'm ready to prove the sexy-smexy, smokin' hot Ruby Vixen wrong."

The crowd cheers again, and I clutch tightly onto the ring. If I fall, I'll break my leg or something. Harnesses aren't allowed, because Alexander thinks that we deserve whatever pain comes with failures. And falling? I just better not.

"I'm going to need a volunteer. Someone tall. Strong. Someone filthy fucking rich, because my Ruby's blood is far more superior than anything you've ever tasted. She's never had a bite before, so you'll also get to sink your teeth into her sweet, virgin flesh. How does that sound? Who wants to show her how much fun it is to be tasted by someone worthy?"

"Fucking stupid," I mutter under my breath. This is probably the only time I can speak my mind, high above the stage and surrounded by music loud enough to stop any vampires from hearing. They can pick up on the softest whisper. A heartbeat. Sometimes, I even think they can read minds, though Opal denies it. I don't know the vast capabilities of a vampire, but I do know that they're powerful, especially when hungry.

The crowd goes absolutely wild, more so than last night, and I clench my teeth, putting on my stage smile. My cheeks will be sore later, but if I dare break my performance and show how awful I feel...I can't think about it. The pain isn't worth it. The crowd needs to believe I want them. They want me to beg for their attention.

"Ruby, Ruby, Ruby!" Alexander chants, raising his hands above his head. The crowd chants along with him and the music changes to alert me of the start of my routine.

I reposition myself, sliding my butt off the hoop until I catch my knees and hang upside down. My turquoise wig billows like a cascading waterfall but stays in place. The rhinestones sparkle on my bodice and thong bottoms, and I swing up and lock my hands to the ring, using it to flip and spread my legs into the splits. Flexibility is a turn-on for vampires. I'm sure they're all fucking and biting me in their heads, wishing this was more than a soon-to-be topless performance.

"Baby doll, I don't think these fine patrons want a taste of La Vega's most stunning and delectable woman," Alexander says from below, faking the dumbest frown with his fat lip popped out as he blinks dramatically. "Perhaps you should just exit the stage."

"Fuck no!" a deep voice shouts. "I want a taste. You're gorgeous, Ruby! Sexy! I want to sink more than my fangs into that supple body. Give us a peek of your juicy pussy!"

Alexander feigns shock, covering his mouth. "Now, now. Is that a way to treat my exquisite baby doll? If you really want a delightful performance of your fantasies, prove it with more than your words. Show her she's worth the cost."

The vampire growls and flips off Alexander. "Fucking impossible."

"Not my problem if you're unworthy. Go to The Pala and play with their donors. It might suit you better." Alexander waves his hand at the guy as security drags him back, stopping him from retaliating. It wouldn't be the first time someone tried. Alexander doesn't play games or make exceptions in the price he keeps for the back row vampires to drink from me on stage. Releasing a dramatic sigh, he glances up at me. "Go on, baby doll. These gentlemen can't see how exceptional you are. We might as well just cancel the rest of the show."

The crowd groans and growls, vocalizing their displeasure.

I swing back up and climb onto the hoop, sitting sideways and using the strength of my glutes to keep me in place. "Oh, no! Please, Master Aris. There must be something I can do. I've been waiting all of my life for the perfect vampire to bite me." I project my voice, ignoring another male vampire calling my name, vying for my attention. "I can't be a bite-virgin forever. Please, master, please!" The crowd devours my begging as if they can taste my blood. It's a silly part of the act, considering I've been bitten over a thousand times at least, but whatever plays into their desires.

"What do you think?" Alexander asks, lifting a brow as he searches over the audience. "Should we let her try to convince you?"

The crowd roars and cheers, calling my stage name. Playing Ruby Vixen gets me through the torture of what's about to come—probably some asshole who dry humps me at vampire speed while sucking on either my ass, thigh, or boob. I've never had anyone choose anywhere else. Because of this, I shut down and think about what kind of meal Opal will have the donor staff prepare to celebrate another successful night while my persona Ruby Vixen moans and screams in pleasure, ensuring our guests come back for me.

My stomach flips, wishing tonight could be different. But the crowd roars in excitement.

"You heard them, doll face! They want to see what you got." Alexander throws his hands out, pretending to be responsible for the metallic confetti exploding through the air. "The highest bidder will get to sink their fangs into the hypnotic Ruby Vixen right here on this stage in front of everyone. Let's show her she has nothing to be afraid of. One of you fine vampires will gladly pay the price and make the whole room succumb to jealousy."

The music rises in volume, and I lose myself to the song, the sultry beat helping me focus on the routine and not the madness breaking out in the crowd. My aerial ring finally comes to a stop above the bed. I twirl my fingers, reaching behind me to press the small snap that'll release my top, giving the crowd what they've truly come here for—a glimpse of me in all my bitable glory.

Whistles and yells hum through the air, and I remain swaying with my fake smile, concentrating on the bright lights instead of the crowd. Cool air gusts around me, sending my hair away from my boobs, giving the club the perfect view of my hard nipples. Opal ensures the place is cold on purpose.

I slowly, seductively spin around the ring and stretch out my arms toward the bed, striking my final pose. The music lowers again, and I wait for Alexander to return to the stage, but he remains in the crowd.

"Hey, Ruby Bloody Vixen! Sexy girl! While those fuckers keep you waiting, why don't you hop on down into my arms?" A tall vampire flashes his fangs at me. His bald head gleams in the stage lights, and he flicks out his tongue. "Let me suck on those sexy-ass titties."

I remain smiling and ignore him. If I give him even an ounce of my attention, he'll take a mile. By his appearance, he looks like a backrow player, here on credit, and far from someone able to pay whatever cost Alexander has on a couple minutes of my time.

"Ruby! Come on, baby doll. Don't be a bitch. I'm far more superior than those assholes fighting over there. I know you don't want to be bought like a prostitute. Just jump into my arms, and I'll get you out of here. We can have a fucking fantastic time." The vampire traces my silhouette like he can imagine putting his gross, dirty hands on my body.

I don't know exactly what he's implying by what I think is a back-world term with prosti-whatever it was, but he makes it sound like my performance is intended to end with more than a bite. He'd have to be invited as a guest to a private show for something more, and thank God that isn't happening. If his hands are this dirty, I'd hate to know what is under his torn jeans.

"Don't ignore me, baby. I'll take good care of you," he continues, wiggling his fingers.

I can't control my annoyance and flip back up. My head rushes for a moment, forcing me to blink a few times. Where is security? He did mention there was a fight of some sort, but I can't see anything past the stage.

"You blood slut. Look at me when I talk to you." The vampire climbs onto the bed, causing it to roll a foot. He jumps into the air and tries to grab me but I'm still high enough above him. "Come on. They're finishing up."

I lick my lips and flick my gaze around. If security is busy, then where the fuck is Opal? No one ever makes it this far on stage. This guy is turning belligerent with his anger at me not giving him even a glance.

"Fucking Ruby. Come on!" the guy growls.

The music suddenly cuts off and the lights go out. My hoop jerks and freefalls a couple feet, startling me. I tighten my hands around it in fear, knowing what's going to come. The bastard vampire can reach me, and sure enough, a cool hand wraps around my ankle. I screech, swinging the ring on the wire. Kicking my leg, I try to knock the vampire away, but it's impossible. No one can hear me either with the cacophonous fight breaking out in the audience.

A siren blasts through the air, nearly sending me crashing right into the vampire's arms. I catch my glow-in-the-dark hoop and dangle a foot above him. If someone didn't hit the switch to reel my ring back toward the platform above, he would've gotten me.

"Hayley, Alex needs a distraction. I have to make it rain. Get ready." Opal tosses me a small bag, and within it, a glittering dagger. It must be serious if she refers to Alexander by his casual name instead of taking the time to be formal.

The spotlight jerks across the stage. One of the technicians manages to regain control. The world remains dark around me, and I lick my lips and wait for Opal to whistle, drawing the crowd's attention to me.

I click on my hidden microphone, wishing I didn't have to do this. It's one thing to bare my body to a bunch of vampires. It's another to tempt them with my blood. The psycho below me still remains in his spot, the security personnel choosing to handle the bigger threat the rowdy crowd poses. They must do so since I'm out of reach and in Opal's care. Not that I can complain about it to Alexander even if I wanted to. Unless I'm on the verge of death and cutting off his income, he doesn't really give a shit about me.

I force my mouth to smile, listening to Opal whistle again, louder this time. Clearing my throat, I project my voice loud enough that no one will be able to ignore me. "Master Aris, you were right. I think the whole room might want a taste of me. I'm so happy for your excitement!"

My friendly, sweet voice quiets down the room, and another spotlight lands on Alexander. He adjusts his sparkling suit jacket and manages to compose himself, tucking away his dagger. Four members of his security team surround him, and they guide him back to the stage. This isn't the first fight I've experienced during a performance, and I'm sure it won't be the last. There is something about Vampire Nights that gets to the crowd. Possibly because this is one of the few places that vampires of all statuses mingle or maybe it's the excitement of watching the best donor show around. Either way, I'm just glad heads haven't rolled.

"Oh, my baby doll. Of course I was right. So much so that one of these assholes thought he could buy you right out from under me. The audacity!" Alexander whips his attention toward someone in the crowd and winks, acting as if the offer hadn't gotten under his skin. No one messes with Alexander Aris's girls unless they want to find themselves forced to the shadows out on the La Vega Strip.

I fake a gasp. "Which asshole?" Swinging on my hoop, I stretch forward and spread my arms wide like I'm trying to get a better view of the audience. "I'm so flattered that I want to blow him a kiss."

Alexander chuckles, playing along with our impromptu change in the performance. "I think I have something better in mind. There are a helluva lot of bastards here tonight who would kill for a taste of you. Why don't we let them?"

I form an O with my mouth and cover it with my hand. "Are you suggesting what I think you are?"

He wags his brows. "Damn right, baby doll. Someone's gotta learn a lesson." Turning toward the crowd, Alexander strides to the edge of the stage. "Rule number one here in Vampire Nights is my pretty collection of precious gemstones belongs to the crowds. My Ruby Vixen is here for your entertainment and enjoyment. All of yours."

The crowd reacts with a cheer, and I clap and bounce, listening to the crowd going wild, probably loving watching my boobs jiggle. I blow a kiss to the crowd and smile, flipping around to balance my feet on the ring.

"Which is why I have an idea. If you all can show Mr.

Asshole at table three in seat two that Ruby Vixen isn't his damn personal blood donor, then she will give you all a taste of her mouthwatering blood. What do you say? Do you want her to make it rain?"

Shit happens so quickly that I miss seeing the vampires move and go after the asshole Alexander speaks of. A growl, followed by a scream, rips through the air, only to be cut off. Light shines over table three, revealing what happens to those who try to pull bullshit in Alexander's hotel. And now, the guy who wanted to buy me lies dismembered on the table.

Holy fuck. They really took it far tonight. Usually it's just a couple stabbings or getting the shit beat out of them.

Another spotlight sweeps across the crowd, showing off the packed club as they cheer. I clap my hands and keep my performance smile plastered on my face. I can't give even an ounce of fear or disgust by the awful sight.

"My heroes!" I yell, swinging on my hoop. "What would I do without you brave, badass bastards standing up for me?"

Alexander winks at me, giving me his approval. It helps ease the nerves in my stomach. I should've been off this stage already and on my way back to my room. Hopefully, he gives me some sort of bonus. Extra dessert. A night off. Who am I kidding? I'll probably end up having to incorporate this into future shows.

"What do you think, Master Aris? Was that as good for you as it was for me?" I ask, spinning around. Seductively drawing the blade across my thigh, I tease the crowd. "Should I reward them?"

Alexander swivels on his feet and taps his finger to his chin. "What do you think?" he asks the audience. "Are you ready for your prize?"

Voices ring through the air and the room explodes in rainbow light and confetti, turning the club magical. From my spot, I catch a glimpse of only one woman among the crowd. It's not because our show is geared toward only males either. We have three guy performers. It's just that there aren't many women in La Vega. No one I've asked knows why exactly. All I know is that men outnumber females for blood donations fifteen to one, and among vampires? I have no clue. Opal is the only female vampire on staff in the entire Aris Hotel.

"You heard them, baby doll!" Alexander shouts, flinging his arms into the air. "Make it rain!"

I snap out of my thoughts, breaking my gaze away from the crowd and to the blade Opal had given me. God, I hate this. It's one thing to let some bastard sink their fangs into me. It's another to cut myself open. I only get away as a bite-virgin because Alexander ensures to give me his blood to heal me and keep me scar-free unlike many of the donors who work the casino, restaurants, and bars. I'm used to it. It no longer hurts. But purposefully nicking my veins and trying to perform through it is hell.

What can I do, though? If I fuck up, Alexander will punish me. The show must go on.

The cable tethering my aerial ring pulls me from the stage and over the crowd. I trace the point of the blade teasingly across my boobs and down my stomach until I reach my bottoms. Cutting off the side straps, I let the fabric fall, showing off my even tinier sequined G-string and listen to the crowd catcall and whistle as if my thong wasn't enough.

"All right, you fuckers! Open wide!" Grinding my teeth in my fakest smile, I slice the blade over each of my forearms from my elbows to my wrists. It stings so badly that I squeeze my eyes shut, concentrating on getting my hoop to spin as quickly as possible.

My blood flings over the audience, raining across the crowd until the lights dim and the hum of the sprinklers sound through the air, sending more blood spraying from above. The crowd goes wild, and I focus on the music, using it to complete my performance. The general population blood Alexander serves to those who can't afford a live donor coats my skin, truly turning me into Ruby Bloody Vixen.

The cheering crowd goes ballistic and the music thrums wildly. I wave and blow kisses, ignoring the cold dread running through me. I just want Opal to reel me in again. I want the night to be over. I pose on my hoop, sitting and dangling my legs. The crowd moves and dances below, licking up all the blood they can.

And then something smacks right into my chest and lands on my lap.

The shock of seeing the severed cock stuns me for all of a second, and I screech and fling it off, sending it back to the crowd. I've never had anything thrown at me before, and getting hit with the cock...? What the actual fuck.

I'm too focused on my stomach clenching to see the asshole from earlier materializing below before it's too late. Swinging the severed head by the hair, he chucks it at me next, hitting me hard in the stomach, knocking the wind from me. I lose my balance and fall backward. I think I blackout for a moment, because one second I'm freefalling, and in the next, I'm in the asshole's sticky arms.

He grabs my chin and tries to capture my attention. I blink, staring up at the lights, knowing better than to make eye contact. He will get into my head and manipulate me to do something against my will. It's one of the damn powers some vampires have, though many aren't talented enough to make it stick.

"Look at me, Ruby. Come on. Don't make this hard," he says, spinning so quickly that the world blurs.

I groan, dizziness washing over me. "You threw a dick at me."

He laughs and leans in close, trying to capture me with more than his gaze this time. I do the only thing I can think of. Snatching his lip between my teeth, I bite down as hard as I can. He yowls and rips his head back, but not before his blood drips across my tongue.

He growls. "You little bitch—"

I don't get a chance to move or react. Blood splashes my face, and his eyes bulge as a dagger jabs through his throat. His hold loosens, and we both fall to the floor. I gasp, trying to find something, anything, to protect myself with.

A male vampire stands above me and smiles, showing off his fangs. His neatly styled caramel-streaked light brown hair is combed away from his forehead, giving me the perfect view of his high cheekbones and expressive brows.

He definitely has front row potential as his muscles bulge against his fitted suit. Reaching down, he grabs my hands and pulls me to my feet. I stand in shock, wobbling, trying to summon a coherent thought.

"Here, drink. You look like you're going to faint." Biting his arm, he offers me his wrist, letting his blood dribble into my mouth.

His sapphire blue eyes turn the color of gunmetal with the flicker of silver lighting his gaze. I can always tell a hungry vampire when I see one, because their eyes sparkle with the electric light. His hungry eyes are hypnotizing, and I can't stop staring at his soft features. He might be more pretty-boy than ruggedly hot, but his smile really does something crazy to my body, and I like it far more than I should.

I watch his tongue glide across his full bottom lip, and I swear he mouths the words, "so good," as he grins wider.

I hum and grip his arm, the taste of his blood warming me up and sending tingles across my body. I've never drunk vampire blood apart from Alexander and Opal's, and something about his taste awakens every cell on my body. His gorgeous smile turns him from attractive to sexy, and I can't stop from caressing my hand over his shaven cheek. I don't know if it's due to the healing properties of his blood or what, but I suck harder, wanting more and more.

My nipples harden and I shift on my feet, his blood getting to me on a level I have never experienced with my caretakers before. I tighten my fingers and watch him watch me, wishing he'd be bold enough to pick me up.

"Good girl," he murmurs, touching my face. "I got you, vixen. You're going to be okay."

The hotel's siren blares, and the lights turn off. A commotion breaks out on the other side of the curtain. I realize the other fucker who tried to steal me was heading toward the backdoor. I was too disoriented to see him take out one of the security guards.

"Looks like I gotta go." The vampire eases his arm from my mouth and replaces it with his lips. He kisses me softly, surprising me. "Mmm, but I wish I didn't. Your mouth is exactly how I imagined your lips to taste watching your stunning performance."

I react to his words by kissing him back, the flavor of his lips as good as his blood. "Don't leave." What am I saying? His blood must be influencing me, turning me into a pleading little donor. I've seen it happen with Pearl, another performer, and Alexander.

The stranger gives me a sexy smile that smolders my insides. "Sorry, vixen. I wish I didn't have to, but it's not safe for me. You saw what happened to my guard when he was trying to buy you on my behalf. Your master would hunt me down if I tried to take what doesn't belong to me too."

My eyes widen as his words sink in. He admitted to trying to buy me. What the hell? I don't even know how I feel about it. It snaps me out of my lusty haze, and I try to find a reason to explain why he would. Why he thought it was something he could do. "You caused all of this?" I don't know why my words come out as a question. Or why I say anything more at all? One of the biggest rules of surviving a vampire is never giving them a reason to keep engaging in conversation.

The strange man doesn't respond or try to explain himself. I doubt he would anyway, even if footsteps didn't sound from somewhere behind me. He disappears, leaving me staring at the empty space in front of me.

"Hayley! Damn it! Get your ass over here," Alexander yells, flying into the small hallway with Opal and another guard behind him. "What the fuck? How could you let that asshole put his hands on you? You almost cost me—"

"Master Alexander, don't blame—" Opal hisses and steps back, touching her reddening cheek. Alexander slapped her too quickly for me to follow.

"Don't fucking get involved." Glowering at me, Alexander flashes his fangs. "Come on, Hayley. Time to go. You have some fucking explaining to do."

I hang my head in silence. There is no point in arguing.

Alexander locks his fingers around my wrist and drags me away.

I SIT ON the small swing seat in a metal, human-sized birdcage not even tall enough for me to stand. The casino floor buzzes with life as vampires gamble and socialize.

Without a clock or even one of the tinted windows to peer out, I can't tell what time it is or how long I've been locked in this cage on display. All I know is that I'm tired as fuck, hungry, and bored out of my damn mind. I still can't believe Alexander blames me for the bastard who knocked me off my aerial ring and ran away with me. Apparently I should've been more aware and avoided being put in the position in the first place.

He swears that if it happens again, he'll let the fucker keep me for a while so that I learn my lesson. Because no vampire will kill a potential food source without good reason, and because I have a tracker that glitters like an earring on my ear, he purposely let me think the worst.

I should be more pissed, but all I feel is defeated. Maybe Alexander is right, and I shouldn't have let my guard down. Then again, what the fuck was I supposed to do? It was a damn severed cock and then a head. I can't move as fast as a vampire.

This blows.

A soft whistle hums through the air, drawing my attention away from my glittery nail polish. I shift my gaze and peer around the crowded casino, my heart fluttering for a moment. The image of the handsome stranger who gave me his blood flicks to the front of my mind, and I wish I knew his name. Alexander never even questioned how the douche vampire died or how I healed. I should appreciate my luck, but I'm afraid it'll bite me in the ass harder than Alexander's biggest high roller guest who travels from another territory to stay here twice a year.

"Little bird, do you need someone to set you free?" The raspy voice comes from somewhere to my right, tightening my chest. It's not the stranger from the last show. I thought he might lurk around and approach me again, but he hasn't. And after that kiss? I'm out of my mind. Alexander would beat me if he knew I was giving out affection for free.

I remain frozen, rocking on my seat. The feather bikini I wear is the itchiest and the least favorite out of my costumes, especially now.

"It's okay to respond to me. Your master isn't around, and the security will be busy in a moment." A figure shifts in the side of my vision, moving closer but still keeping his distance.

This isn't my first time in the cage, nor is it the first time a vampire approached me and tried to start a conversation. But there are rules I must follow, and after getting thrown in here in the first place, I'm sure Alexander would blame something else on me. It's my job to never give anyone a reason to give me more attention than necessary. Conversing with this man would do just that. So would eye contact.

He whistles again and clinks something metal against the bars. "I suggest you answer my question, little bird. My offer to free you will only last for another minute, and

I don't think you want to be in here when shit goes down. You see, your master had one of my crewmembers killed on the job last night...but you're already aware of that, aren't you?"

I frown, twisting my fingers together. Who the hell is this guy?

"You can consider it a courtesy of Knox. You don't want to disappoint your hero, now do you?" the guy adds, finally shifting into my line of sight. "He'd hate for his favorite girl to get hurt in the crossfire when he's not here to save you."

Knox? My whole body hums at the name as it registers in my mind that he must know the guy who saved me last night.

Unfortunately, risking injury couldn't be worse than the punishment Alexander would inflict on me if he realizes I've left my cage.

"All you have to do is tell me you want out, little bird," he continues, tapping something metal against the shiny gold metal bar. I think it might be a weapon. Fuck. "Ten seconds."

I whip my attention to him, my heart pounding in my ears. I should be used to handsome vampires drinking me in like I'm about to become a fine-dining experience, but something about him gets under my skin and not necessarily in a bad way. Maybe it's because he lets me look at him without trying to stick his hand into the cage or because he doesn't threaten me with the knife in his other. Maybe it's because he smiles. Regardless, I can't help drinking in his features. He doesn't look either front or backrow, and his ruggedly handsome face complements his simple yet tough attire. A glint of something dangerous lies in his golden eyes, a shade lighter than his brown hair. Rubbing his hand over his well-kept beard, he outlines his angular face, giving me a glimpse of his jawline. Muscles flex and bulge across his body like my gaze gets to him the same as his gets to me. God, help me. This is bad. I'm entranced without him even trying to open my thoughts to control me.

"Time's up, little bird. It's a shame. Knox will be disappointed." The vampire vanishes, disappearing completely. My heart skips. I didn't expect him to abandon me.

I open and close my mouth in surprise and get to my feet, hunching over a bit as to not hit my head. Now that he no longer stands in front of me, I can think. That was the strangest thing. I'm usually not so curious, but he mentioned the stranger from last night. Who the fuck are these guys? What did he mean about me getting caught in the crossfire? His comment sinks in about something happening, and I peer around the casino, spotting strange vampires loitering. They're not any regulars I've seen, and one reveals a gun.

Shit. He wasn't lying or messing with me. Something is going on, and fear clenches my chest as I think about all of the donor staff. They'll be the first to get hurt. I can't let it happen.

Clearing my throat, I scream, "Fire!" It's the code word all donors are supposed to use when they think there's trouble to alert security.

Opal materializes in front of my cage, her dark blue eyes flashing with silver. Her concern stiffens her movements. I wonder how far she was away from me and if she noticed anything before my yell.

"Opal, hurry. Shit's about to go down," I say, gasping.

I shake the door, rattling the lock. I flit my attention to the casino behind her, spotting a few security guards blurring across the floor. Several patrons gawk in my direction, trying to figure out why I'm yelling.

"What do you mean? Where?" Opal asks, clutching a dagger at her side. Her holographic wig sweeps around her head as she whips her attention to glance at the casino floor.

I rattle the cage again. "Everywhere. Let me out. A man warned me that there was going to be—"

Several ear-piercing pops echo through the air, startling me. Widening her eyes, Opal quickly unlocks the cage and pulls me out. She picks me up into her arms, carrying me like she has done at least a couple dozen times over the years, and even before I became the star of the show of Vampire Nights. She's been caring for me all my life for as long as I can remember.

"Once we hit the elevators, I want you to go straight to your room, okay?" she says, blurring the world around me with her speed.

She sticks to the outer wall and crosses under the bridge leading to the strange metal tower with a lookout deck over the city. Four of its wide legs cut through the ceiling with a service counter beneath it. I've never been up there, but I can see the tall, triangular tower from my room, which according to Opal, is a replica of a back-world monument. The carpeted floor turns into shiny stones with a fake painted sky above, and I peer down the crowded shopping area made to look as if it's outside. I always imagine if that's what it's really like somewhere in the world because the street I can see from my window is nothing like it.

"When you get there, send an alert to the other girls. I'll be up as soon as I can." Opal sets me on my feet. "Remember, keep your head down. Don't look at anyone.

And hurry."

I don't make it far. The man from earlier cuts me off and aims a gun, stopping me in my tracks. I scramble backward and into Opal's arms. She automatically shifts me behind her protectively and hisses. Blood peppers his forehead and a streak runs into his beard. I panic in fear. What if he hurt a donor? What if he hurts me?

"Please, don't hurt us. We're just getting out of the way," I say, regretting my words immediately as Opal hisses in my ear.

"I warned you, and you rejected my offer by ignoring me. We have rules, and since you're on the casino floor, you gotta go with the others." The man waves his gun, motioning in the direction of the check-in lobby.

"Why are you doing this?" I ask, meeting the man's dark eyes, the brown turning gold with the flash of silver lighting his gaze. "Just let us go."

Again, Opal warns me with a hiss. "Ruby, stop. I will handle this."

Growling, he points his gun at her. "Shut the fuck up. I'm talking to the donor. Unlike with you bastards around here, I prefer to hear them speak freely."

My eyes widen, but I don't respond. Neither does Opal.

"Go on, little bird. Beg me one more time to let you

go," he teases, a quirk stretching his smirk.

I know I shouldn't give in and instead obey Opal, but my mouth disagrees and refuses to remain shut. "Please, I couldn't accept your offer. But now we can. Please, let us go."

"Sorry, ladies. I can't do that now. I don't want any fucker to question my allegiance if I tell them to let you by. You lost your chance two minutes ago, little bird. Not to mention you disrespected me by calling for help. The invitation was only for donors. Your mistress will cause problems for us, and we might need her." The man wags his eyebrows, enjoying this too much. Not because of me but because he seems to enjoy pissing Opal off. Keeping his gaze locked on mine, he adds, "I didn't want to have to do this, so don't hold it against me. Your master needs a message from the Bella Crew."

Opal tenses, standing tall, not letting the man intimidate her. "Tell him your goddamn self and keep us out of it. You don't need us. At least let my donor go. She's a target."

He sucks in air through his teeth, pretending to think about it. "No can do." Aiming the gun toward the ceiling, he fires, startling us and making those guests nearby scramble and run to hide. "I think I like her too much. Don't worry your possessive little head though. I'll protect her. Now walk your ass back to concierge. If you're lucky, maybe you won't be chosen as retribution for the act against the Bella Crew."

My heart beats wildly, threatening to spill onto the floor. Opal holds her hand out to me and pulls me into her side, draping her arm over my shoulders. My bare feet slap against the pristine tiles, glittering under the crystal chandeliers over a long check-in counter.

At least a dozen vampires in all different styles of clothing aim various weapons at several of Alexander's security personnel. I don't understand how some of the most powerful vampires in this hotel could be cornered by men who look like they belong in the backrow at the club. The wealthy covens are immediately recognizable with the way they carry themselves, dress, and have their own security following them around. Whoever this supposed crew is, I don't even think they belong to the same coven or maybe not one at all.

Opal struts past a few vampires who catcall and whistle, trying to get her attention. She puts up with just as much bullshit as a female donor does, but she can handle herself. If she couldn't, Alexander would've never put her in the position to care for us, which he considers one of his biggest assets.

"What does Asshole Aris have that turns you into his

obedient little bitch?" one of the guys asks Opal. "I have something that you'll enjoy more."

I catch sight of the vampire grabbing his junk through his pants as if offering to fuck Opal could sway her into turning against Alexander. I've never in my life seen her persuaded by cock, and I highly doubt she'll start now.

Opal stops and confronts the guy, pulling a blade from a hidden sheath in her jacket. "I guarantee my toy collection is far superior over that pathetic excuse for a dick you are so embarrassingly proud of. Now speak to me like that again, and you'll be on your hands and knees with your ass out and ready to take my fucking monster cock strap-on. Do you understand?"

The guy releases a guttural noise, charging forward. Opal reacts and sweeps his feet out from under him before kicking him in the ass with her heel. Stepping onto his back, she threatens to impale him with her sharp stiletto, and I tighten my jaw, stopping my mouth from smiling. Because damn. I've never been so impressed in my life. Opal takes shit from no one and isn't second in command to Alexander just because. I've never been prouder to be one of Opal's gems in my life.

I sometimes imagine what our lives would be like if it were Opal in complete control around here and not Alexander. He doesn't mistreat us often as long as we behave, follow orders, and bring in the wealth and power he needs to protect us, but he's an asshole. I fear him deeply in my bones more than I don't. Opal has never done anything except push us to our limits to prove that we're capable of things we hadn't realized. She rewards us while Alexander takes on the role of the punisher.

"Someone stop this bitch!" the guy yells, trying to reach up to grab Opal's foot.

A gunshot booms through the air, startling me. A tall, wicked-looking vampire with long black hair, a thick, muscular build with biceps bigger than my thighs, and a strange face tattoo I've only seen on the Strip dwellers who venture into the casino during the day, created by what Opal says is some sort of special UV ink that lasts a couple years on a vampire's skin and not like the tattoos given to each of us to mark us as property of Alexander Aris.

I rarely remember even having one as it was done in white ink on my lower back in a small swirling heart design. I was younger too, just turning a teen. Alexander instilled how important it was because when I grew boobs and started looking more like a woman, life in general became a bigger threat.

Why it's hidden never made sense with his reasoning, but I couldn't question it. Everyone has them with a lifetime contract. It could be far worse—I mean, this asshole looks like a baby tried to draw a tree or something on his cheek and around his eye to his forehead. I consider myself lucky that mine looks like a teensy pretty scar.

"You know help comes at a price, Beau," the freaky vampire says, waving his gun. "What do you have to offer?"

The vampire growls and flashes his fangs. "I'll give you a fucking month of free work, Walcott. Just get this bitch off before she tries to fuck me with her heel."

Smiling, Walcott aims his gun at Opal. "As much as I want to see a woman like you put Beau in his place, I put my men first. So, you have five seconds to get in one last kick. If you fail to let him go after that, I will shoot you."

Opal leers and lifts her stiletto, only to stomp it right into the guy's ass, piercing his butt cheek through his jeans. He howls and swears, rolling over, but Walcott doesn't do anything but give Opal a smirk as she click-clacks a few feet away, tugging me with her.

"Go stand with the others," Walcott says, motioning to the group of vampires by the counter.

Opal takes my hand, but Walcott snatches me by the wrist and yanks me away. He points his gun in Opal's face and growls. I expect her to try to attack him, the fear of her getting hurt or worse scaring the crap out of me, so I wave my hand.

"It's okay, Mistress Opal. I'll be fine," I say, my words coming out a whisper. I only use her formal title to show her I won't do anything stupid to get myself in trouble.

"That's too bad you have such an obedient little bitch. I was looking forward to teaching you both what it means to stand against me." Walcott dares Opal with his stern gaze to act out against him. She wouldn't though. Unlike with the other fucker still clutching his now bloody ass in silence a few feet away, he didn't hassle her. She is a smart woman and handles things as they should be instead of acting out in defiance.

Opal swivels on her heels and disappears at vampire speed, materializing at the edge of the crowd. She folds her arms across her chest and messes with her earring, the sign that she's putting out an alert to Alexander.

Something smacks me hard on the ass, making me jump. I whip my attention from Opal and Walcott as annoyance washes through me. I should know better than to react, but damn it. I can't believe he had the nerve to spank me with the side of the barrel of his gun.

"Go stand over by Monroe. You're mine until your master shows," Walcott says, growling under his breath. "If he doesn't, I'll take you until he's man enough to face me."

Fucking no, I'm not his. Opal would never allow it. He's disgusting and far from attractive like the other vampire who offered to help me. I don't tell him as much though. I know better than to stand up for myself. I'm a blood donor and nothing more to most of these vampires.

I slowly nod my head and stride away from Walcott, wanting to get space between us. It's not until I flick my gaze at the vampire extending his arm to me that I realize it's the guy who brought me and Opal here in the first place. Monroe. His name is Monroe. I repeat it in my mind a few times as my nerves loosen with his presence. He makes me less nervous than Walcott.

"Little bird, Knox isn't going to appreciate that you've drawn Walcott's attention...or mine for that matter. You should've fluttered away like I told you to when you had the chance." A muscular arm slides around my bare waist, tugging me closer.

I shiver under the soft sensation of Monroe's fingers caressing along the waistband of my bikini bottoms. A part of me wants to resist and try to stomp on his foot for touching me without an invitation from Alexander. Another part of me begs to release the breath I'm holding and relax. He's hot but insane, and I'm not sure how to feel. Unfortunately, the sensible part of me wins, and I ignore him the best I can, letting him drum his fingers on my hip while keeping my eyes on the shiny tiles. It's not like I haven't been touched by a man or a vampire before. I've been through worse. I'd rather gentle touches and testing boundaries than getting smacked, hit, screamed at, and threatened to be thrown to the vampires of the Strip—vampires I'm pretty sure are a part of this weird crew. I don't think they're coven brothers. At least not official ones under the La Vega city laws barely followed by anyone. These guys seem to have some sort of alliance, and that's all.

Leaning closer, Monroe shifts the pink hair of my wig away from my ear. "You ever been with a man before, little bird? Most donors recoil at a vampire's closeness. You're shifting closer. You like my hand on you, don't you?"

I swallow and ignore him, trying my best not to look at him as Walcott instructs a few other vampires to get in line. Silence fills the casino, and I peek at the entrance to the lobby and notice how vacant the hotel has become. I don't think it's ever been this empty.

"It's all clear," a guy in a dirty T-shirt, jeans, and well-worn black boots calls, shouting to Walcott. I spot a few more guys in the same type of attire, lurking near the slot machines glowing and chirping with catchy tunes. It's the only noise outside of the low murmur of voices.

"Listen up, staff of Aris!" Walcott yells, aiming his gun toward the ceiling.

Weapons like his aren't legal in La Vega, but he's obviously no law-abiding citizen. None of these guys are. It's not like Alexander is either, but with his power and wealth from the casino, a lot can be bought. I guess the same goes with brute force.

"Your fucking showrunner seems to need a little incentive to show his ass." Walcott grins at a few of the guys and stomps his way closer to the group of vampires. Opal is the only woman among them, and she remains stiff and expressionless. "So I'm going to need someone to help me bring him out. Do I have any volunteers?"

Monroe tightens his fingers to my hip. "You're going to want to keep your gaze on the floor, little bird. You might lose a couple feathers otherwise."

What the fuck is he talking about?

"I—I can go find Master Aris," Harvey, the head concierge, says. He straightens his shoulders and steps from the crowd. All of the vampire staff are trained to serve others, and he would be the first to always jump to making sure things are in order.

"What a suck up," Monroe says, breathing a cool breath in my ear.

"It's his job," I whisper, wishing my mouth would

learn to control itself.

Monroe leans in, brushing his lips to my ear. "He's going to regret his job and decision to speak up in three, two, one—"

Harvey's scream rips through the air, practically sending my soul from my body. I automatically twist and hide against Monroe's chest like the freaked out blood donor I am. Alexander is going to whip me if he sees me in this stranger's arms, but my human fear instincts yell like crazy, wanting me to hide behind someone stronger and more powerful than I could ever be.

"Fucker Aris!" Walcott shouts. "Come out, come out. If you don't, your overeager minion will lose his other arm next. Then his legs. Maybe even his cock. I'm going to need something to shove down your throat to choke you with."

I gasp, my eyes welling with tears. I don't know Harvey that well because I've never been allowed to interact with anyone apart from Alexander, Opal, and the rest of the performers, but I've seen him every day for as long as I could remember. And the sound of his pain? I think I'm going to be sick. He doesn't deserve to go through this.

A cool hand covers my ear, and Monroe presses my head against his broad chest. The sound of his heartbeat picks up, thrumming in a quick, rhythmic beat that helps keep me from dry heaving. It's not like I could throw up if I wanted to on an empty stomach.

"Get ready for another round," Monroe whispers, turning me slightly to wrap both his arms around me. Why does his embrace feel so good? I can't recall a man ever hugging me like this. They're always far rougher, pulling my hair to bite me.

I feel his body harden between us. He likes embracing me as much as I do, and there is nothing he can do unless he lets go to stop him from pressing his cock against my stomach through his pants. I freeze at his boner flexing, and I can't help wanting to reach between us to let my hand act as a barrier. He's enjoying my closeness way too much, which doesn't help my own wandering thoughts. I would be lying to myself if I wasn't curious about what he looks like naked. It's one of the things I get anxious about when performing in private for guests of Alexander. I've seen a lot of cock, and there is something about a nice one that makes things easier. And now? I could use his attraction against him. I'm not naïve and clueless. I use my sexuality every damn day to bring in stipends to this hotel, and Monroe loves every second of this.

Maybe I can use it to my advantage.

I shift, pressing closer to his body, squirming just enough to get him to slide his big hand over my shoulder and down the length of my spine until he reaches my lower back. I risk giving him the wrong impression and rub my hands over his back like I can't help myself. His scent engulfs me—like mocha and whipped cream, or one of the desserts Opal lets us have after a good performance. I bet he'd taste like it too. I've had some vampires taste so good that my mouth waters. He'd be one of them.

"Please," I whisper, keeping my voice low. I stretch up to grind his hard-on with my body. "Please make him stop." I say my words more like a prayer, but I hope Monroe understands that it's only him I'm speaking to.

Harvey screams again, his voice so high-pitched that it stings my ears. "Master Aris! Please!"

God, please.

I don't think I can listen to another round. "Please, Monroe. What can I do to get you to intervene? I'll do anything."

"Why do you have to tease me like this? There's only one way to make him stop, little bird," Monroe mutters, bowing down and closer to my ear again. He glides his tongue over my lobe. "Your master needs to come."

Fucking Alexander. Where the hell is he? Why won't he show up already? I knew he could be an asshole, but this is unbelievable.

"Next goes his leg!" Walcott shouts, his booming

voice echoing through the lobby.

I whimper, my fear instincts going crazy. "No," I say, shuddering and squeezing my eyes shut. "Please, no."

Monroe grips me tighter, humming into my ear like he enjoys everything about this twisted situation. And why does my body choose to keep flush against him? Not to mention my mind pays particularly close attention to his every movement and breath. Fuck. I just want to run away and hide. I'll spend a year in the damn birdcage if someone would make it stop.

Once again, Harvey hollers, his voice ringing through the air. I cover my ears, trying to stifle the noise the best I can. Then his screams suddenly stop, leaving his voice still reverberating through my ears. Growls echo through the air, and another few gunshots pop. I can't stop myself from twisting in Monroe's arms to look at the rest of the lobby.

I gag and cover my mouth, my stomach clenching at the sight of Harvey in a bloody pile on the floor. Both of his arms sprawl across the tiles in a streak of blood, as does one of his legs. A tall, even buffer figure stands before Walcott, holding Harvey's head. My bottom lip quivers, and Monroe tries to pull me back to him, but I finally find the will to resist.

I already can't un-see what Walcott did to Harvey, so

there is no point in trying to hide any longer.

"That's enough, you bastard!" the new vampire shouts. "You've gotten your restitution for your crewmember." Swinging his fist, the vampire punches Walcott in the face, sending him reeling back.

He growls. "But—"

Yanking a blade from his jacket, the stranger throws it at the scary vampire, sinking it into his gut. "Shut the fuck up and get out of here. You've made your point and failed to take advantage of the situation, so I'm going to do it for you."

Monroe releases a loud whistle. "Tell his crazy ass, Sawyer!"

Walcott glowers in our direction, looking like he might try to shoot at us, and I can't stop from hiding behind Monroe's bulky form. Straightening his back, Monroe meets Walcott's glower with his own, and he flips him off, daring for him to try anything.

Walcott whips his attention to me and blows a kiss. "Don't think you're getting away from me so easily," he mouths, his eyes flashing silver. "I'll find you later."

Monroe growls under his breath in response. I don't get a chance to even react before Walcott disappears.

"He won't touch you," Monroe mutters, once again standing close to me.

The new vampire, Sawyer, throws Harvey's head toward the group of utterly silent vampires, getting them to finally move and react. Opal flips her long, holographic hair over her shoulders and steps away from them, braving to face the guy, who seems to be another head asshole.

"Mr. Noble, I do hope you realize that a simple phone call to Master Aris to discuss the situation would've sufficed." Whoa, she knows his name. "I'm sure whatever restitution you felt you needed for the dismemberment of one of your allies could have been properly done in a more professional environment. Now I have to train another of Master Aris's staff members to fill a position that Harvey had been in for over a century. You do understand that this has accomplished nothing for you." Opal places her hands on her hips, arching one of her brows. "And quite frankly, I'd have expected such an ordeal from a Strip dweller, and not someone of your status."

I intake a sharp breath, my fear getting the best of me as Opal stands before the massive man. She doesn't even reach his shoulder in her high stilettos, the beast of a vampire probably towering close to seven feet. He would stand taller than seven feet if he wore heels like Opal.

I shove the weird-ass thought to the back of my mind.

Sawyer clicks his tongue. "You run things your way,

and I manage things my way. Now where is Aris? We have some things to discuss."

Like Alexander has been waiting somewhere in the shadows, the bastard materializes a few feet away from Sawyer and Opal. I heave a breath in anger. He gives no one a second look. He doesn't look fazed at all, and I know in this moment that he obviously didn't care enough to intervene.

I step forward, trying to control my emotions. Monroe grabs my wrist, surprising me, but Opal hisses at him and snatches me from his grasp. She lifts me into her arms and hugs me close, whispering that she has me into my ear. I relax, trying not to make a scene or draw attention to myself, though I can feel the weight of Alexander's stare on my back.

"Mr. Noble, why don't you and your crew join me in my suite? I'll have Opal call some of my most exquisite girls for a private performance, and we can let this nonsense pass?" Alexander winks at me, remaining easygoing. "What do you say?"

Sawyer narrows his eyes for a moment like he's considering denying the offer, but a handsome smile crosses his face. "Now that's the kind of accommodations I'm talking about." Whipping his attention toward me, he adds, "What about Ruby? Is she part of your truce offering?" He must've been at the show.

Alexander flashes his fangs and smiles. "You may have anyone you'd like."

I STAND IN the wardrobe of Alexander's suite, staring at my reflection in the brightly lit vanity mirror. Garnet, Pearl, and Topaz hover in front of the rack of costumes. Those aren't actually their real names, but the three sisters choose to keep their stage names all the time. Many of the performers do.

Me, on the other hand? I can't. It'd be too awful being Ruby all the time. She's the one who deals with this madness. It helps playing a role and immersing myself in it, so it doesn't haunt me when I take off my wig and become an unknown donor.

Mya struts into the wardrobe with Jasper, the only male performer invited to this private affair, and the two of them come up beside me. Mya grabs one of the tubes of red lipstick and smooths it over her full lips.

"We're lucky Mr. Noble only invited a handful of his crewmembers—at least, that's what Mistress Opal said. Looks like it will be one-on-one for mostly everyone. Jasper is only here as backup. No one wants a male tonight." Mya smacks her lips together and winks at herself. "They're all decent too. No one absolutely repulsive."

I puff out a breath and comb my fingers through my pink wig, deciding not to change it. The last thing I need is for one of the vampires to think that just because I swap them out a couple times a day that they can ask me to take it off along with the rest of my clothes.

The long, colorful hair is what keeps my wild emotions at bay with my act. With it on, I'm always Ruby Vixen. And Ruby Vixen isn't afraid of vampires or showing her skin. She's not afraid to kiss strangers and let them bite her wherever they please. Tonight, Ruby is brave enough to suck a dick if she has to. Hayley—me—on the other hand? I don't want to be here. I don't want to be tested and treated like Alexander's baby doll that he shares with others. As long as I have my makeup, wig, and glittery costumes, I can survive anything. Ruby does things so I don't have to. It's what makes this life bearable.

"That's good," I muse, finalizing my makeup with the same red lipstick Mya used. I turn toward her and drape my arms over her shoulders, meeting her brown gaze. "You ready, Crystal?" I ask, using her stage name. "Do you want to lead the way or shall I?"

She crinkles her nose and kisses each of my cheeks. "How about together? Maybe we can get a pair of friends who want to hang out with us both."

A girl can dream.

I hold out my hand to her. "Doesn't hurt to try, right?"

Linking her fingers through mine, Mya mirrors my show smile and we walk hand-in-hand from the wardrobe and into Alexander's massive bedroom suite. Music hums from the living area, and Mya spins next to me, making me laugh. The other girls stroll behind us while Jasper jogs ahead to open the door. His ass glitters with his sequined speedo tight enough to leave nothing to the imagination, but that's the point. It's why most of my costume consists of strings and sparkly rhinestones. Luckily, vampires prefer the temperature a bit warmer, so I'm never freezing my nipples off except on stage.

Alexander claps his hands in two quick successions, beaming us a smile as we enter the living area. I flit my gaze quickly around the room, trying to catch a glimpse of all the different men, but I'm too afraid to linger on any of them long enough to drink in. Giving anyone even a second of attention before it's requested could cause problems.

"My baby dolls, why don't you give our guests a little show by turning around?" Alexander says, twirling his finger. He wears an elegant black suit with a rhinestone-encrusted tie. Not stage-worthy for him, but bold enough to draw attention. His smile lights his face, hiding his emotions toward his guests. If I didn't notice the silver sparkle of his vampire nature in his green eyes, I might think he was happy about this private party.

Mya playfully spins me and giggles, waiting for me to do the same to her. I can't stop the laughter from bubbling out of my mouth. It feels so good to play around, even under the intense gazes of the six guest vampires.

"Gentlemen, pick your companion. Please remember that my girls are dear to me and must be treated as the gifts they are. Do not expect anything apart from their blood unless you plan to return the favor—if and only if they agree. Do you understand?"

Sawyer leans forward, the growl escaping his lips stealing my smile. "What do we look like? My inner circle knows how to treat a donor and a lady. You might think we're fucking savages or some bullshit, but—"

"My apologies, Mr. Noble. It wasn't my intent to offend you. It is in my nature to protect what belongs to me, and some assume that an invitation as such means more than a meal. That kind of expectation comes at a cost not many can afford and is not included in my gesture of hospitality." Alexander remains expressionless with his words despite the obvious jab at Sawyer and his crew.

I expect a fight to break out between them, but Sawyer leans back on the couch and crosses his muscular arms over his chiseled chest. He dips his chin in silent agreement to Alexander's terms.

"Good," Alexander says, combing his fingers through his brown hair. "I will return in an hour after I handle some personal affairs. Please note that you are being monitored, and I expect you to sign the agreement that you will ensure no more of your men enters my hotel with the intent to cause harm. Next time, I won't take things so lightly."

Once again, no one responds to Alexander, and I realize that all of this is only for show. Anger burns inside me that he purposely let that bastard Walcott have his way in the casino when he's powerful enough to handle a gang of assholes like the Bella Hotel crew, or whatever. Alexander owns this hotel and the one connected to it for a reason. He helped start the Vampire Uprising over a century ago, long before I was born.

With his power and influence, he helped bring La Vega to its intended glory. He, along with the other leaders on the Strip, turned a massive amount of humans into vampires, biting them with venom and letting them run wild with blood hunger. The act decimated humanity but made it more manageable for vampires to take control. It allowed them to wall in the big cities and start a new, better world before donors could destroy the place they must live for eternity. Vampires don't die naturally, so I sort of get it, but I always wonder what the back-world was like. I wonder what it would be like if humans still controlled the world. I can't even imagine what the city was like under the control of humans, though.

Half the hotels were destroyed in the chaos when vampires decided that the human population needed culling. There are no longer donors on the Strip at all, and vampires work for or play for blood from the running hotels' gen. pop. that live within the hotels and are controlled by the most powerful leaders running La Vega. At least, that's what Opal once said.

It's strange to think of any other life, but from the old posters I once found with Mya as a teen, I know La Vega was once a city of lights, partying, gambling, and a vacation locale when it was still Las Vegas. Taking the city apart to rebuild it as La Vega was what really solidified the fact that humanity would never be the same. Opal swears it's a good thing, but I can't help wondering the truth of her words.

It takes the door to Alexander's suite slamming shut to knock my thoughts from me. I hate the first few minutes of scrutiny from the guests the most because of the awkward silence that comes with vampires whispering too lowly for us to hear. It wasn't until last year that I realized as much. I used to think Opal and Alexander could read minds. I once tried to think a response to them, and the two of them thought I was ignoring them because of it. Opal still doesn't let me live that one down. She fought Alexander to save me from a beating because of my curiosity.

Trying to ignore the heavy silence, I close my eyes and listen to the soft music. I sway my hips and twist my hands in a way that accentuates my body by stretching my torso with my movements. The five of us girls make our way closer to the vampires, and I find myself dancing in front of Sawyer as if Mya and the others planned who was going with whom without consulting with me.

I spin in front of Sawyer and dip low, arching my back and seductively give him a view of me bent over.

"What did I say, Sawyer? She's fucking hot, right?" The familiar voice snaps through me, tugging me back to the performance last night and the whole reason why I ended up in the damn birdcage on display. "The fucker was worth the sacrifice to have her within reach. She's an amazing kisser."

I can't stop from turning around and meeting Knox's gaze. He smirks at me and wiggles his fingers. My whole body buzzes at the reminder of our kiss, but no one comments about it. He noticed my reaction, though, because his eyes flash and his nostrils flare. A smile softens his beautiful features even more, and I break his stare before I find myself on his lap. That would be bad. He might already be possessive, and Alexander doesn't tolerate that.

"If I didn't agree, I'd fucking punch you in the dick for the bullshit you pulled, Knox." No fucking way. Monroe's voice draws my attention away from Knox and to him. He winks at me, shooting a mixture of emotions through me. "But damn it." Wiggling his fingers, he motions for me to give him my attention. "Come here, little bird. I'd love to continue what we started in the lobby. I'll keep these fuckers back."

My feet automatically carry me a step forward. I can't deny him, even if I wanted to, without facing some sort of punishment. I'm here solely for whoever wants my entertainment.

"Pretty vixen, don't give him the pleasure." Knox surprises me by reaching for my hand. Tugging me closer, he pulls me from Monroe's reach. "Come sit with me. I want your company."

Two hands lock around my waist and yank me forward and away from Knox's attempt to get me to sit with him. I land on top of Sawyer's hulking body and stiffen, nervous about being in the middle of three vampires who all want my attention.

Nerves tighten my chest at the quick intervention before I could join Knox. I'm not used to so many wanting me when the other performers are just as beautiful. It's like I've turned into a competition, but I don't get to choose who I let treat me like theirs for the next hour. And Sawyer? I'm not sure about him. He's bold for stealing me away from his crewmembers, and I kind of like it. It makes it easier, since they might've started fighting or asked me to pick. I can't make that type of decision. Someone would be angry, and Alexander would take it out on me.

"I requested Ruby, so you two are going to relax and not smother her." Sawyer's arms lace around my stomach, the chill of his skin sending goosebumps over my body.

"You asshole," Monroe mutters, but he doesn't try to snatch me away.

"Seriously. I kissed her first. She should be mine." Knox reaches out and caresses his fingers across my bottom lip. "Isn't that right, sexy vixen?"

I don't respond and pull my hair in front, giving Sawyer access to me to see if he'll bite me.

"You know she can't agree with you, Knox. Aris owns her and she'd never claim otherwise." Sawyer hums and sniffs my shoulder, his mouth so close that his lips send tingles over the spot. "Right, Ruby?" I've never been addressed directly so much during a private show.

"Mmmhmm," I reply, choosing to keep my comments to myself. I roll my hips and offer a soft moan, my reactions to him calculated and imprinted in my mind from everything Opal taught me about how to get a client to come back over and over again. It's the regulars who pay the higher prices, even for just the chance to be near me. It also will help redirect their conversation. They can't think about anything besides what they want to do to me, which is better than them arguing with me in the middle.

It works. Sawyer continues to explore my stomach.

"You like my attention, don't you?" Sawyer whispers, now ignoring Monroe and Knox.

"Mmmhmm." My voice comes out low and breathy, and I continue to grind on his lap until I feel his body awaken beneath me. Planting my feet to the floor, I spin to face him.

Sawyer grabs at me again, tugging me back to him until I straddle his lap, my knees planted on the couch cushion on the outside of his legs. The heat of Knox's gaze smolders over me, but I keep my eyes trained on Sawyer, not looking into his silver-flashing irises directly but close enough that he knows I won't give anyone else attention while in his possession. It's what I'm trained to do. If one of Alexander's guests thinks for even a second that they're paying him for me to look at someone else, I'd end up with a worse punishment than the cage.

"Isn't she so sexy?" Sawyer asks, tracing the silhouette of my body with his hands. "Flawless on every level. The way she moves..." He licks his lips.

I bite my bottom lip between my teeth and comb my hair over my shoulder, exposing my throat. "I'd love for you to taste me." While many donors ask vampires if they want a taste, I would never. I know they want a taste. It's about them thinking that I want them to want me.

Sawyer's fangs click as he extends them. The automatic reaction of his vampire nature excites my body more than it should, and I can't stop the soft moan from escaping my mouth. With some vampires, the act of a bite can be more than just them getting sustenance, and with how hard his cock is flexing between my legs, I can guess he's the type to want to turn a bite into something more intimate.

"If you don't give her what she wants, then I will," Knox says, leaning closer. He risks the safety of his hand to stroke his fingers over my arm.

I tense and freeze, fear rising inside me. Vampires are possessive as fuck when they have their sights set on a donor, and it's clear that Sawyer already has silently claimed me for the hour. Because with the way he looks at me, I sense it's more than about just tasting my blood. He desires me on many different levels.

"Oh, she's going to get everything she wants," Sawyer says, stroking his fingers along my jaw.

I swallow my nerves, trying to calm my racing heart. Knox continues to run his fingers across my wrist without Sawyer trying to murder him, which helps ease my anxiety. They were all aware that because all of them prefer female donors that two of them would share.

"Would you like a taste?" Topaz's soft voice comes from my left as she dances in front of Monroe. It's now that I realize the others all have chosen companions except for her, and it's probably because these three vampires have their sights on me.

Monroe ignores her, his gaze burning into the side of my face. If Sawyer hadn't locked me in his stare, I would shift to look at Monroe. I'm used to having dozens of vampires' attentions on me, but this feels different. It feels as if the three of them won't accept anything else, which will be a problem if they bite me and drink. They could take too much.

Topaz must sense what I do, because she dances closer and unclasps her top, dropping it right onto Monroe's lap. I expect him to finally take her up on her offering, but he still doesn't respond to her. And shit. If her boobs don't steal his attention from me, I don't know what could.

"Come here, baby," a masculine voice says. "Come join your sister and me. There's enough of me to give you both attention. Don't let that fucker's rejection get to you."

This time, I do break Sawyer's eye contact to glance at a burly vampire sitting on the loveseat with Garnet. He holds out his hand, curling his fingers to get Topaz to go to him instead. I expect Monroe to finally react and grab her, but he doesn't say anything. And now I'm weirded out. Who dismisses the chance for a personal donor?

I watch in silence as the other vampire leads the two dancers out of the living area and into one of the bedrooms. Mya and Pearl have already taken their guests to other bedrooms as well. I frown, accidentally breaking my performance expression and meet Monroe's eyes. They crinkle in the corners, the golden color of his irises lighting up silver with his hunger.

"What is it, little bird? Are you upset that I denied your friend?" Monroe asks, reaching out to stroke his hand over my arm. "Because you shouldn't be. I prefer to give my attention to you."

My breathing quickens, and I don't respond. I don't trust my voice not to give away what runs through my mind. These three vampires turn my body out of whack, and I don't even know what to do. So I remain silent, pull myself together, and do what Topaz did. I click the quick release button on my bikini top and let it fall onto Sawyer's lap. Like Opal has said a million times before, if I'm ever scared, uncertain, or need a moment to figure out what to do, then show off my boobs. It will give me a couple minutes to think.

"Damn," Sawyer whispers, his fingers leaving my jaw and traveling down my neck. "Is that where you want me to taste you, Ruby?"

His use of my stage name kicks my good senses back

on, and I smile and fall back into my performance.

"I'd love it if you bit me anywhere you please," I say, linking my fingers around his, guiding his hand lower to give him the silent permission he seeks to touch my boobs.

"Don't fucking do it," Knox mutters under his breath. "She's mine."

Uh-oh.

His words set Sawyer off, and I realize there is only so much a vampire can handle before they get truly possessive. And it's obvious that Knox wants me for himself.

Sawyer blatantly ignores Knox's comment and caresses the pad of his thumb across my nipple, sending an explosion of tingles through my body. I release a soft moan and shift, trying to think through the sensations buzzing over my skin.

I blindly reach out and touch my fingers to Knox's cheek, the stubble coarse against my fingers. "There is enough of me to go around. I'd love to taste you again. Maybe somewhere different this time. I haven't forgotten that you are my hero."

Another tip to surviving a possessive vampire? Offer to suck their dick. And if Knox's blood tasted as good as it did, his cum will taste similar. At least it's one perk for telling a hungry vampire to fuck my face to get him to chill out.

Knox intakes a breath and groans at my insinuation. "Show me where."

Easy bastard. I knew it would work. Opal's advice has never let me down before.

"You lucky asshole," Monroe mutters, scooting closer to Sawyer as he continues to strum his fingers over my boobs like he can't get enough. And maybe he can't. It's not like females are readily available. It could've been years since he's touched a woman's body.

"I'd love it if you would bite me anywhere you desire too," I say, offering my hand to him. "Master Aris will be upset otherwise. I insist."

Silence falls between the three of them as they take their gazes away from me and look to each other. Without having to hear them or see their lips moving, I know they have a quiet conversation with each other. And it makes me anxious. Usually, vampires are quick to agree with my suggestions.

Sawyer turns back to me first and slides his hand lower until he pulls my body flush to his and he can whisper in my ear. "Tell me, Ruby. What happens when your master becomes upset?"

A dozen responses cross my mind, but I lean back and smile, shrugging my shoulders. "I won't have to worry about that, now will I? Master Aris will see the bites, which will make him happy."

Something indecipherable flickers across Sawyer's gaze. "You can tell him we didn't want to."

Goosebumps prickle over my skin. I blink a few times and frown, unsure of what to say. It's my job to please Alexander's guests, especially these guys because he saw them as a threat and this is supposed to help maintain peace and to stop future attempts to attack the hotel. Not giving them what they want isn't part of it.

"We know you're acting," he adds, sliding his fingers into my wig.

What the fuck?

"Acting?" I giggle and tilt my head to the side. "No. I want you to bite me." I bring his hand back to my boobs, getting him to touch me again. "You touching me feels so good."

Sawyer releases the sexiest noise, the rumble from his throat surprisingly turning me on. "You shouldn't tease me. I want you far more badly than I realized, but I know better. You're here because you're one of Fucker Aris's gemstones."

"So tell us. What happens if you don't do your job?" Knox asks, keeping his voice low.

Again, I shrug and smile. "Nothing. This isn't a job. You heard my master. He doesn't force us to do anything we don't want to."

"Is there a problem, gentlemen?" Jasper's soft voice snaps the three vampires' attention away from me.

Monroe moves too quickly for anyone to react and slams Jasper's back into the wall, shaking the picture frames. I gasp and try to get off Sawyer, but he tightens his hold on me, not letting me try to interfere.

Leaning in close, Monroe captures Jasper's gaze, locking him in place. "Don't fight. I'm not going to hurt you. I just want to know something. What happens if the performers don't do their jobs in taking care of the guests?"

Jasper tightens his jaw, unfazed by Monroe's attempt to get into his mind. "Nothing happens. Master Aris takes exceptional care of us."

Monroe releases him and shakes his head. Materializing in front of me, he leans over and touches my chin. "You've all been given blood."

"Of fucking course they have," Knox says.

Jasper quickly returns to his corner, choosing to remain silent instead of confirming Monroe's assessment.

Reaching out, I grab the front of Knox's shirt, surprising him. I bow toward him and smile at the change in his expression. I need to do something to distract him. If they know I'm acting, Alexander will think I've failed. He put the responsibility into my hands to make these guys happy.

"Master Aris does it to protect us. Like I said, he cares and makes sure we aren't forced to do anything we don't want to." Bringing my mouth to his ear, I add, "Plus, he's watching. So please. Give me what I want. Let me care for you."

Like my closeness triggers his deep-seated desire, he tugs me from Sawyer's lap and kisses me, reminding me of our strange and exciting moment backstage after he stopped the asshole from running away with me.

My body reacts at his closeness, the memory of his blood coursing through me turning me on. It usually takes a lot to get my body to react, my mind always guarded because I know what kind of predators I'm dealing with, but this time? The attraction is real. It's exciting.

Fuck. It's dangerous.

I pull away, my wild heart racing. Shoving my hands to Knox's chest, I push myself away and flip, landing on my feet.

He gets up, standing over me. "Ruby, I—"

"Is there a problem, baby doll?" Alexander's voice cuts through the room, startling me.

I shake my head. "No, Master Aris. I was just—"

"About to give these gentlemen exactly what they want?" he asks, his stern expression as sharp as the lash of his words.

Swallowing, I bob my head. "Yes, sir. I was only trying to figure out how to properly care for three. They all want something from me."

Alexander narrows his eyes. "Remember, only two bites."

"I know, sir. I will still ensure your guests are taken care of." My voice barely comes out a whisper.

"That's not necessary." Knox clenches and unclenches his hands.

"Do you not want her?" Alexander asks, stepping forward, his fangs peeking from beneath his top lip. "Has she been unsatisfactory? If that's the case, I will remove her immediately and bring in someone up to your standards."

I suck in a small breath. Alexander doesn't take rejection lightly. He prides himself on having the best of the best girls around, and if someone denies a moment with me? God, this hasn't happened before.

Now I'm scared.

Fuck.

Sawyer growls and stands up, his muscles bulging as he flexes. "She's perfect. Exceptional. Don't mistake this asshole's shortcomings and shyness on the donor."

Tipping his head back, Alexander howls a laugh. "Fuck. You hear that, baby doll? Show the bastard there is no reason to be shy with you. Show him exactly what a gift it is to be a guest at the Aris Hotel."

I force myself to smile. "Yes, sir. I'd be happy to."

Turning my back away from Alexander, I face Knox. His eyes search mine, his chest heaving. I stand on my tip-toes and brush my lips to his ear. "Please, let me do this. Please."

"But I don't want you to be forced into this by fear. I can tell you're only doing it for him." His whisper tickles my ear, and I'm afraid Alexander heard his comment. But if he had, he doesn't react.

I meet his gaze and smile, hoping he believes me. "I want to, handsome. I told you already. You're my hero."

He doesn't argue, and I lean in to kiss him.

"Thank you," I whisper, offering another smile.

Slowly swaying my hips, I dance my way to the floor and get on my knees. I hate that Alexander watches me from behind. I can feel his gaze on me. I always knew he was a monster, but I thought there were bigger monsters outside our hotel.

Now? I'm not so sure.

Maybe I shouldn't be so afraid of the world on the Strip. Maybe there is a life outside being one of the Aris Hotel's showgirls.

Who am I kidding? This is my life. I'll never be free.

OH, FUCK.

Oh, shit.

My mind screams that I should grab this beautiful vixen's hands and stop her from unfastening my belt, but my damn cock throbs and my body refuses to obey my brain. My heart thrums in rapid beats, and I flick my gaze toward Sawyer and Monroe. They look jealous as fuck that Ruby smiles up at me from her knees.

I've thought about her since last night and how she kissed me back instead of slapping me like I expected, and my dreams turn into a real-life fantasy. I should've taken her when I had the chance. It would've been worth the risk of getting dismembered like the asshole I hired to be on my security personnel.

Ruby's warm fingers sliding into my jeans snaps my attention away from my thoughts. Only the sexy sight of her pink tongue gliding over her cherry-colored lips as she wets them remains on my mind. It's been forever since a woman's gone down on me, and the anticipation stops me from focusing on anyone else.

My balls tighten with a shock of pleasure. I moan and lock my fingers through her hair. The sensation of her hot mouth sucking in my cock erupts pleasure straight to my core. It's been so damn long since I've had my cock sucked that it takes everything in me not to blow my load already. But fuck. Her mouth is like a portal to paradise. I would try to fucking kill Aris right now if I knew he couldn't overpower me. I know my limits, and it wouldn't only be him I'd have to face. He has a dozen allies, all who each run other hotels on the La Vega Strip. I know better than to start a damn war for a donor who gives fucking incredible head.

Damn. There goes my cock and brain arguing again.

All I can think about is how I want Ruby to be mine.

Her startling turquoise eyes meet mine as I watch her, and I can't stop from stroking her cheek. I wonder if her body tastes as good as her lips do. The thought of wanting to reciprocate hits me hard and fast.

"Can I take you to the bedroom? I don't want to be part of the performance for these fuckers anymore, pretty vixen," I murmur, combing my fingers through the pink wig.

She responds by sliding my cock from her mouth and biting her lip. "Whatever you want, handsome," she says, using my waist to help herself to her feet.

I tuck away my cock and ignore the stares of Sawyer, Monroe, and the bastard Aris. I expect one of them to try to stop me, because I know that they've already put their sights on Ruby, especially after last night, and the three of us have been arguing over her since despite knowing that she belongs to someone. And since Aris denied my first offer—which was almost out of my reach—I know there isn't a number I could provide that'll get her.

Maybe that's why my brain reluctantly goes along with my desire. Because damn. I'm not sure I'll ever get this opportunity again. Fucking moral dilemmas. I'm usually a decent guy as long as someone doesn't fuck with my wealth, power, or allies. I'm not some psycho donor collector that snatches humans from the general population to cage, nor am I the reason some donors resort to relying on the hotel owners for protection in exchange for a place to survive the rest of their miserable lives. Getting my cock sucked by Ruby should've been a line I didn't cross, because I damn well know she's doing this out of fear of punishment. I should've tried harder, but the second she touched my belt, I fell to her mercy. I'm still there.

"Jasper, why don't you offer these two gentlemen a drink while they wait for their turns?" Aris says, his voice humming through the air.

And fuck. I want to spin around and flash my fangs at the thought of treating Ruby as something he can pass around.

I twist and look at Sawyer and Monroe, but I don't even have to glare. It's obvious that they only liked the idea when Ruby was dancing and being playful for us, but now that this bastard makes it sound like Ruby is something merely here to be used, it gets under all of our skin. I want her to be mine, but I don't want to own her. There is something sexier to me about her having freewill to decide. The challenge is more fun.

Of course, I still have the need to kidnap her. My brain tells me it's different, though.

"Jasper will be good enough for us. Let Knox enjoy your generosity. He's been deprived of a sexy woman for years." Fucking Sawyer. He's asking for me to bitch slap him. "Why don't we go to your office? I'd like to go over a few things to ensure our affairs are in order."

Okay, so maybe less of a bitch slap and more of a whack on the back.

Aris glances at me for a second, but I don't let him watch me for long, allowing Ruby to guide me into what looks like the master suite. It's far nicer than my suite in the Bella Tower across the Strip but only because the hotel was trashed long ago. I don't give a fuck about some graffiti or holes in the walls. It's just a place to sleep when I'm not busy keeping assholes in line.

The second Ruby clicks the door to the suite closed, I envelop her in my arms and lift her off her feet. I can't stop myself from kissing her how I want, not even caring if her mouth was all over my cock.

"Fuck, I want to taste you," I murmur, striding across the room and to the king-sized bed. "Will you let me?"

Ruby smirks and rolls on top of me, straddling my waist. "You can bite me anywhere you please, handsome."

I intake a sharp breath and shake my head. Her words snap me out of my lust-filled excitement. I wasn't asking for her blood, and hearing her so casually say I can bite her reminds me that she's only with me right now because of Aris.

I groan and sit up but don't nudge her off me. The blinking camera in the corner of the room shows me that she wasn't kidding before about being watched. And damn it. Once again, I'm facing a moral dilemma.

Ruby touches my cheeks, drawing my attention away from the camera and back to her. "Is something wrong?"

I tighten my jaw and shake my head. "No, it's just—you're so beautiful. I want you more than I should."

"Thank you," she says, biting her bottom lip between her teeth. "That makes me incredibly happy. Master Aris will be pleased."

"Shit," I mutter under my breath.

She catches my whispered swear, and her face falls. Even confused and grimacing, Ruby is incredibly beautiful. "You don't like that?" Her voice shakes with her words. "You don't want him to be pleased with me?"

Fuck.

Pushing her back, I grab the blankets and pull them over us, trying to shield us from the view of the camera. The last thing I want is for her to think she's doing something wrong or that I don't enjoy her closeness. I've never dealt with anyone like her. The blood donors at the Bella give to a general pool that is dispersed among the guests and permanent residents like me. There are a few personal donors, but they're not exclusive. It'll fuck with the alliances of the Bella Crew, because we have an agreement when it comes to power, and power lies within donors.

"Ruby," I whisper, clutching her cheeks in my hands, getting her to look into my eyes. "I know you're only here because you're being forced. I went along with this because I could tell you're afraid to be disobedient in front of your master."

"I'm not afraid. I'm doing what I want," she says, smiling again. This time, her eyes don't light up. "And I love hearing you moan for me. If you don't want to bite me, then let me finish what I started. I want to taste you."

I groan and squeeze my eyes shut. My damn cock loves the sound of that to the point I let her wiggle lower and lace her fingers around my girth again. "Ruby," I whisper. "You have no idea how badly I want you. I want to kiss you and fucking have my way. I want you to sit on my damn face and drown me in your pussy juice."

She intakes a small breath. "Okay."

Shit. How do I even respond to that? "You don't mean that, do you? You're saying what I want to hear."

Releasing a small laugh, she shakes her head. "You're different than the other guests of the Aris Hotel. It confuses me, but I'm not against playing out your fantasy. I've never sat on someone's face before."

My balls ache so bad that I'm starting to think they're going to fall off if I don't do something about it soon.

Growling, I inhale a few deep breaths. I might regret this, but I just can't read her well enough. It would be easier if I could open her mind and ask her to be honest. Her eyes widen at my reaction, and my chest tightens. I've scared her. I should be used to it. Donors are naturally afraid of vampires. But with Ruby? Fuck.

I sigh and caress my fingers through her hair. "I'm sorry. I'm just a bit frustrated. I don't think you understand that it's okay for you to be yourself around me. I'm not here seeking pleasure or blood."

She twists her mouth to the side. "Why are you here then?"

"That's a difficult question to answer." I could lie and tell her that I'm here because after seeing her on stage last night and getting a chance to steal a kiss that I haven't been able to focus on anything else. While that's partly true, the real reason is that we're here getting a feel of the Aris Hotel. We're taking notice of how things are run and what Alexander Aris does to secure his power. And Ruby is a part of it.

"Okay," she says, keeping her voice low.

I shouldn't have expected her to argue with me. She's

too obedient to do as much. So instead of focusing on things I know she won't budge on, I change the subject. "Let's just say that you've caught my attention. Your performance was incredible last night."

Like a switch flips inside her, her face lights up with a real smile. I thought she was beautiful before, but she's absolutely stunning. It's obvious that she prides herself on her performance, and now I want to figure out what to do and say to keep her relaxed in my arms.

"I could watch you all night. It's an honor to even be in your presence right now, especially..." My voice trails off at the thought of her mouth around my cock again.

She giggles and pats my cheeks. "I'm glad you liked it."

"I fucking loved it," I say, smiling.

My fangs click under her scrutiny, and her gaze darts to them. Reaching up, Ruby pokes her index finger to my right fang, pricking herself. She traces her bloody finger over my bottom lip, setting me off, and I suck harder, wanting a better taste. I hadn't planned on drinking her blood or getting a blow job for that matter, but I'm damn set to go wherever she leads. I should fucking care whether or not she's doing this because this is her job, but right now, I've lost all my fucks. She's taken them from me and refuses to give them back until she's finished.

Lowering herself back down, she rests on her elbow and slides her hand into my pants again. "My master will expect to see a bite on me," she whispers. "Please, do it."

My breathing quickens, and I groan at the sensation of her mouth sucking my cock again, sending an explosion of ecstasy through me. Grabbing her wrist, I sink my fangs into her arm, doing what she begs of me. Her sweet blood fills my mouth, setting my whole body off, and it only takes her a minute more to bring my desperate balls to their peak. My muscles tense, and I grunt and clutch her head, gasping as she lets me cum in her mouth. She only slows down when I tighten my fingers, and I just stare at her with my jaw slack as she wipes her lips.

"You taste amazing. Just like your blood." Her smile widens with my reaction, and she shifts the blankets off us, reminding me that there is a world outside of this bed.

"You didn't have to do that," I murmur, my thoughts racing.

"I wanted to. You're different." Ruby flashes her brilliant smile at me. "Plus, you're my hero. I don't have anything else but my body and blood to offer you. Had you not saved me last night, my punishment would've been far worse than a few hours in the birdcage."

The sound of a door slamming shut draws my attention away from Ruby. She stiffens in my arms but doesn't pull away. Voices hum through the cracked door, and I hug her closer, wishing with everything in me that I could make it out of here alive with her in my arms. Her blood was unlike anything I've tasted, and I can imagine waking up with her as mine every damn day. Is it love? No. More like obsession. I feel my sudden possessiveness growing with my deep-seated nature. I want her to be my girl. My good girl to take care of and treat the way she deserves and not hurt her like the fucker Aris does. If he didn't, she wouldn't be trembling in my arms. Even his nearing presence scares her.

She straightens her back and turns away from the door, focusing on me. Like she doesn't want to be caught doing nothing, she plants her mouth to mine and kisses me, sliding her tongue into my mouth and setting off my cock again. If she continues, there will be no turning back. I want more. I crave more. It would be so easy to snap the thin string of her bottoms and align my body with hers. I groan and dig my fingers into her tight, toned ass. Her hand reaches between us, and I moan, my mind turning into putty just for her. As long as she keeps touching me the way she does, I'll fucking do what she wants.

"Time's up, Knox," Sawyer says, knocking on the doorframe. "Everything is set. We got the deal with Aris. Five percent not to fuck shit up and an additional four percent to keep other crews off his property. It would've been five, but he offered a permanent reservation at table one at Vampire Nights. I couldn't resist." By percent, he means exclusive Aris Hotel donor blood, which we can charge triple the damn stipends for among the Strip dwellers.

"Four for you, five for me," I say, smirking at Ruby. She remains smiling like she's trained her face to hide her emotions with it. "I accept."

"Fuck that, you horny bastard. Four for each of you and one for me, plus dibs on the table." Monroe slides past Sawyer and crosses his arms. He wiggles his fingers at Ruby. "I plan to sit front and center every damn performance just to see your glorious tits, little bird. What do you think? Do you want me to? I'll be your fucking hero." He winks, flashing his fangs.

I growl under my breath, his comment feeling like he flicks me in the nuts. "Talk to her like that again and you won't have eyes to appreciate her killer body."

Ruby shudders in my arms, and I glower at Monroe, wishing the bastard would stop checking her out now. A shadow materializes behind him, and I realize it was Aris that set her off and not him.

"I do hope you've enjoyed your time with my baby doll," Aris says, sweeping his gaze over the room. His eyes land on Ruby, and I watch him assess her, zoning in on the bite mark I left on her wrist. He smiles and nods at Ruby, and she relaxes, her fear melting away.

She slides off of me and kisses my cheek. "Thank you for being such an amazing companion, Mr. Knox."

I adjust my pants and zip up. Grabbing her wrist, I stop her for a second and pull out my com device. "May I leave you with a gift?" I don't know how it works here, but it's a courtesy to tip blood donors for their services—the ones I've had aren't under permanent contract and choose the position. For Ruby? I know whatever arrangement she has with Aris is far less accommodating.

She offers me a smile and crinkles her nose. "I have no need for gifts as I have everything I could possibly want with Master Aris, but you may make a donation to the staff on this floor."

I tighten my mouth and nod. "You are an exceptional woman, Ruby. Your master is a lucky man."

Ruby saunters ahead of me and straight to Aris, bowing her head and waiting for him to tell her what to do. Leaning down, he whispers something in her ear, and my insides twist at her reaction. Whatever he said leaves her wide-eyed and more freaked out, and I wonder if he used me as a test.

"Please excuse me," Fucker Aris says. "I need a couple

minutes with my girls. I'll meet you gentlemen outside."

Draping his arm over Ruby's shoulder, he guides her out of the bedroom. I don't even get two feet before Sawyer materializes in front of me. He growls under his breath and swings his fist, punching me in the gut.

"Why the fuck did you offer her a gift?" Sawyer asks, keeping his voice low. "Aris just told her that she better hope that you insist and give her a tip anyway."

Shit. Anger rolls through me, and I charge toward the living area, ready to fucking fight and steal Ruby away from that worthless asshole. Monroe blocks my way and dodges my fist, not letting me punch him in the gut.

"Move, asshole. I'm taking her with us." I growl and square my shoulders.

"Don't fucking start, Knox. She's not yours. Don't equate a blowie to her wanting to be your girl. She did it because it's her job. Don't be stupid and ruin things. I like my damn appendages attached to my body, and I'm afraid I'll lose them because you can't keep your fucking cool." Monroe shoves me back, risking me trying to punch him again. I'm older, more powerful, and a skilled fighter, trained during the Vampire Uprising to handle all the dickholes who thought they could just do whatever the fuck they want. He only challenges me because I rarely actually fight. I prefer to be more of the brains instead of brawn.

It also means I know he's right. Ruby was putting on a show, which was my hesitation in letting her suck my dick. But damn. It doesn't change the fact that I'd treat her a helluva lot better.

"Just do what I said and send her a gift. Aris thinks he can use her against us, so fucking let him remain on his power trip." Sawyer drapes his arm over my shoulders. "It'll be sweeter when he falls. He underestimates us."

I pull my shit together and offer him my fist. "You better be right."

Sawyer lifts an eyebrow. "I am."

Now if only I could speed shit up. I can't wait to see Alexander Aris fall. And when he's on his damn knees, I'll take the fucker's head. This city will be ours.

"GREAT SHOW, MY gems," Opal says, beaming a brilliant smile. Her short neon wig glows in the streak of black light from the stage.

I wring the donor blood from my hair, wishing I didn't accidentally taste the metallic concoction during the finale. Alexander surprised me by setting off the blood rain just for the hell of it. He likes to keep the audience excited and have a few unpredictable changes to keep them coming back for more. And unfortunately, I'm afraid it's going to rain every night from now on.

"Crystal, Garnet, Jasper, Diamond, Aquamarine, and Amethyst, go ahead and return to your quarters. You're excused for the night." Opal kisses each one of the performers as she passes them, giving them a hug and ensuring they know how well they've done. She glances at the rest of us. "Quartz, Topaz, Emerald, Pyrite, and Ruby, I need you to clean up, take an hour to relax and put on the leopard costumes. Master Alexander has a special client that needs entertainment over a meal and has a thing for big cats."

I inwardly groan, wishing that for once, Opal would choose someone else over me. I'm sure I'll have to crawl around the floor and purr like a good big kitty until some fucker pounces and pins me for a bite. I know I headline at Vampire Nights, but I'm exhausted and starving. Alexander will force us to wait to eat until the private party so that his guests have the luxury to do so for us. He doesn't do it to make us feel like we're equals. He does it because apparently many vampires enjoy it like we're some sort of pet, which if we're in leopard print, it's definitely the case. If they feed us, we'll show more attention. Usually, that wouldn't be true, but my stomach growls and I can already bow in defeat at the feet of whoever offers me a bite of whatever. I don't even care.

Opal hugs and kisses everyone but me, and I can't exactly blame her. I don't think she's ever tasted gen. pop. blood, and she has far higher standards than the fuckers that enjoy licking it off of me.

Reaching into her pocket, she pulls out a small foil-wrapped protein bar. I nearly lunge at her but refrain because even though she wouldn't hurt me like Alexander would for being a bit aggressive, I respect her and don't want to get any blood on her tight white dress.

"Eat it slow, my gem. I know you're starving. Just don't tell Alex." She keeps her voice low. The use of her nickname for him, which she only ever uses in private, gets to me. I don't know why, but in this moment, it feels too affectionate, and I'm still pissed at him for only giving me things he knew I hate all because I suggested Knox donate a gift to the staff. I knew that it would go to waste if he gave it to me because I don't get to keep anything. Whatever.

I nod and give Opal air kisses in appreciation. She smiles and motions for me to head toward the showers, and I stuff the bar into my mouth, disobeying her suggestion to eat it slowly. I regret it immediately. Not because it makes me sick, but now I just want more. My stomach burns and complains, making it hard to focus as I cleanse my skin and wash my hair.

The others remain in the showers after I dry off, and I ignore Jasper sneaking past me to fuck Emerald. The two of them celebrate every show with a bang, and I don't know whether to be happy or jealous. I wish I could have the kind of connection they do.

I push the thought away and return to the dressing room. The scent of something savory and buttery wafts through the air, twisting my stomach in hunger. I bow forward, clutching my middle.

"Hey, you." A familiar voice sounds through the room, and I jerk my gaze from the floor and to Sawyer sitting in one of the vanity chairs, his tall frame making it look tiny in comparison to him.

I clutch my towel around my body. "You shouldn't be in here. Master—"

Materializing in front of me, Sawyer cuts off my words with his hand, quieting me down. "I ran into Opal. She mentioned that performers can't deny gifts, so I brought you something for your enthralling finale."

I heave a breath, trying to get my body under control. "You got me a gift?" Why would he do that? What does he get out of it? "I don't understand."

"What's not to understand? You did an incredible

job, and I have the need to give you something for it." Holding up his other hand, he shows me a paper bag with the logo of the Aris Hotel printed on it. The triangular statue looks just like the one I can see from my room window if I crane my neck enough, and it makes up the A while the rest of the letters are in a fancy script, hand-drawn by Opal what seems like forever ago when she talks about it.

"You brought me food." This is a first. It's like the delicious scent wafting around me turns my brain to mush. It doesn't help that my stomach growls uncontrollably. Vampires have given me all sorts of gifts like flowers, jewelry, clothing, and shoes but never food.

He shrugs. "I thought you might be hungry. I know I always am after a workout." His fangs flash with his words, and I can just imagine him guzzling blood, glistening with sweat, and looking...my damn thoughts. Why do I have the sudden urge to see him without a shirt?

"Oh," I whisper, my emotions getting the best of me. "I don't know what to say. I mean, thank you."

He cocks his head and chuckles at my reaction. "You're tearing up? Had I known you'd like this so much, I'd have filled this entire damn room."

I blink my eyes, getting them in control. Laughing in embarrassment, I stretch up and get him to bend closer, so

I can brush my lips to his cheek. "That would be a little much, but the staff would appreciate the leftovers. I'm only allowed to eat so much."

Something strange and indecipherable crosses his expression, but I don't know him well enough to figure out what's going through his mind. Footsteps sound from the concrete hallway, and I hear Alexander yelling into the showers for the others to hurry up.

Sawyer whispers that he'll see me around and vanishes, the haunting sensation of his lips caressing mine sending goosebumps over me. I stare at the closed door, clutching the bag of warm food in my hands. I'm torn between opening it and shoving whatever it is into my mouth or turning it over to Alexander.

My growling stomach wins, and I rush to pull out a buttered rosemary roll sitting on top of a takeout container of some sort of pasta and meat—things I never get much of and something only the personal donors of the wealthiest get to enjoy.

I tear into the roll and moan, the fluffy, warm, light texture so mouthwatering that I shove the whole thing in my mouth, chewing and swallowing as fast as I can. The door swings open, startling me, and Alexander stands in the frame and flares his nostrils. I quickly extend my arm, holding up the bag to him, praying that I've left no crumbs on my face.

"This was a gift from Sawyer for my performance, and he asked to see me eat one of the rolls. Please forgive me. I didn't know what to do." I hang my head, letting my towel loosen and fall from my wet hair. My heart rams against my ribcage under the intensity of Alexander's scrutiny, and I lick my lips and swallow. My stomach now tumbles and threatens to make me sick.

Alexander hums under his breath. "Baby doll, you did fine." His voice remains low as he strolls closer to me. "Don't worry. I'm not angry with you."

I release a breath and tilt my head up to meet his gaze. "Thank you. It was unexpected and after what you said about Knox—"

One second I'm in front of him, and in the next, my back slams against one of the wall mirrors, shattering it with the force. Pain stings my skin, and I gasp, trying to keep my cry from echoing through the room. Alexander extends his fangs and growls in my face, his eyes flashing like crazy.

My body slackens under his stare as he traps me in his mind manipulation. My insides scream, my heart threatening to explode. Fuck. I didn't expect him to get into my head. I should've known better. I wasn't injured, so there was no need to drink his blood. He probably came by for that reason. He always gives us his blood before private affairs. I'm so stupid.

Alexander's eyes turn solid silver, glowing against his ashy complexion. "Hayley, are you lying to me ab—"

"Ruby, I forgot...I'm sorry, Mr. Aris. I forgot that I was still holding the wine. It's as exquisite as she is. I remember it fondly." Sawyer stands in the doorway, holding a glass of red liquid that he hadn't had before.

He offers me a smile and wink, straightening his shoulders when Alexander releases me from his gaze and turns around. The two of them have a silent staring match, and I heave a few breaths, getting myself under control.

"May I watch her enjoy my gifts? I hope this isn't too much of an intrusion." Sawyer lifts an eyebrow, daring Alexander to say something otherwise. I don't know what kind of arrangements they have, but it's something that Alexander doesn't want to fuck up, because he shockingly nods his head.

Straightening his suit jacket, Alexander forces his tight mouth to smile. "Perhaps one sip won't harm her. I don't usually allow alcohol before a private show." Or at all. I've never had anything slightly intoxicating. Or flavored. Water is the only thing I get plenty of.

"You're very generous to allow me such a treat."

Strolling forward, Sawyer trains his eyes on me, drinking me in as I stand in only my towel, my hair now on display. It's like he needs to memorize every inch of my makeup-less face even more so now.

He closes the space completely but doesn't hand me the glass to take. Instead, he holds up the fragrant glass to my mouth and whispers for me to take a soft breath to truly enjoy it. The strong smell overpowers my senses, and I can already imagine what the wine tastes like, the subtle hint of something sweet in the notes almost hypnotic.

Tipping the glass, Sawyer offers me a sip with a smile. The liquid warms my insides, the intoxicating taste lingering on my tongue even after I swallow.

"Thank you," I murmur, offering him a smile. A real one. Something about how he stayed nearby and intercepted what could have been a terrible beating awakens something inside me. "This was very kind of you."

"It's my pleasure." Stroking his finger along my shoulder, he gently touches my burning skin. His finger coats in my blood as he carefully picks out a piece of glass. "I'm sorry if I put you in an unfortunate position with your master. I do hope he realizes how lucky he is to have a woman as stunning as you around."

Alexander growls under his breath, his muscles tensing with Sawyer's jab. "She is my most prized performer, which is why I am strict. I care about her wellbeing." Biting his arm, he steps closer and holds it out to me. "Perhaps this is something for you to think about before offering gifts that could hinder her performance."

Things go from uncomfortable to painful as the two of them act as if this situation isn't about to explode any second. I clasp Alexander's arm and suck his bite mark, saying a silent prayer that nothing happens with me in the middle.

Someone claps their hands, startling me, and I release Alexander and meet Opal's gaze. The other performers stand behind her, devouring the drama unfolding, and I manage to get a couple feet between me and Alexander, taking a second to slide into my vanity chair.

"Take your discussion out of my dressing room. My gems need to get ready." She narrows her eyes at Alexander. "Your clients have checked in at the lobby and require your presence. I'll see to it that we're all set and ready to go upon your call."

Alexander snatches the glass of wine from Sawyer and squishes the bag of food in his grip. "I'll see to it that Mr. Noble's gift waits in your room, baby doll. And don't wear your wig. Our guests want something more natural."

I open my mouth to argue, but Alexander disappears before I have a chance. I'm left staring at my reflection in the mirror. He's punishing me because he can. He's taking the one thing from me that gets me through these private shows.

Now I have nothing. I hate him more than ever.

"I'll leave you in my baby doll's hands, Misters Grey." Alexander offers a short bow and vanishes through the suite door.

I twirl my arms, faking a smile at the gentleman across from me. "I'd love it if you allowed me to show you one of my new dances."

The leader of the Grey Coven grins and nods his head, swiping his sleeve over his blood-stained lips instead of using a napkin. "That sounds like an excellent idea, baby doll." His use of Alexander's pet name for me skeeves me out more than it should. "I've been dying for a close up of your magnificent body."

His coven brother with curly, wild black hair chuckles from his place. He holds up his palms to me and pretends to grab my boobs. "I think your hands are too small for those tits. Maybe she should give me a go first. I could give her a ride that'll put her out of commission for a few days." Extending his fangs in excitement, the bastard winks at me. "What do you say? You look like you could use a vacation."

I blink, trying not to react. All I want to do is gag and run out of here. I'm used to men treating me as an object. I am an object and plaything to them, but Alexander failed to mention his stipulation of what is acceptable.

I run my fingers through my golden brown hair, hating that it's too short and thin to cover my body like the long tresses of my wigs. I can barely hide my reddening face. "As fun as that sounds, Master Aris has rules in place, and I hope you understand that I can't break them." I tilt my head and show off my neck. "How about you take a taste instead? I'd love to feel your lips on my skin."

Mr. Grey turns to his wild-haired brother and narrows his eyes. The two of them share an obvious conversation I can't hear, and I slide my chair back, preparing to get to my feet. Moving faster than I can follow, Mr. Grey towers in front of me and locks his fingers through my hair, yanking my head back and forcing me to look at him. I clench in pain, my eyes watering, and I press my hands to his chest, trying to keep space between us.

"Mr. Grey, there is surveillance in this room," Quartz, the silent male performer, says from his spot in the corner. "I hope—"

Mr. Grey's strong grip releases me, and I struggle to

realize what's unfolding in front of me. Quartz hollers, his yells echoing through the room, and Topaz screams. Blood splashes over her light-colored, leopard-printed costume, staining it muddy-red, and I reach for my fork, my fear instincts raging wild and unbidden, stealing away my good senses and turning my body to survival mode.

"Stop!" I scream, rushing across the small living area. "Stop, you're going to kill him!"

Mr. Grey snarls and whips around, spitting out a hunk of Quartz's flesh. The performer crumples to the floor, and screams ring through the air. Jabbing my hand, I surprise Mr. Grey by stabbing him in the eye with my fork. I screech and scramble away, dodging out of his reach as he charges me. Fear tightens my chest, and I slam into the hard chest of one of his other coven brothers.

A cold hand clamps onto my stomach and the vampire grabs the side strap of my bikini bottoms, tearing the fabric. I shriek and flail, kicking my legs and fighting his strength the best I can.

What the fuck is going on? Where is Alexander?

I then realize that the cameras have been ripped from the walls and another vampire—one of their security guards—blocks the door.

"Be a good little bitch and hold still. If you don't stop fighting, I'll make it hurt. Your master said we can do whatever the fuck we want as long as none of the females die." He growls in my ear and brings his hand up to my throat, cutting off my airway.

I try to open my mouth to scream, but I can't. The edges of my vision shadow, and I focus on the bloody floor. This is beyond punishment. This is cruel torture and the worst thing Alexander has ever put us through.

I tense, feeling the vampire's other hand rip at my other side strap, scratching my skin in the process. Tears burn my eyes, and I hope he kills me before anything else. I won't stop fighting. He's going to destroy me.

A loud gunshot rings through the air, and the vampire roars and drops me to the floor. I hit my palms to the carpet and claw away, rubbing my knees on the coarse material. My hands slap against a pool of blood, and all I can think about is finding somewhere to hide.

"Fucking get down! Don't fight or we'll take all of your damn heads." Something thuds to the carpet, and I whip my attention to Sawyer's bellow as he tosses the head of the Greys' security guard on the floor.

"This is a private party—" The wild-hair Grey coven brother screams, his voice turning from sharp to muddled.

I gawk in shock, my whole body trembling as Knox cuts out the man's tongue and then shoves it back in his mouth and forces it down his throat. Mr. Grey's face turns red, and he snaps his fangs, trying to cough it back up.

"Like I said. Fucking get down!" Sawyer shouts again, aiming his gun at the ceiling. He pulls the trigger, sending dust raining over him. "Time is up, gentlemen."

The coven leader straightens his back, scowling. "Where is Alexander Aris? This was his gift to us. If this was a setup, he will have a huge problem on his hands."

Sawyer flicks his attention to Monroe, pulling a blade from a hidden holster in his jacket. "A problem, huh? Is that what you think? The only problem I see is you thinking you could get away with pulling this kind of bullshit."

"The girls are ours for the night. We have done nothing wrong," Mr. Grey continues to argue. "Now, I'd advise you to leave us be."

Monroe tips his head back and howls a laugh. "Leave you be? Are you shitting me? The only thing I'm going to do is teach you what happens when you think you're some kind of entitled prick who wants to wet his dick in something that doesn't belong to him."

A shadow falls over me, and I flinch in fear. "Hey, Ruby. You okay?" Knox whispers, squatting down beside me. "Here, take my jacket."

The tough leather material engulfs me as he drapes his jacket over my back, covering up my exposed body from my ripped bottoms. He doesn't touch me or try to lift me up, waiting in silence for me to make the first move. Like his closeness screams safety, I hold my arms up and let him help me stand. I find myself pressing into him, hugging him like he's the only one who can ensure protection.

"I'm sorry that asshole hurt you," he murmurs, stroking his palm over my back.

"He tr-tried to rape m-me," I say, my voice shaking. "I didn't want to. That's not in the rules."

Knox growls, easing back to look into my eyes. "He's going to pay for that."

My lip quivers. "No, I will. Master Aris will make my life hell. He didn't even let me wear my wig. He was trying to punish me." I don't know why I say it or why I bring it up, but it's like I need to say the words out loud, so I know that it's not in my head. "I'm dead. He's going to take my final donation."

Knox intakes a sharp breath, his eyes flashing silver with his anger. It wouldn't be the first time Alexander drained a performer. Even though I'm a headliner, it doesn't make me safe. It makes things harder. Every one of us is replaceable. My mom is the biggest example. She used to be a performer before she had me. I can't remember much about her, but Opal keeps a collection of pictures in her room of all of the past performers. All I know is that she did something that tested Alexander too much. It's one of the reasons why I carry this life-long fear.

"Can you stand okay?" Knox asks, turning his attention to watch Sawyer and Monroe force all of the vampires into a line against the wall.

Even though there are seven of them—the Greys and what's left of their security—they don't fight. The Bella Crew must be more powerful if that's the case. No vampire ever backs down otherwise.

I bob my head and ease away, showing him that I won't fall over in hysterics. Now that I've caught my breath, my body turns numb to everything. My mind shuts down, and all I can think about is the sensation of sticky blood under my feet.

"Go to the others and wait in the room. We'll be done and get you out of here real quick." Knox motions to the archway leading to the suite bedroom.

Topaz and Emerald cling to each other, their shoulders shaking with their silent sobs. Quartz's dead body remains on the floor a few feet away, and Pyrite kneels beside his fallen friend. I swivel on my feet and meet Knox's gaze, shaking my head. I don't want to go to the room. I want to stay here with him.

"I want to stay," I whisper, looking past him at Sawyer and Monroe glowering at the group of vampires. Shifting, I flick my fingers at the others. "Go into the room and call Opal, okay?"

Topaz and Emerald grab onto Pyrite and pull him with them, closing the bedroom door and cutting them off. I wring my hands together, feeling the heat of everyone's gazes on me. Tugging the jacket closed, I inhale a soft breath of Knox's scent, letting it settle my nerves.

"You sure you want to be here, little bird? You know what happens when someone fucks up and does something we don't like," Monroe says, raising his eyebrow.

I swallow and dip my chin. Raising my hand, I point at the fucker who tried to rape me. "I want to see him pay for what he tried to do to me." I don't know where the demand comes from, but letting the words fill the air lessens the tightness in my chest. "I want them all to pay for what they did to our friend."

"You've got to be kidding me!" the coven leader hollers. "You're not going to take commands from a fucking donor, are you?"

Sawyer hands his gun to Monroe and pulls out a blade from his belt. "No, we're not. What we're going to do is give our girl what she wants. If she wants to see you pay, she will get the show of her life."

Growls echo through the air in response.

"You fuck—"

Swinging his arm, Sawyer jams his blade into the chest of the closest security guard and sends his heart splattering to the floor out of his back. Silence fills the air as Sawyer pulls the knife back, letting the blood drip onto the carpet.

I can't stop my head from nodding in approval. I shouldn't enjoy watching a vampire die, but something about Sawyer doing it on my behalf sends my mind whirling. What if this is his way to give Alexander a message. He called me their girl, and it's strange and exciting to even think about it. I have so many questions and thoughts, but right now, all I can think about is wanting to see them unleash their power and wrath on this disgusting coven. I've never had someone stand up for me like this before. Why do they anyway? I don't fucking care. I'll do anything for them.

"Next one of you fuckers who tries to talk or argue will lose your head. Do you understand?" Sawyer says, aiming his knife at the throat of the vampire who tried to rape me. "Do I make myself clear?"

No one responds.

Monroe aims Sawyer's gun and shoots a security guard in his leg, making him holler. The fact that they go after the hired help doesn't go unnoticed to me. I know they're doing it for a reason, but I don't know why.

"Yes," they all say, stiffening and breaking their scowls under Monroe's closeness.

He grins wickedly, his handsome smile lighting up his golden eyes. Rubbing his hand down his thick beard, he says, "That's what we want to hear."

Knox touches his hand to my lower back, guiding me to walk with him and closer to the Grey Coven. Even scowling, he's attractive—maybe more so because his features sharpen in a way that accentuates his jaw and cheekbones. I drag my bare feet, my human fear instincts screaming like crazy to run away. I would do as much if Knox didn't slide his fingers through mine and pull me close.

"Now, who's up first? Which one of you fucking assholes thought he could get away with putting his hands on my vixen?" Knox asks, knowing exactly who it is. I think he wants the guy to admit it. I want the fuckhead to admit it too. I want to see him cry and sweat and regret everything.

Silence fills the air.

"You better give yourself up and beg our girl for mercy. If you don't, every damn one of you will be taking your cocks home in a to-go bag." Sawyer slaps the bloody blade to his palm. "We're not joking. You need to learn a damn lesson. The Bella Crew doesn't tolerate rapists. I don't give a fuck if you thought you had the go-ahead from Aris."

"Pfft, that's not enough, Sawyer," Monroe says, getting close to the guy who tried to rape me. "A to-go bag? Nah, dude. They will take each other's cocks home in their asses to shit out later."

Wow, is he twisted.

I stare in stunned silence.

I never thought I'd want to agree with something that sounds so awful, but I want the fucker to pay.

"Is that good enough for you, little bird? I can be creative," Monroe says, smiling again. He's far too happy planning his punishment, but I love how excited and sexy he looks, ready to cut a dick on my behalf.

I nod my head, my mouth still refusing to speak. All I can do is hug my arm around my waist and clutch Knox's hand, using him to keep myself from wobbling on my weak knees.

"Last chance, fuckers," Sawyer says, aiming his knife at the coven leader's groin.

"Damn it, Cornelius! I'm not losing my fucking dick because you can't keep yourself together and accept the damn consequences for your need to ruin every donor you put your sights on, you son-of-a-bitch," the coven leader snaps, swinging his arm to punch the asshole in the gut.

He turns to Sawyer. "I'll fucking hold him still if you promise not to take mine. Please. Not all of us are demented rapists. I don't need to flex my damn control and power over a pussy to feel like a man. I just wanted blood. We never get live donors."

This bastard. I hate them all.

Sawyer glances in my direction, but I don't react. My muscles tighten and flex, and all I can do is watch the coven leader grab his brother's pants, rip them down to show his flaccid cock, and then grab him from behind, pinning him to show he was serious.

Cornelius hollers and yells, thrashing his body, swinging his sad excuse for a dick like a mini-propeller. Gnashing his fangs, he tries to bite at anything and everything, but he's not strong enough to break his brother's hold.

"Hey Ruby, would you like to do the honors?" Sawyer asks, stepping on one of Cornelius's dress shoes to stop him from kicking one of his legs.

I gape, my mind whirling. Do I want to see the fucker punished? Hell yes. Do I want to get anywhere near his naked body? Hard pass.

I crinkle my nose. "I can't. They'll blame me."

"Fuck no, they won't, but I get it. Don't worry. I got you. I'll touch this nasty dick on your behalf." Sawyer winks at me and turns back to Cornelius.

The asshole vampire won't give up, and it takes Monroe stepping on his other foot to restrain him. I can't take my eyes off the vampire's naked junk. Knox stares at the side of my face, watching me watch his two friends as they get ready to do something crazy. Something I can't even process. You have to be twisted as fuck to come up with a punishment like this. I realize that their brand of crazy gets to me in a good way. If I hadn't had a moment to just be near them and see their civility, I might be freaked out. Sick even. Now? I just want Sawyer to hurry up. I want that dick to stop whirling in circles. I want to hear the sound of the bastard's pain.

My feet take on a mind of their own, and I shuffle closer, tugging Knox with me. He hugs his arm around me like he's preparing for me to lose my mind when Sawyer follows through. The other vampires stand in stiff silence, bracing for what surely is one of the worst things that they think could happen to them.

Wiggling his fingers, Sawyer grabs Cornelius's cock and stretches it. He screams at a pitch so intense that I flinch. Monroe whips Cornelius's belt off of him and shoves it in his mouth, trying to gag him. I squeeze Knox's hand tighter until he gets me to hug his side instead.

Sawyer tips his head back and laughs, releasing his grip on Cornelius's cock. "You're such a fuckhead. Did you just shit yourself?"

Cornelius heaves a few breaths, his fear turning into relief when he realizes Sawyer let him go. I've never seen a vampire cry, and I don't know how I feel about it. And the fact that Sawyer doesn't cut off—

Moving faster than I can keep up with, Sawyer yanks Cornelius's cock again and swipes his sharp blade through the shaft. Blood pours from the severed member, and Cornelius screeches and thrashes, bucking his body until he manages to look down at the one-inch bloody nub and passes out.

"Be fucking thankful I left you with an angry inch and your damn balls," Sawyer snaps, kicking the unconscious vampire in the stomach. Waving the severed dick, he whacks the Grey coven leader in the face, leaving a bloody mark on his cheek. "If I ever see you guys around here again, it'll be more than your dicks that you'll need to worry about. Now take your damn brother and guards, and get the fuck out of here. Leave Aris out of it. Understand?"

"Yes," Mr. Grey says, motioning to the other to grab Cornelius and the dead guards. "May I take my brother's member?"

Sawyer scoffs and holds it out. Closing his hand, he uses his vampire strength to crush it into a pile of guts. He flicks them into the coven leader's face with a laugh. "That's the best I'm giving you. Now take the back way from the hotel. Monroe will see you out."

The vampire coven disappears along with Monroe, leaving me alone with Knox and Sawyer. The two of them drink me in without saying a word. I struggle to put my thoughts together. I can barely grasp what just happened.

And then my gaze lands on Quartz's body.

"How could Master Aris let this happen?" I murmur, pulling away from Knox. "What did we do to deserve this? I don't understand."

"Ruby?" Knox says softly, remaining by my side.

I finally manage to break my stare from Quartz. "It's Hayley. My real name is Hayley."

"Hayley," both Knox and Sawyer say in unison, repeating it to me as if discovering that my name isn't actually Ruby is the wildest thing of the night.

"It won't be like this forever," Knox says, stroking his fingers on my arms.

I laugh. I can't help it. His comment is the most ridiculous thing I've ever heard. "Yes, it will. This is my life. It's only going to get worse." Because now that I'm out of immediate danger, I realize just how bad this situation is. "Alexander set me up for punishment. He's been especially hard on me lately, and while I appreciate what you've done...I'm terrified. I don't know what the hell I'm going to do. He's going to murder me. He'll blame me."

Knox growls under his breath. "It wasn't your fault."

"None of this would've happened had I minded my place and done as I was told despite everything." It's how I was raised. Shut up. Keep my eyes down. Obey. Know who owns me. It's those things I should've just gone with. "If Alexander finds out you guys did this on my behalf..." I can't even think about it. Tears burn my eyes, and I cover my face with my hands.

"What are you talking about? We didn't do shit for you. These assholes had a debt with the Bella Crew," Sawyer says, his voice deep and serious. I almost believe his lie.

I sniffle and wipe my hands to my cheeks. "He can open our minds. He'll find out."

Sawyer and Knox glance at each other, remaining expressionless. They converse in silence as they let my words sink in.

Sawyer's jaw twitches. "Then I'll make sure he can't. Mind manipulation is my specialty."

My heart pounds in my chest, crashing hard enough I think it might break free and throw itself at the vampire. "You're going to erase my memory?"

"And the other performers'...if that's okay," Sawyer says, meeting my gaze. "They will only think that the

Greys killed your friend and then ran because they were afraid."

"Will you make me forget all of this?" I wave my hand around. "Please? I just want to forget this night ever happened."

Sawyer glances at Knox again and the both of them nod in agreement. Knox takes my hand and says, "If that's what you want."

I bob my head. "I do."

Cupping my face too quickly to react, Sawyer leans in, filling my vision with his handsome face. Knox remains close, holding my slackening body, and I lose myself in Sawyer's sky blue eyes, a few shades lighter than Knox's.

"Don't break my gaze," Sawyer commands, his eyes turning silver.

The world melts away.

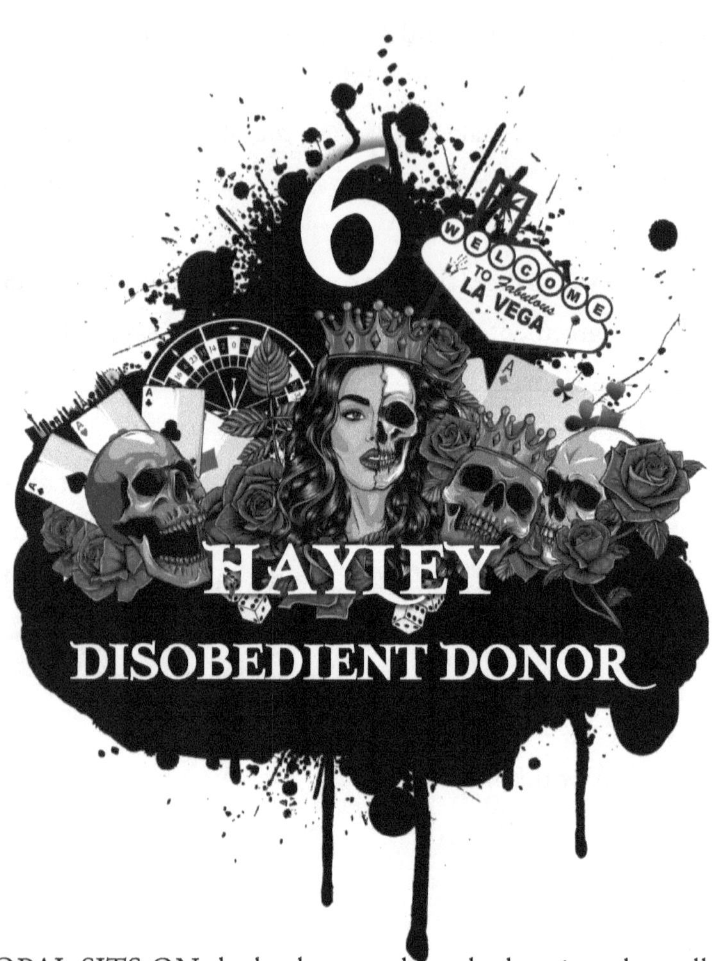

OPAL SITS ON the leather couch pushed against the wall of the huge gym we practice our routines in every day. Her eyes shine red and tears leave streaks down her usually perfect makeup. She was the one to find us around Quartz's dead body, and I'll never forget her reaction. She's always been so strong, but losing Quartz was harder on her than us. He's only been part of our performance a year. She knew him longer because she spends every day with the donor children for fun and she chose him to join us. My heart hurts for her.

I'm just thankful the private performance didn't turn out worse than that. Opal said there was a glitch in the security feeds. I'm lucky the Greys ran when they did. Quartz's death saved me from one of the bastards. He ripped my bottoms and wanted more than I was willing to give.

I shudder at the thought.

I still can't believe that Alexander's guests had the nerve to disobey him and get too rowdy with us or that he isn't as upset as Opal. He basically reminded us that shit happens and we're resilient. The show must always go on...but maybe tomorrow.

This is the fourth time in the last five years for a show to ever be canceled. I'm sure the whole hotel and Strip could hear Opal and Alexander fighting, but he finally relented, chalking things up to the fact that the new guy needs training.

And while Alexander was quick to replace Quartz in the show with another guy, who still looks like a teen, Opal grieves. I'm glad she stood up to Alexander about everything. I've never seen her so angry and reactive, but it was enough to get him to leave her in control of what happens tonight.

If only she wasn't crying. I don't know what else to do for her besides trying my best in rehearsal.

I adjust my harness and stare at the top of the silk rope where Mya stretches her legs into the splits. She looks stunning above me, gracefully spinning and moving as if the rope is a part of her very being. The others practice a floor routine, and I prepare to scale up the rope to join my best friend.

"All right, my gems. I think we've had enough for the day. Great job, everyone." Opal's voice hitches, and she remains in her seat. She's usually hands-on in her directions, but losing one of her gems hurts her as much as it hurts all of us. "I want you to spend the rest of the night doing anything you want. Just stay out of trouble, okay?"

I frown at her words. I can do anything I want? The others look as confused as I am, because we have a schedule.

"Go swimming. Play with the kids. Walk the casino. Do something to keep your minds off this bullshit, okay?" Opal adds. Whoa. I can't believe it. We're usually told to remain in our rooms.

Mya slides down the silk rope and lands on her feet. "You sure you don't want us to stay?"

"Nope. Master Alexander is gone, and you should enjoy a bit of freedom. You deserve it after everything." Opal shifts her gaze to me and purses her lips. "I have some arrangements to make and will be within reach if you need anything. Just love up on each other for me, okay?"

Extending her arms, she waits for each of us to give her a hug. She spends an extra minute with Pyrite, and the two of them cry in silence. I blink the tears from my eyes and turn away, not wanting to intrude on a moment where they need each other. Quartz was Pyrite's best friend. They have been inseparable since Quartz joined our team.

"I don't know about you, but I love the idea of going to the pool and soaking in the hot tub," Mya says, draping her arm around my shoulders. "Want to join me? Maybe there will be someone hot to flirt with."

I smirk at her and shrug my shoulders. "Yeah, sure. That could be fun."

There once was a time where the pool and hot tub were outside, and humans could enjoy lounging in the sun. But then all humans turned into blood donors, and Alexander remodeled, enclosing all hotel amenities to be safe for vampires. It's always weird for me to see old pictures of the Aris Hotel. But the walls of tinted glass do help make it feel like we're outside. I've never been, so it's not like I miss it. I'd probably burn the same as a vampire in the sun's rays.

"Could be? Come on. It will be amazing." Mya guides me toward the showers to get cleaned up. "I know exactly what we can wear." We don't have bathing suits, but we have plenty of costumes that can withstand getting drenched in blood, so it's easy enough to pick some similar.

"You want to look good enough to eat, don't you?" I say, laughing.

I raise my eyebrows at her devious smile. When Mya's given an inch, she will take a mile. But it's easier for her. She purposely doesn't show off to ensure she never gets a solo part of the performance and just adapts to every situation thrown at her. It helps that she chose to join the show. Unlike me, who was born into it, she traded her freedom to ensure her family would be safe. That's where we're different. She had the choice. As for me? I don't even know what that feels like. Everyone's always made the decisions for me.

"Hell yeah. We never get to have fun with someone we like. And who knows? Maybe there will be a hot personal donor one of us can entertain." Mya drags me faster to the showers, and she rushes to rinse off and change.

Handing me a black, rhinestone-studded one-piece,

we both change and fly together from the gym. She grins at me the whole time we race through a short section of the lobby, surely gaining everyone's attention, but I keep my gaze trained at the floor, refusing to look around.

"You have no idea how nice it is to hear you laugh, Hayley. It feels like it's been forever," Mya says, slowing down as we reach the glass door to the pool.

I sigh a small breath, trying to maintain my smile. "It's been a weird few days."

"Alexander has been tough on you," she mentions, hooking her elbow with mine. "I think those new guys get under his skin. I overheard him talking to Opal last night, and he fears that you've given them the wrong impression."

I cock my head and look at her. "I've only been doing what I was told. I knew he was punishing me. He wouldn't let me wear my wig last night."

Mya blinks, her eyes widening with my words. She knows what wearing my wig means to me, and the fact that I couldn't channel my alter-ego made last night even worse. It's easier to think of things happening to Ruby and not me.

"Oh, babe. I'm sorry. I had no idea," she says, throwing her arms around me. "Maybe there's something I can do to get his focus off you."

I slouch my shoulders, not wanting her to take any heat from Alexander on my behalf. "I—"

A figure materializes behind Mya, startling the comment from my mouth. I take an automatic step back, my fear triggering Mya to turn around. Her body relaxes at the sight of the vampire, and she tosses her pretty ginger hair over her shoulder.

"Oh, hey! I didn't know you'd be here, Govan," Mya says, her voice turning sweeter. She boldly reaches out and caresses his arm with her fingers.

"I saw you leaving the gym. Had to fight off a dozen assholes who were trying to follow you." The vampire, who I recognize from the Bella Crew, smiles with his teasing words. Usually, a line like that wouldn't be serious, but it might actually be true. Vampires love a chase, and we were running. "Did Alexander loosen your chain a bit? Please tell me yes."

Tipping her head back, Mya giggles. She reaches for his hand and swings it back and forth. "Only if you tell me you have a friend with you. This is our first night off in over a year, and I'm not the only one in need of entertainment."

My heart skips, my muscles tensing. She's talking about me. Shaking my head, I say, "I'm good. I don't need you to call a friend or whatever."

Govan doesn't turn his attention to me, practically ignoring my existence. His eyes flick behind me, and I sense someone staring at my back.

"She's right about that. I've got my girl covered." Cool arms drape over my shoulders from behind as Sawyer's familiar scent washes over me. His vanilla-citrus fragrance helps relax my nerves, and I can't stop the excitement washing through me as I remember how he brought me food after the last show.

I tip my head back and look up at his tall frame. He smiles down at me, showing off his fangs, and something strange washes through me. It's hard to explain, but it's like my attraction is twice as much as yesterday. I shouldn't even be feeling this way, especially after giving Knox a blow job. The last thing I need is to find myself in the middle of a feud.

"Your girl, huh?" I ask, teasing him with a smile. "Don't let anyone hear you. Master Aris would punch your dick or something." The 'or something' meaning that he'd probably take out his anger on me. I regret saying the comment, because instead of taking it lightheartedly, Sawyer's blue eyes darken and he scowls.

"He'd regret trying," he mutters, tightening his arms around me.

Mya's brows scrunch together, and she shifts awkwardly on her feet. This went from playful to dark real fast. Forcing herself to laugh, she draws my attention away from Sawyer. "Relax, Ruby. You heard Opal. Alexander isn't here. Let's just have some fun. These guys are tough. Isn't that right, Govan?" She flutters her lashes at the vampire and winks.

"Damn straight." Swinging his arms, he surprises her by picking her up and tossing her on his shoulder. "Now come on. I want to get you wet."

Her laughter at his innuendo echoes through the quiet pool house until a splash cuts off her voice. It's now that I realize the place is empty. There are usually at least a dozen vampires with donors hanging around, but I don't even see the pool staff.

Sawyer moves and stands in front of me, blocking my view of the rows of empty lounge chairs. He reaches out and touches my cheek. "I hope it's okay if I'm here. I wanted to apologize for last night after the show. I didn't mean to piss Aris off. I heard what your friend said, Hayley."

Goosebumps prickle over my skin. He knows my real name. How the fuck does he know my real name? I've never told him.

"I want you to know that you don't have to worry about him either," he adds. His blue eyes capture mine, drawing me in.

Something strange blossoms through me the longer I stare into his blue depths, and I feel as if he's looked at me like this before. My muscles slacken, and a small blip of panic ignites inside me. He's getting into my head. Fuck. What the fuck?

Leaning closer, he whispers, "Remember for me."

Like a bunch of missing pieces click into place, I blink as memories flood back to me. The blur of a night surrounding Quartz's death clears, and I gasp and clutch Sawyer's cheeks, sharing his breathing space. My heart beats erratically—my mind and body trying to catch up with each other. He saved me. Knox and Monroe too. I asked them to wipe my mind, so Alexander couldn't get into my head, but it looks like he made it so that he could bring the memory back.

"Sawyer," I whisper, pressing my fingers harder into his skin.

"I didn't want you to lose everything from last night, so I only put a block in place that I can remove...though I erased all the terror you felt. You shouldn't have to live with that." His hand travels over my side and to my lower back, pulling me flush against him. "You're my girl. I already struggle not to steal you away."

I lick my lips, his admission of his possessiveness

sending a wave of mixed emotions through me. I know I should correct him, because he doesn't own me and never will. Alexander would ensure it. Another part of me wishes that he did own me. I wouldn't mind it. He's shown me what it's like to be under his protection. It's addicting almost, knowing what he and the Bella Crew would do on my behalf. I want them to destroy every asshole for me.

But would they really?

I don't even know. We've only met a short time ago.

"I wish." Something intense comes over me, and I stretch up and close the space completely, brushing my lips to his.

He reacts with a moan, sliding his hand lower until he grabs my ass, sending tingles through my body. I part my lips open, inviting him to glide his tongue into my mouth, and he kisses me deeper. I comb my fingers into his hair, loving how soft his strands are. Kissing him is like kissing someone who wants to give me more than they take, because his sensuous kiss is more passionate than demanding, and so full of desire that I feel his cock hardening against my pelvis.

I automatically reach between us and stroke my hand over his shaft, feeling the thickness of his girth. He's bigger than Knox, thicker too, and I shouldn't have expected anything less considering how tall and broad and buff he is.

He moans softly, taking my hand and lacing his fingers through mine. "Hayley, you don't have to do that."

I ease away, frowning in confusion. No one ever stops my wandering hands, and I want him to feel as good as he makes me feel. "But you like it."

He chuckles and grins, his handsome face lighting up. "I fucking love it, but it still doesn't mean you have to do anything. I'm not expecting you to."

I can't stop the smile from crossing my mouth at his admission.

"What?" he asks, the soft features of his desire hiding the cruel protector he is for me.

He cut a dick off and threatened a coven on my behalf and without asking for anything in return. I couldn't have asked for a better punishment for the asshole who tried to hurt me. And while I still feel bad about the knowledge, he is right about not feeling the terror. Alexander would make me live with it. Sawyer wants to protect me not only in body but also in mind. I can't help wanting to do something more for him.

I shrug. "Nothing. It's just...you're different. For once I want to do this, and you deny me. Everyone expects this from me and doesn't complain. Well, except Knox didn't want me to do anything either. Is this some kind of law with your crew?" The second I mention Knox, I regret it.

Sawyer's jaw tightens. "You like him, don't you?" It must be a big deal if he doesn't mention the other stuff I said.

I consider lying like I always do when a man asks me something I know he won't like the answer to, but with Sawyer, I decide to be honest. It's too dangerous to lie when he can open my mind. Also because I've seen him more than any of Alexander's clients and guests within a week's time.

"I do, yeah. But I also like you." I might as well be honest about everything while I'm at it. "...and Monroe. I've never met anyone like you guys."

Something shifts in his expression, but he doesn't get angry. If anything, his features soften even more. He chuckles and shakes his head with whatever thought crosses his mind. "I want so badly to beat the shit out of them and keep you all to myself, but I also don't want to hurt your feelings. This is confusing as fuck."

How do I respond to that? "Oh." It's like my brain wants me to stay silent in case.

Groaning, he kisses me again. "I won't ever hurt them though. Not because of my interest in you. They're like my coven brothers even if we can't form an official alliance because of the fucking ruling vampires and the La Vega

Leadership." Leadership? I don't think I've heard of them before.

"Oh." Come the fuck on, stupid brain. He's going to think something is wrong with me if I can't articulate my thoughts. I kiss him again to give me an extra moment to figure out what to say, and I meet his gaze again. "I'm glad to hear that. I wouldn't want to get between you guys and risk getting kill..." Okay, bitch brain.

My comment sends silver flashing in his eyes, but he doesn't scowl. He surprises me by laughing.

"If you were in between us, killing you is the last thing that would happen," he murmurs, squeezing my ass again. "If anything, we'll never let you leave."

Holy shit.

My body hums at his words, and warmth blossoms up my chest and neck. His smile widens at my reaction, and he touches my heated skin with his cool fingers. I bite my bottom lip between my teeth and squirm under the intensity of his gaze.

"You'd like that, wouldn't you," he murmurs, his eyes flashing silver again.

My muscles relax as he taps into my mind again. "Yes," I say, my mouth speaking without my mind's consent. "I feel safe with you three."

He breaks my stare and shakes his head, pulling away

to put space between us. Turning his back on me, he laces his fingers through his hair and stares at Mya and Govan splashing in the pool.

I close the distance again and touch his shoulder. He spins around, and I automatically recoil, my chest tightening. I can't help it. It's instinctual for me to try to protect myself when a vampire moves that fast.

"Fuck, I'm sorry, Hayley. I wasn't going to hurt you." Sawyer slowly reaches out and touches my hand. "I wouldn't."

My lip quivers as I try to get myself under control, but it's hard once something sets me off.

"I just—I want you. I want to steal you away from Fucker Aris and keep you safe and treat you like my queen. I can't explain it without sounding like a psycho. It's just that there is something about you that gets under my skin and won't let me go." He tightens his jaw and flicks his gaze past me. "You make me want to do stupid ass shit, and it pisses me off that I can't. I just—I have to go. I'm sorry. If I stay, I'll do something crazy."

Sawyer kisses me again, cutting off my chance to ask him to stay. He disappears, leaving me standing alone and confused. Mya cocks her head at me, watching me peer around at the space in front of me like if I stare long enough, Sawyer will come back.

"Hayley, come join us!" Mya calls, waving her hands in the air.

I shake my head and turn around to leave. Why do I feel so rejected? I know better than to let him get to me like this. I belong to the Aris Hotel. I shouldn't even consider going out of my way to spend time with a man that could cause my end—not by his hands but by Alexander's.

Peering around once more, I head toward the entrance to the casino. I don't want to bring Mya down or make her come with me.

If only a shadow didn't move from the real trees beside me. I don't have a chance to react as someone covers my head with a bag. Strong fingers grab onto me, and I'm stolen away.

I'M GOING TO DIE.

I can feel it in my body and soul. My mind races as my stomach flips, threatening to make me sick. No one tries to stop whoever relocates me. If they notice, they don't care. They're letting this asshole get away with me.

"If you try to fight or scream, Ms. Aris, I was instructed to gag and restrain you for transportation." The strange voice instills dread in my core. "Please know that I don't want to hurt you."

I heave a few breaths, my silent sobs racking through me. Who instructed him? What's going on?

And then the strangest thing happens. The air turns from warm to cold and then the man sets me onto some sort of leather bench. Voices and loud music echo around me for a second, and then something booms, cutting off the noise. Maybe a door shutting? It sounds different.

Someone sits beside me, touching their knees to my leg. The vampire yanks my hair as he pulls off the cloth bag, finally letting me see what the fuck is going on. I tense at the tinted windows around me. We're in a limo. A fucking limo. I've only seen these vehicles from high above in my tower.

I gasp and cling onto the seat, looking for anything to grab ahold of. The driver, hidden behind a painted partition stomps the throttle, sending the limo barreling forward down the busy street of the strip. There are very few other cars on the road, because not many vampires own them and it's illegal for a donor to drive. I tense as the driver doesn't even swerve as the Strip dwellers scramble to get off the street and out of the way.

"Ms. Aris, I apologize for frightening you, but it was imperative to remove you from the hotel without notice.

Mr. Aris noted that there would be problems otherwise due to some interest you've gained recently." The man shifts beside me, his movements stealing my attention from the outside world.

It's hard for my mind to grasp what's going on.

"Mr. Aris would've brought you himself, but to ensure the safety of The Pala's staff, he advised this was better. Mr. Pala agreed. It's not often that performers are given this kind of opportunity, and you will do your master proud, bringing in extra stipends and blood through the new alliance between him and Pala." The vampire offers me a smile, keeping his fangs in check. He adjusts his navy tie and loosens it around his collar.

I just gawk at him, trying to process his words. A new opportunity and alliance? More stipends and blood? What the hell is going on? No one told me anything, and I wonder if Opal knew of this plan. She would have surely put a stop to whatever the fuck this is.

"I don't understand. Have I been sold?" I try not to react, keeping my gaze on my glittery nail polish. "How far is The Pala? I've never heard of it."

The vampire chuckles. "Sold? No. You are quite the commodity. Consider yourself to have been...rented. You will be traveling to The Pala for twenty-four hours once a week. Mr. Pala will be pleased to bring in more guests with you."

I release a breath. I thought Alexander sold me and didn't give me the chance to say goodbye to anyone. I wouldn't put it past him. He's been pissed at me lately. Now that I know I'm not, I relax a bit in my seat. The Strip looks even more incredible from the ground, the lights of so many different hotels dazzling me. I don't even notice most of the Strip dwellers because we move too fast. Mya is going to freak when she finds out that I got to leave.

The limo comes to a stop at a magnificent entrance to a hotel as pristine as the Aris Hotel, and a donor man in a black uniform opens the limo door. His eyes dart to me and then to the ground, his surprise prevalent in his expression. I doubt he expected to open the door to find a female in a tight glittery costume.

The vampire growls and snaps at the startled donor, and he rushes away and vanishes through a door off to the side of the building. Composing himself, the vampire offers me a smile and steps out first, extending his hand to me to help me.

Dozens of loitering vampires stare in my direction—most of them dirty and unkempt, clearly Strip dwellers who survive on credit and violence to get by. I drop my gaze to the ground, my fear over the sudden attention stabbing right into me. I'm usually fine under hundreds of vampires' scrutiny, but out here somewhere unfamiliar? No fucking way. I really wish I hadn't been taken in this damn tiny costume. It could've been worse though. Mya could've given me a G-string and mesh topped outfit.

"You are safe, Ms. Aris. The guests are only excited to see you." The vampire strides forward, tugging me along.

Another donor in the same uniform as the guy that ran away opens the door to the hotel. He greets the vampire with a smile, but keeps his gaze on the floor. "Welcome back, Mr. Perry. I hope you've had a lovely night on the town."

Perry grins and pats the donor on the shoulder. "You bet. I got to escort this magnificent woman here on Mr. Pala's behalf."

I force myself to smile, trying not to look around too much. Voices murmur in the grand space, more sleek and luxurious with a water display and an open lobby with a view of several floors. I don't know what the rules are here or what is expected from me. Every vampire that controls a hotel has their own laws.

"Lovely," the donor responds. "Do have a good day."

Perry nods again and guides me along and past the huge monument of the word 'love.' It was obviously from the back-world and unchanged like the rest of the lobby.

We enter a red-carpeted casino, humming with catchy slot-machine tunes and glittering with flashing lights. Music pulsates through the air, and I recognize one of the songs. I can't stop myself from swaying along to the beat. It keeps my mind off of all of the hotel guests acting as if they've never laid their eyes on a woman before. I'm sure there are some around here. Every hotel has their own donor population, and a hotel would fail without them. With women, new donors can and will be born. I hate to think about it, but that's one of the few things that keeps donor women alive. Vampires are protective of those who can help expand their blood source population.

"There are just a few rules for you around here, Ruby," Perry says, swinging my hand to get my attention. "Do not interact with any guest who doesn't carry a platinum card. They are our best and most well-respected guests. They need to feel their importance."

I nod my head. That's not so different than one of Alexander's rules.

"You must also do as you're told. The only thing off-limits is sexual acts, so if a guest tries to initiate it, you will hit this button on your com device." Perry shows me a diamond bracelet with a deep ruby inlaid in the center. "This will alert your floor staff, so they can intervene to make the proper arrangements. You do not work for free.

We understand how charming and attractive many of our guests are, but it is in the contract that any private time must be paid for. Do you understand?"

My body cools at his words. Is he insinuating what I think he is? It sounds like I can be bossed around up until they demand sex, and if they do, they have the option to buy it with me. No fucking way. It's one thing to feed some of Alexander's guests and occasionally give a hand job or to suck them off. But sex? No. "That's not one of my duties at the Aris Hotel. I'm a stage performer. I thought I'd be doing that."

Perry scrunches his brows and chuckles. "Might I remind you that you're under Mr. Pala's control for the next twenty-four hours? You do what we say, and if you disagree, we will make you. This is not open for discussion. Mr. Pala paid an exponential amount to acquire you, and he expects a return on his investment. You will perform, show our guests a good time, and keep your mouth shut."

Oh no. Oh fuck.

I thought Alexander could be bad, but whoever Mr. Pala is sounds so much worse. My stomach twists at the thought. I can't do this. I can't just let a bunch of vampires think they can do as they please with my body. Alexander's clients could be pushy, but up until the Greys, it's been more social. This sounds like it'll be my job to let a bunch of wealthy vampires fuck me one after another.

I clench my jaw, a million thoughts rushing through my mind. Tightening my hands into fists, I bite my nails into my palms. "I understand," I whisper, feeling as if my world crashes around me.

Twenty-four hours. I have to live with this for twenty-four hours a week. I can...I can't fucking do this.

I summon my bravery and jerk my gaze from the floor to peer around. I'm about twenty feet from the archway to the lobby leading to the exit. If I make a run for it—what the fuck am I thinking? I'll never make it. If I try, he'll do something to me. I know it.

So I start sobbing. I can't help it.

Tears burn my eyes, and I gasp in breath after breath. What have I done to deserve this? It seems like I'm asking myself that question more frequently. My voice echoes over the music, drawing even more attention. A couple vampires leave their seats at the slot machines and shift closer, treating me like I'm a spectacle for their entertainment. And technically, I am.

"Aw, baby. Whatcha crying about? Come to daddy. I'll give you something to truly cry about," a gruff, older-looking vampire says. Streaks of gray highlight his black hair. "It seems like you got yourself a naughty girl, Perry. Do you want my belt? She looks like she needs it."

Another vampire chuckles. "I'd love to see that. I'd pay for it."

What? I can't believe what they're saying. It's like the room of vampires turn into sadists, now getting off on the idea of seeing someone beat me.

"Gentlemen!" a booming voice yells through the air. "Come one, come all. You look like you're enjoying the sneak peek of our upcoming show."

Someone whistles, the ear-piercing sound ringing through the air. "Fuck yeah!"

A short, bald vampire pushes through the crowd, using a glittering, jewel-encrusted cane like a scepter. He grins, his fangs extending, and his gaze narrows on me. I recognize him. I've seen him before at the Aris Hotel. I might have even participated in a private dinner with this vampire.

And what I can recall of him, I know he's a perv and was always expecting more than just blood. I've fortunately never been in that position with him. Garnet has a thing for men like him and always volunteered.

"I'd love to introduce you all to Nasty Natalie, our bratty, in need of punishment, little bitch who needs to learn her place and how to be your good girl." Mr. Pala steps closer and towers over me, meeting my gaze.

My heart falters the second I realize what's happening. He captures me in his manipulative gaze and leers, showing off his fangs. My muscles seize under his eyes, and my whole body screams to look away, to fight, to do anything to see to it that he doesn't get into my head.

"Stop crying," he mutters under his breath, his command stealing my freewill and replacing it with his own.

My eyes dry as my tears stop, and though agony clutches my chest and I still feel like I'm on the verge of dying, my body doesn't give it away.

"Now, now, Nasty Natalie. Our guests want to see you punished for your bad behavior. We've welcomed you into our beautiful home, and you don't appreciate everything we have to offer. Nasty girls get the cane. Do you understand?" Mr. Pala's sadistic grin widens, and he releases his hold on me, sending me sprawling to my knees.

I don't get a chance to brace myself as something hard smacks my ass, and I fall forward onto my hands. Laughter and hollers fill the air, the crowd going wild. Mr. Pala pumps his fists and twirls his cane, pretending to swing it like a bat. I can't cry or do anything, my mind foggy despite him releasing me from his manipulative glare.

"What do you think? Was that good enough?" he asks the crowd.

"No!" the crowd shouts. Men laugh and play fight each other, moving in closer and closer to me.

Mr. Pala thuds his cane to the floor in front of me and touches it to my chin, forcing my head up. "You heard them, Nasty Natalie. They want to see you punished real good."

Shaking my head, I try to crawl backwards and away from Mr. Pala, but there is nowhere I can go to escape. I'm surrounded within a circle of assholes, shouting obscenities and wishing for Mr. Pala to do monstrous things to me with his cane.

I want to die. I've always feared death until this moment, but I don't want to survive another second of this brutality and humiliation. I don't want to find out what twisted things Mr. Pala can think up next to entertain the men in his casino.

"Who wants to see how red I can make that ass of hers?" Mr. Pala asks, strolling behind me.

Oh, God. Please, God. I whisper my prayer under my breath, hoping that something, anything, manages to grant me mercy in this universe. My mom used to pray with me before bed before she was drained, and it used to help me then. But now? Nothing can even hear my pleas over the raucous crowd.

I squeeze my eyes shut and dig my nails into the carpet. I expect to get my ass beaten with a vampire's strength at any moment. I expect the crowd to join in to feast on my blood. I hope if they do that they'll drain me so I never wake up to live through this again.

Gunshots ring through the air, the quick pops startling me, sending me to the floor. Blood splashes over me as the crowd of onlookers gets ravaged by bullets spraying everything in their way.

"This is a hostile takeover!" A familiar voice shouts before gunfire rings through the air again. It's not someone I want to hear, but Walcott's interruption just saved my ass. "If you're caught running, you will lose your legs. If you're caught hiding, I'll gouge out your eyes. If you don't fucking get on the floor and bow down to me, you'll lose your heads. Do you understand?"

I fall to my side and curl in on myself, trying to make myself as small as possible as vampires drop to the floor around me. Mr. Pala growls under his breath from close by, and I listen as he mutters for help into his com device, calling his security. Only static responds.

Heavy footsteps thud nearby, and a black boot stomps on Mr. Pala's hand, crushing it. Unlike at the Aris Hotel, Walcott wears a full face mask like the ones I've seen vampire guests wear coming in during the day, desperate enough for entertainment to face the heat of the sun. Their sun sensitivity doesn't kill them, but from seeing a fight outside through the tinted glass doors of the entrance, I know it scorches the hell out of them.

Walcott grinds down with his steel toe, grinning as Mr. Pala shouts in pain. I release a breath, hearing the sound of his agony so satisfying that it takes everything in me not to sit up for a better view.

"Would you like me to stop, Mr. Pala?" Walcott asks, his deep voice growling the words.

"What is it you want?" Mr. Pala asks, grinding his teeth. "Stipends? Free credit? Rooms? Donors? I can provide that."

"A man after your heart, dude." Monroe's familiar voice shoots a bolt of energy to my core. I can only see his reflection in one of the shiny mirrored pillars with a sign for one of the card tables. "But I think he can do better than that."

I roll over slightly and peer up at him, stepping to stand tall beside Walcott. Several other masked vampires lurk around the casino, pushing and forcing all of the staff and guests toward the main carpeted walkway.

"Just name it," Mr. Pala says, his voice rising in pitch. "I can arrange it."

"Until your precious allies come to the rescue," Walcott says, thudding the cane near Mr. Pala's head.

"They won't. I won't call them. I swear." Mr. Pala rests his elbows on the floor. "Please. I have power and influence. Just tell me what you want."

"What about her?" Monroe squats down beside me, and caresses his finger along my cheek. I can only see his golden eyes, but they crinkle in the corners with a hidden smile.

Mr. Pala groans. "She doesn't belong to me. I have an arrangement with Alexander Aris. If you take her, he'll find her. It would be a mistake. Please. He'll not only take my head, but he'll also take yours. No one will get anything they want."

Is he really trying to convince them not to take me? Is Alexander so terrifying that even Mr. Pala fears him? I can see it, but I don't know the extent of it.

"An arrangement, huh?" Monroe asks, taking the cane from Walcott. He presses it to the side of Mr. Pala's face. If he pushes hard enough, he could break his skull. "Tell us or I'll move on to someone more willing. Your second in command would be thrilled."

Mr. Pala growls and bucks under the pressure of the cane. "Wait! Wait! Every Monday to Tuesday morning she is under contract to perform here. You can have it. I'll provide the room. Please."

Monroe hums and stares at me a bit longer. "What do you think, little bird? Would you prefer me to take your contract instead?"

"Fuck yes," I say, my voice surprising me as I speak out loud.

Holding his hand to me, he helps me to my feet and offers me his jacket to cover up my skimpy costume. I peer around the casino, shocked by the sight before me. The Bella Crew wasn't lying when they threatened to hurt anyone who tried to run or hide.

"We won't be taking a room here, though. We're not as stupid as the man whose security ignored their jobs to get their rocks off on watching you and your cane." Monroe thuds it to the floor again. "I have to say though. Your performance gave me an idea."

I press my lips together into a thin line, studying the thoughts crossing his face and darkening his expression.

"I love nothing more than a good punishment. What about you, folks? Who wants to see this little bird in action? I know I do." Monroe twirls the cane and offers it to me.

"You heard him, assholes, get on your knees and tune in for the greatest show in La Vega courtesy of The Pala!" Walcott shouts, throwing his hands out. Kicking his boot under Mr. Pala, Walcott forces the vampire to his hands and knees and shocks the hell out of me by ripping his pants at the seam, forcing him to bare his pale ass.

Murmurs whisper over the catchy music of the slot

machines, and the once scared crowd now becomes enthralled with the change in Mr. Pala's twisted show. My head pounds with my heartbeat, and I grip the cool gold of the cane, listening to the Bella Crew start to chant for me to beat his ass.

"No one messes with my girl," Monroe whispers under his breath, touching his palm to my lower back. "Teach him that, little bird. Teach him what happens when you touch what doesn't belong to him."

Bending down, Monroe slaps his hand on Mr. Pala's ass, leaving behind a bright red handprint. He smiles with his fangs, encouraging me, and I summon my nerve to do what the crowd wants. What Monroe wants. And right now, what I really fucking want.

Because this asshole hurt me. He humiliated me. He thought because he bought a contract with Alexander that he was entitled to do whatever he pleased with me.

Well, fuck that. I'm going to make him reconsider ever thinking about doing this to any woman or donor again.

Swinging the cane like a bat, I use all my strength to whack him hard on his ass. The crowd cheers, the sadist fuckers not even caring who gets hurt as long as it's not them. Like with my stage performances, I let the crowd infuse me with their energy and I hit Mr. Pala again and again until he falls to his stomach. My whole body trembles with adrenaline, and Monroe scoops me into his arms and tugs his mask from his lips, kissing me. Electricity zings between the two of us, his kiss rough and passionate, driven by the craziness unfolding around us.

"Make sure he doesn't forget his place," Monroe shouts. "Make him feel his mistake for days."

I clutch onto Monroe and watch with wide eyes as a few of the guests from the crowd force Mr. Pala back to his knees while pressing his head to the ground. Walcott spits on the cane and slickens it, aiming the end at Mr. Pala's ass.

I close my eyes and bury my face into the crook of Monroe's throat. The world blurs, and only the faint holler of Mr. Pala reaches me as the glass door of The Pala closes. Cool air blows my hair from my neck, and I don't say anything or try to look around until Monroe slows down.

A bright red convertible idles in the valet drive, and Monroe sets me onto the front seat and quickly buckles a harness over my chest. Hopping over the doorframe, he gets behind the wheel and hits the throttle, sending the silent car barreling forward and onto the Strip.

I shift and look at him, my heart still pounding in overdrive but not with fear. "How did you find me?"

Tapping a button on the dash, Monroe turns on the auto-pilot and removes his hands from the wheel. "I saw Sawyer's dumbass leave your cute ass at the pool and was about to approach you when I saw Perry grab you. I knew some bullshit was going down, so I called in a favor with Walcott. He was itching to fuck some people up. Knox and Sawyer are watching Aris now. He won't even know. You're safe, okay? We'll hang out at the Bella until it's time for you to go back."

I lick my lips and swallow. "I don't want to. Please, just..." My voice fades. What am I saying? I can't just ask some vampire to hide me. I have friends—family—at the Aris. It's my home. Without me, they might take the brunt of Alexander's anger. And Opal? She would be devastated.

Monroe rests his cool hand on my knee. "You know I want to. I want to drive out of this fucking city and take you with me, but things are complicated."

I sigh. "Why? What is it about Alexander that scares you all? You fucking cut tongues out and force people to swallow them."

Chuckling, Monroe leans closer, touching my cheek. "You're hurting my ego, little bird. No one scares me."

I lift an eyebrow. "Mmmhmm. Keep telling yourself that."

He flashes his fangs with his smile. "You're going to get yourself in trouble, teasing me like that. I like it far too much."

"Your kind of trouble doesn't scare me. It excites me." I bite my lip between my teeth. "I don't think I've ever felt this way, you know."

"What way, little bird?" He lowers his voice, peering into my eyes.

I kiss him softly. "I don't want to jinx it."

Because for the first time in my life, riding in this car with a crazy-ass vampire who unexplainably punishes people on my behalf, I feel free.

If only it could last.

I PLOP DOWN a microwave on the dresser of my room and hunt for an outlet to plug it in. I had to search around the entire floor to find this ancient piece of shit, but there was no way I was going to offer Hayley the single banana an old man on the donor floor offered me along with a goddamned frozen dinner in exchange for a new TV and access to La Vega After Sunrise, one of the vampire-only porn feeds that streams to the hotel.

"I hope you like...whatever the fuck this is." I tear the box open and pull out a tray of what looks like brown jelly and peas...maybe. It's been so damn long since I've even looked at donor food, let alone tried to make it, but I want to prove that I can handle taking care of the woman of my dreams.

"It looks like shit," Hayley muses, grinning from her spot on the edge of my unmade bed. I wish I had cleaned up, but I hadn't expected to bring anyone here. "Maybe I'll just eat the banana. I'd have thought porn was worth more than this."

I groan and shake my head. "Fuck. I'll find something else. You're right. Bodie was probably hiding the good stuff from me."

Tipping her head back, she laughs, the most musical sound escaping her lips. "Monroe, I'm playing. The stew doesn't look that bad. My standards are low when I'm this hungry."

I growl and stab the film on the tray with my knife. "We need to fix that. Your damn stomach's growl is more intimidating than Sawyer. You look ready to lunge at me."

She laughs again, pushing to her feet. Strolling the three feet it takes to reach me, she snatches the tray from my hands and pops open the microwave. I study everything she does, feeling dumb as fuck that I couldn't remember how to use this bullshit. She doesn't tease me about it though.

"You'd probably enjoy it. You look like the type to enjoy handfeeding me." She waves the banana, teasing me.

I try to take it from her to prove that she's absolutely right but for the worst reason, because watching her peel that damn phallic fruit and part her lips to take a bite—the little tease. She does know the reason I'd gladly feed her, and she's enjoying fucking with my horny-ass way too much.

"Mmm," she hums, slowly, sensually taking another bite. "So good."

I play-growl and snatch it from her hand, using my vampire speed. I love how instead of just letting me and acting afraid like I've seen her dozens of times, Hayley tries to grab it from me. I hold it above her and out of her reach. She narrows her eyes, flicking her gaze to the banana, to my face, and then over my body.

The little minx surprises the hell out of me by jumping up and clinging to my waist. Swinging her leg up, she hooks it over my shoulder and hoists herself high enough to steal it back. I stand frozen as her thighs squeeze my neck and I can't stop from sucking in a breath of her sweet, delectable-scented skin, her pussy so close that I could rub her with my nose and make her cream.

She flips to her feet before I even get the chance. Grinning, she takes a huge bite of the banana. "Be thankful I didn't lunge at you. I can and do bite."

Damn. "I like that kind of thing, little bird. Being a bit...primal. And so you know, I thought you were going to offer to feed me too," I tease, giving her a long once-over, studying her reaction. I flick my tongue at vampire speed, showing exactly what I mean.

Her skin flushes with my words, and she giggles and turns away, letting her golden brown hair veil her face. The microwave dings, breaking the silence, and I beat her to it and pull out the hot tray and set it at my desk. I pull out the chair for her, motioning for her to sit down. She rubs her lips together and hesitates, indecipherable thoughts crossing her mind.

"Are you hungry?" she asks, pushing her hair over her shoulder, teasing me with a peek at her smooth, scar-free skin. "I could feed you while I eat if you'd like."

I'm going to fucking regret this later, but she's been through too much that I don't want to treat her as anything less than my queen until I have to take her back. She's so used to trying to please everyone because she's afraid of what happens when she doesn't, and I don't want that for her. I want her to know that I fully believe that reciprocation must be earned, and I don't think I've done enough yet.

"I'm good, Hayley. I have some gen. pop. in my fridge. We have plenty of that shit around here." I nudge her to take a seat, but once again she doesn't give in.

She shifts her gaze to the desk and back to me. "I'm...I'm sorry. I'm not used to eating in front of a vampire without offering anything in return. Please, I'd love to feed you, even if it's only a taste. Let me repay you for everything you did for me. It's what I want to do."

My mind and stomach battle it out. She looks obviously uncomfortable at the thought of eating in front of me and letting me take care of her. And I really, and I mean really fucking want to taste every inch of her. On the other hand, I want to break the cycle of her thinking that she must repay me for doing something for her.

Grabbing my hand, she twists me toward the chair and pushes me down, not giving me a chance to deny her. My cock hardens as I stare in silence as she lowers herself to my lap and shifts to hang her legs over the armrest.

A smile graces her gorgeous face, and she leans in and kisses me. I groan at the pleasure aroused in me by her mere closeness and give in to her desire to treat me as if I deserve her affection.

Combing her fingers through her hair, she tugs it from her shoulder and slides her costume down, exposing her skin to me. "It's okay to bite me. Please. Let me do this for you, Monroe."

I lick my lips and nod, lowering my head until I brush my mouth over her warm skin. She squirms under the sensation, her ass rubbing me in a way that makes my body ache with lust and need. It takes her a moment to finally turn away to look at her food, and she intakes the sexiest small breath hearing my fangs click as I extend them.

And damn. I want to explore her body with my hand. I can already smell how fucking deliciously turned on she is, even if she doesn't give much away apart from her subtle movements as she picks at her food with her fingers. I nearly break the silence to apologize for forgetting the damn fork, but I can't get myself to do anything other than softly lick her skin and listen to her breathing quicken in anticipation for my bite.

"You're so beautiful," I murmur, caressing my fingers over her arms as I gently shift her on my lap. "Thank you for offering to take care of me. I won't take it for granted."

Quickly sinking my fangs into her shoulder, I moan so fucking loud at the taste of her blood filling my mouth. I've never tasted anything so exquisite in my life. My whole body buzzes, and I mold my lips over my mark and suck, listening to her pounding heart and savoring the sensation of her hand rubbing across my leg.

She wiggles uncontrollably with my bite, and I can't stop from adjusting her again until I know she feels how hard she makes me. Like she can't take another minute of my attention, she stops eating and reaches between her legs, stroking her fingers over my zipper, slowly pulling it down.

I gasp and pull away, licking my lips. I can't trust myself if she continues. I want more. I'll take more, and right now, I don't know whether or not she actually wants to give me what I want. This could be out of habit as I know Fucking Aris has burned it into her very nature to do what she thinks a man wants without consideration to what she wants and desires and needs.

"Hayley," I murmur, locking my fingers around her wrist, stopping her. "You don't have to do this."

"I want to." Her breathy voice strikes my balls with another bolt of pleasure. "You want me to."

Fuck me.

Standing up, I set her on her feet and gather her hands between mine. She frowns, her face screaming at me that she thinks I don't like what she's doing because I made her stop when it's far from it.

"I'm sorry," she whispers, her lip trembling. "I—what did I do wrong? Did you not like it?"

I knew it. Her question is confirmation enough that she thinks I rejected her. It's in this moment that I want so badly to fly across the Strip, find Aris, and beat the shit out of him for the mental fuck he instilled in her.

Her eyes glass over, her heart picking up speed. "I'm sorry, Monroe," she repeats.

I whip my head back and forth, taking a breath. My boiling anger toward Aris is getting misconstrued. She thinks she's done something wrong and it's far from that.

"Don't apologize. It's unnecessary," I say, inhaling a breath to control the tone of my voice.

Dropping to my knees, I grasp her hands tightly, choosing to look up at her instead of down. I want to be as close to her level as I can be. I don't know what it exactly is about her that has me wanting to bow at her feet, but I do know that donors aren't beneath me. That's one of the things the Bella Crew is about. We don't need fear and control to keep our donors supplying blood. They do so because we respect them. We protect them and will fight to keep them even when the bastard leadership of La Vega tests us over and over, trying to take what doesn't belong to them.

I wasn't always so vicious and violent. But it's what it

takes to even maintain an ounce of power in this wild domain, uninfluenced by any other territories. Most have dozens of cities and power split between a few select, run like a business. I've never been far from La Vega—I was fucking born here before the Vampire Uprising, and I'm not leaving the city that should've always been mine.

"You did nothing wrong, but I want you to know that this isn't the Aris Hotel. I know you've had it fucking beat into your head to obey and ensure whoever you're with is satisfied. I know you feel like you've done something wrong because I stopped you. And I fucking know that you're probably starting to question everything you know." I touch my fingers to her cheek, searching her eyes. "You don't have to. I want you to know right here and now that as much as I want you—and I mean, I really fucking want you more than anything, I haven't earned the right. I want you to want me. I don't want you doing things out of habit. I'm not one of Fucker Aris's guests or clients. You're not a donor who needs to submit to me because I stole your contract. You will not submit to me until I deserve you. I never want this to be about power and possession because that's what you know. I want it to be about you giving up control because you trust me to take care of you how you need, little bird."

Hayley tilts her head and searches my eyes, her brilliant turquoise gaze drinking me in as she processes what I've just said.

"There are vampires in this world that want power just to have power. They mistreat and take the beauty and gifts donors bring because they know they will never earn them any other way. I'm not like that. My crew isn't like that. We cut out tongues, break bones, and take heads to prove as much." I lean closer, sharing my breath with her. "And we do it on behalf of donors. I'll do it on behalf of you."

Hayley's expression softens, her face brightening with a smile more stunning than anything I've ever seen on her. She closes the space completely, wrapping her arms around me as she meets me with a kiss that gets me in a good way. I slide my tongue into her mouth, tasting the savory flavor of her tongue.

My body hums and aches, begging me to throw her onto the bed. It takes everything in me to chill the fuck out. I need to get out of my room with her. If we stay, I know I'll go against what I just said about wanting to earn her submission to me.

I stretch her lip with my teeth and kiss her once more, showing her how hard it is for me to put space between us. "Let me give you some of my blood and introduce you to the Bella Crew. I know the others want to meet the woman who has grabbed me by the balls and makes me want to fight harder than ever."

Her smile falters, her fear obvious. "Okay."

"I think Sawyer and Knox might be back too. They're going to want to see that you're okay," I add, testing her for a reaction.

I really would fucking prefer she ignored those two bastards, but I have no right to tell her to do so. Just as they know they have no right to try to stop her from showing me attention. It's a weird-ass arrangement, but our alliance is more important than anything else. If any of our crew thought something was threatening it...fuck. They won't.

"Okay," she repeats, remaining guarded with her feelings.

I wish I could listen to her thoughts to know what goes on in her mind, but like with everything else, I need to earn her trust, and I plan to.

Biting my wrist, I offer her my blood, which she accepts without question. She knows the reason I offer without having to ask, because there is no way I can let her keep my bite mark no matter how hot I think it looks on her. It'll also ensure her mind is safe from being manipulated. After what happened at The Pala, I fucking want to give her my blood every hour of every day to ensure no one can force her to comply like that again.

Releasing the sexiest whimper, she sucks harder, causing me to tighten my hand through her hair. I lean in and kiss her jaw, savoring her mouth on me. I haven't done a blood exchange with someone I was so utterly attracted to that my damn fangs extend automatically. I swear if she even thinks of touching my cock in this moment, I'll blow a load in my pants. She's that fucking good.

"You're so sexy," I whisper, keeping my voice low. "You have no idea what you do to me."

Hayley eases away and licks her blood-stained lips. She smiles, her face flushing and heating her skin as my blood already begins coursing through her system. I can't stop from breaking my eyes from hers, the scent of her body growing more potent, inviting me to find out exactly what my blood does to her. It's not always this way, but it's clear that she reacts with the same desire I do while tasting her.

My damn nuts are goners. Rest in blue ball hell, you tight, aching bastards.

"We don't have to go right away, you know," she says, stroking her fingers over my shoulder.

I bob my head, suppressing my lust. "Fuck yeah, we do. If I don't get you out of this damn room right now, we're never leaving."

She opens and closes her mouth. "I don't m—"

I shut her up with a kiss, knowing if she completes her comment, I'm a dead man. I'm sure someone will come banging on the door eventually, and I'll try to fuck up anyone who tries to take this intoxicating woman from me. Staying here is far too dangerous. I need air.

With vampire speed, I race from my room, letting the door slam behind us. Hayley tightens her legs around me, locking her ankles across my lower back. I probably shouldn't do this, but I ease her down a few inches just to fucking feel her body bounce against my cock pinned in place by my pants. All she'd have to do is lift my shirt and she'd see my damn tip flexing and peeking out, but I'd rather it be up than tucked between my damn legs.

She laughs and releases a breathy squeal as I jump from the banister of the second story instead of taking the broken escalator. I land with a thud, bouncing her back up so she hides her face against the crook of my neck. Her body trembles with her nerves, and she hugs me tighter at the sound of a dozen voices shouting as Walcott fucks around with Sullivan, Govan, and Tatum.

Tatum punches Walcott in the dick, laughing and throwing her hair over her shoulder. She's the only female vampire on our crew and a vicious, snarky as fuck babe of a woman. I've known Tatum since after The Divisions when she was turned by a Strip dweller who thought doing so would make her his bitch for eternity. Tatum doesn't fucking play around with that kind of bullshit and took the fucker's heart the next day. It was a week later that she stormed into the Bella and demanded she have a place on our crew. She's been here ever since and handles all the donor affairs. The dude donors around here love her and worship her like a goddamn deity.

Hayley's heartbeat raps against my chest, and I adjust her in my arms and look around the empty casino. Half the machines are shattered and no longer working. The ones that do have been unplugged for a least a decade. If I have to listen to the damn slots ringing in here ever again, I'll toss them all onto the Strip. Because this is our fucking home and territory, and guests aren't welcome here.

Tatum whips her attention from Walcott and to me first, raising her eyebrow as she assesses me. I flash my fangs at her in warning, making sure she doesn't rush to us. Subtle and sweet isn't in her mental dictionary, and she can be even rougher than all of the rest of us assholes combined. There's a reason she's in charge of the Bella and keeping things in check. She'd probably bring a war to our door otherwise. She'd have already tried to murder Aris and Pala, and as much as I want that, we need them alive for now.

"I swear to fucking hell, Tate. You need to chill out and calm down. Hayley startles easily and has been through so much bullshit," I warn, keeping my voice so low that Hayley won't hear. I glare at the others. "That goes for all you dickheads too."

Tatum clears her throat, offering me a sweet smile as she looks at me. "Hey, Monny. Who do you have there?" She sounds fake as fuck, but at least she lowers her voice. "Is that the chick from Aris? Can I meet her?"

Hayley releases a small breath by my ear and straightens her back, steeling herself probably like she does every time she's forced into meeting a new vampire. I study her face, giving her a wink in encouragement, and she swivels in my arms instead of wiggling for me to put her down. And damn it if I don't mind one fucking bit. I'll carry her like this forever if she lets me. I can manage to do whatever the fuck needs to be done, especially with how strong her perfectly muscular thighs grip me.

"Hi, I'm Ru—Hayley," she says, her voice hitching as she decides to tell Tatum her real name. "Thanks for allowing me to stay here for the night."

It took me at least an hour of chanting it to myself when Knox told me she shared it with him and Sawyer. I wish I had been there to hear it for myself. I almost didn't let her know I knew it but thought knowing that Sawyer and Knox tell me everything would be better than thinking we hide shit.

Tatum's sweet expression breaks. The look she gives Hayley, like she's just said the stupidest fucking thing in the universe, gets under my skin. I growl in warning, reminding her that Hayley is my girl and she better not call her out.

Tatum's lips thin. "You're welcome, babe. You can show up and grab a room anytime. No one will fuck with you here. I won't let them. Wanna see my cock collection to prove it?"

Jesus-fucking-Christ. "Tate. Fuck. No one ever wants to see that shit."

Tipping her head back, she laughs. "You're not a woman, so you wouldn't understand, Monny."

Hayley laughs, her face lighting up. "Actually, you have me curious."

Tatum and her cocky-fucking-smile. She sticks out her tongue at me, clearly going to hold this over my head for the rest of eternity. "Told you, fucker."

I open my mouth to comment, but a scream rips through the lobby, and I tense. Hayley clings to me in fear, and I spin around to see Sawyer and Knox tossing some bastard onto the floor. The guy tries to run, but Walcott intercepts and swings a crowbar, knocking the douche off his feet.

"About fucking time! I've been waiting all day for you fuckers to bring in someone for punishment," Govan yells, grinning with his excitement. "Who the fuck do we have here? What has this bastard done?"

Sawyer's gaze lands on mine instead of responding. I guess he hadn't expected me to leave my room with Hayley and bring her downstairs. Combing his fingers through his hair, Knox groans and shakes his head at me. It's too late for me to carry Hayley away since she gets her fear under control and peeks at the two of them.

Knox gets his shit together first and materializes in front of me, forcing his mouth to smile, ensuring he never allows himself to glower at Hayley by accident. "My vixen, what a fucking beautiful, unexpected surprise. Monroe better be taking good fucking care of our girl."

Walcott punches him in the arm, making Knox growl. "Focus, damn it. What's this asshole here for?"

Sawyer stomps forward and towers over Walcott, getting him to back off. "Shut the fuck up. We'll tell you when we're good and ready. Now go grab the restraints. We have some interrogating to do before you all can have your damn fun."

Walcott obeys him and vanishes. The others go to the asshole and surround him, yanking him to his feet.

I adjust Hayley and meet her gaze. "Let me show you around a bit more, yeah?"

She slowly nods.

Tatum groans in annoyance, drawing our attention. "Fuck that, Monny. Come on. Don't take her away. Let us show her what it's like to be one of the Bella Crew." Waving her fingers at Hayley, she gets her to look in her direction. "Wouldn't you like that, babe?"

Hayley shifts her gaze from me and to the fucker on his knees. "I think I would."

"Fuck yeah!" Tatum shouts. She kicks the guy in the ass, sending him sprawling. "It's your unlucky fucking day, isn't it, you scrawny, shitty bastard? I'm so ready to show that sweet little babe of my leaders a good show."

EXCITEMENT RUSHES THROUGH me, the sound of the gorgeous, scary-as-fuck vampire's yells echoing through the air. Tate was the last type of vampire I was expecting to be here as I've only seen male Bella Crew members so far, and I can't help my growing awe in her. She reminds me of a tatted, bit more twisted version of

Opal, though Tate looks nothing like my mistress with her short bleached bob, tight jeans, and leather knee-high boots with red laces. She wears a fishnet top with a red bra underneath, her cleavage on full display like the world around her is her stage and she's ready to make every bastard who tries to fuck with her drop to their knees.

Monroe finally sets me on my feet but doesn't move out of arm's reach until Knox comes up to my other side and slides his fingers through mine. They subtly and quietly exchange positions, Knox now pulling me in close. I step into Knox's side and peek up at him, feeling his gaze on the side of my face. After spending time around all of them, I realize that Knox is hands-off while Monroe enjoys fucking shit up.

"I heard about Mr. Pala," Knox says softly, grazing his thumb over mine. "Are you okay?"

I shudder and close my eyes, trying to push the thought away. Licking my lips, I try to summon my voice.

"My beautiful vixen. I'm going to hurt that bastard myself," he says, engulfing me in his arms. "You don't have to talk about it. Just let me hug you for a second."

His words touch me on a level so deeply that I can't stop myself from sniffling. I sink against him and inhale a breath of his fragrant skin. Going from Monroe's arms and to his unexpectedly was something I needed. It's like knowing they're both here makes me feel even safer. I just wish a part of me wasn't so unsure and untrusting. Monroe said a few things to me in his room that I'm still trying to wrap my mind around. Why me? Why do they have this need to treat me like more than a blood source? I haven't done anything to deserve their kindness and protectiveness—and hell, Monroe wouldn't even let me do anything to try to earn it without my begging.

"I just wish I could forget, you know? Like with the Greys. I know Sawyer unlocked the memory, but it doesn't feel the same as the one from last night. I don't feel anything. It's just there. It doesn't haunt me." I don't know why I admit as much, but something about Knox's closeness opens me up.

He pulls back and meets my gaze. "Because Sawyer manipulated the bad out of your head like you asked. Monroe isn't great at mind manipulation to that extent, so he wouldn't have offered."

"Oh." I guess he's right that I did ask. I couldn't stand living with the pain of knowing that I was put in that position.

"I can call Sawyer over now, and he can help. I can't stand the thought of it taking up your headspace for another moment." Releasing a small whistle, Knox grabs Sawyer's attention, getting him to leave the vampire asshole he stands over.

Sawyer greets me with a smile, not even fazed that some of his crew members groan about having to wait a moment longer. He touches my chin, gently getting me to stretch on my tiptoes to meet him as high as I can for a kiss. The gesture feels so natural, even with Knox tightening his fingers around mine. But he doesn't complain and remains steady and silent. I ease away, the intense emotions settling.

I peek at Knox, but he trains his gaze away. His expressionless face leaves me with no clue of what swirls through his mind as Sawyer kisses me, and I can't help thinking that maybe I need to talk to them. They've been obvious with their interest in me, and I've gone along with it, but there is still a deep-seated part of me that grows nervous and antsy about everything. Am I being careless with letting them pass me between each other? Maybe. Do I care? No. I like it. I had no idea how much I'd enjoy their attention. These guys are feared by many, and I should keep some good senses about them, but I've seen their sweet sides even in the tangle of their psychotic tendencies.

"What's up, my girl?" Sawyer finally asks when I don't say anything.

I turn and look at Knox.

Knox brings my hand up and kisses my knuckles. "I won't speak for you, Hayley."

I kind of wish he would though. My mouth dries just thinking about mentioning what I want Sawyer to do. Not because I'm worried about what he'll say, but I'm afraid I'll break down at having to voice it.

My mouth uncontrollably quivers, and I hate myself a little for it. I should be stronger than this. I've learned how to bottle everything up for so long that I should just accept the horrors of my life. But it's like I finally see how bad the damage done to me is and these guys want to help bandage my wounds and help them heal instead of seeing how much more I can take until I just accept the pain as part of my life.

Sawyer's brows knit together and he scratches his fingers over the back of his neck, ruffling his dark brown hair. "Can I try to guess and you can nod if I'm right?"

I slowly bob my head.

"Do you want me to kick Knox in the nuts for not kissing that pouty mouth of yours to distract you?" Sawyer asks, smirking at me.

I can't stop the laugh that bubbles from my throat. "Sawyer." My voice finally escapes my mouth, sounding stronger than I thought it could be.

Chuckling, Sawyer playfully fake-punches Knox.

"You didn't say no."

Again, I laugh. "No. Please save all the dick punches for assholes who deserve it."

"Damn, Knox. You got lucky, because you know I'd do it for her." Sawyer attempts to whack Knox on the shoulder, but he dodges out of the way.

I step between the two of them.

"Double damn. Did you really just protect him?" Sawyer teases, fake-glaring at me. "I touched a dick on your behalf. Do you know how fucking weird that was?"

A whistle cuts through the air, and Govan winds his hand in a circular motion, trying to get Sawyer to hurry up. Both Sawyer and Knox growl, and Govan flips them off with a grin.

I touch Sawyer's hand, my heart, body, and mind finally chilled out. "I don't want them to get annoyed that you're making them wait to...do whatever thing you plan to do."

"We have eternity, sexy vixen," Knox teases. "Sawyer can take however the fuck long he wants with you."

"I know. It's just..." I lick my lips and turn to Sawyer. "Can you do that thing like you did the other night? I can't stop thinking about..." Mr. Pala's name refuses to leave my tongue.

Nodding, Sawyer cups my cheeks and leans in. His

eyes turn solid silver and his melodious voice hums in my ears. My body slackens and electricity zings through me. I'm not scared and panicking like at The Pala.

I feel relief flood through me and then it's like the pain and anxiety, the fear over what happened, numbs until it feels as if the memory isn't my own but something I witnessed.

I release a breath as Sawyer breaks my gaze, and he gathers me in his arms and hugs me for a moment. Knox still holds my hand, kissing my knuckles like he can't resist giving me the affection he thinks I need after Sawyer tinkers with my mind.

Silence fills the room, and Sawyer sets me on my feet. "Better?" he asks, playing with my hair.

I nod, savoring the lingering energy he aroused in me. "You can go fuck up that asshole now. I'm sure he deserves it."

Tate laughs and claps her hands, locking her fingers to the vampire's hair. "You hear that, you donor thief? She wants to see us fuck you up." Pulling a knife hidden in the thick sole of her boot, she points it at the vampire's cock. "Should I add another dick to my collection?"

I shrug. "Maybe. Is the donor okay?"

"Please!" the vampire shouts, the sharp point of Tate's knife getting him to react with more than just flashing his fangs and growling. "It wasn't my idea. It was just a job. You have to understand. I'm fucking starving out there. You would've done the same damn thing."

"Who hired you?" Sawyer asks, touching Tate's shoulder to get her to back up. "I need a name."

"I—I don't know. Something Vada. Harry? Henry? Fuck. Maybe none of those. Please. I just accepted the free credit at the donation center at the Ingo." The vampire's teeth clench as he stares at Sawyer's blade.

"Vada? There is no fucking asshole coven on the Strip by that name," Sawyer snaps, sinking the blade into the guy's leg.

"Evada," I whisper, recognizing the name. "Henderson Evada. I met him a month ago with Alexander." I should be afraid not to use Alexander's title here, but a part of me wants to pretend that he doesn't have power or control over me any longer.

"Yeah, that's the guy. He's come from out of the area or some bullshit and needs some donors." The guy's fangs peek from beneath his lip. "All unregistered vampire assets are fair game."

Growling, Sawyer swings his fist and punches the vampire hard in the chest, using his strength to shatter the man's sternum.

Blood swells from the wound, and the guy hollers and

shrieks, his voice stinging my ears.

"Our donors are off-limits!" Sawyer shouts, squeezing the guy's heart. "There are fucking consequences for what you've done, and you're going to make a point."

"Wait! Wait!" The vampire bucks and tries to break the restraints.

Sawyer ignores him and looks at Walcott. "Grab the ink. We need to send a message." Turning to Monroe, he adds, "Take his fangs."

"You asshole! Your fucking wannabe coven isn't going to get away with this!" the vampire shouts.

Sawyer laughs in amusement. "Govan, take his hands too."

"What about me, Sawyer? Let me cut a fucking dick," Tate asks, her voice syrupy sweet as she bats her eyelashes. "I'll finally have a dozen for my bouquet."

Nodding, Sawyer says, "Make it hurt."

I startle at the high-pitched wail as Govan wastes no time hacking the guy's right hand off. Knox spins me away and pulls me to him, noticing my reaction.

"Take her to my suite, Knox. I need to talk to her, okay? Grab her something to eat, and I'll be there in a bit." Sawyer turns back to the gruesome scene unfolding before us. "Mark him over his forehead. Nice and big." He motions to Walcott with a bowl of strange blue liquid.

Knox guides my face to him. "Come on. You've seen enough shit."

But this time, I don't want to forget it.

"I can't believe that's what the Aris Hotel looks like from here," I say, smooshing my nose to the glass. "And the Bella's fountain. The view from here is way better than the one from my room."

Knox presses his chest into my back, linking his fingers through mine and pinning my palms to the window. The coolness of his breath tickles the skin below my ear, and I shiver at the sensation of his mouth so close to my throat. Even if I wanted to move, I couldn't, but I enjoy his closeness and how his body rests flush against mine.

"You sound like you've never been on this side of the Strip," he says, sneaking a kiss to my neck. It awakens the memory of our first real moment together and how much he enjoyed me sucking his dick. I wonder if he thinks about it now like I do.

Arching my back, I pop my ass out a bit more, teasing and testing him, needing to see how he reacts to me. I know he was hesitant about the blow job and only let me because Alexander would've turned the situation against me, and I felt conflicted about it, but now? I'm dying to find out if he'd let me do it again. I want him to want me without all the other bullshit.

"I haven't," I finally say, sensually swaying my hips against his hard-on. "This is the first time I've been out of the Aris Hotel." I study the red, white, and blue lights dancing up and down the towering monument across the way. Not far from it, a huge hot air balloon statue sparkles. I've never seen it outside of hotel pictures before.

"You're shitting me?" Surprise lines Knox's words, stealing away the breathiness of his desire. I hadn't realized he'd be so fascinated by my life that I regret letting him in just a bit.

I shrug, bending my neck, testing to see if he'll continue to explore my throat with his lips. "I was born there. My mom was a performer and my dad worked in maintenance before they died."

Knox spins me around, his gaze roving over mine. Releasing one of my hands, he combs his fingers through my hair, cradling the back of my head. His tongue darts over his bottom lip, drawing my attention to his mouth, and I stretch up and kiss him.

"You tear me apart, beautiful vixen. My body craves you but my mind is enthralled by everything you say. I want to know everything about you. I had no idea how much. You're so mysterious and raw. I have so many questions but I don't want to push you." He murmurs his words against my mouth, his admission digging deeply into my soul. No one has ever wanted to know me like this.

I ease my head back and look into his sapphire eyes, blinking with the silver of his hunger and desire. "You can push me. It's okay."

His eyes darken with my comment as he flares his nostrils. "I don't think you realize what kind of permission you're offering me. I have a problem with pushing boundaries with you. I've never had great control."

"Is that why you tried to buy me from Alexander?" My body tingles with his closeness. "Why you didn't put up a fight during his private offering? I know it made you uncomfortable."

He chuckles, though his eyes don't light up. Tugging me from the window, he guides me to a plush chair and gets me to sit with him. "I wasn't. I should've been, vixen. I should've resisted your pleas. I could've figured out another way to please your master without letting you use that pouty mouth of yours, but...I wanted you too badly. I couldn't resist. It's hard for me to resist you even now despite knowing better."

My body buzzes under his intensity. "You don't have

to feel bad. I liked it. I wanted to."

Groaning, he rubs his thumb over my bottom lip like he's thinking about my mouth on him again. "That's my other problem. I don't feel bad. I feel lucky. You're my damn moral dilemma, testing me."

I shift on his lap until I straddle his waist and rest my hands on his shoulders. "I should care too, but I don't. I don't care that you could possibly be my downfall. I know better than being this close. I know the risk and the punishment I will receive if Alexander ever finds out. I just...I don't care anymore. He makes me feel like I'm standing on a cliff and about to be pushed off to fall to my death. But with you? With your crew? I feel like I can fly. For the first time, the pain is worth it as long as I get away from Alexander, even for just a day with you."

"Fuck," Knox breathes, tightening his hands on my hips. He guides my body to grind against him and moans. "Fuck. I'm bad for you. You need to push me away. Tell me to stop."

But I can't. In this moment, with my soul bared and my thoughts running wild, all I can think about is how good it would be to drown in them. At least if this all turns to shit, I can know I wasn't pushed. I jumped headfirst and dove off the damn cliff of my destruction. I'll know whether or not I can summon wings and fly.

Bowing into Knox, I kiss him hard and passionately, refusing to do as he commands. I don't have to obey him. That's the one thing he's made clear. I can rebel, and I've never so desperately wanted this kind of control. I want to know what it's like to finally get my way for once. If he doesn't stop me, I'm going to take my fill and know exactly what it's like to be claimed and possessed by someone who will let me do the same to him.

Knox's fangs click as he extends them, and I graze my tongue over one of the sharp points, giving him a taste of my blood. He moans and deepens our kiss, sliding his hands to my ass to squeeze my body.

I gasp for breath and pull away, sliding off his lap until my knees touch the floor between his legs. Grabbing my hands, he stops me from unbuckling his belt and lifts me into the air by my wrists only to swing me toward the bed. I land on my back and grip the blankets, my world blurring as he drags me to the edge of the bed.

My chest heaves as he towers over me, his eyes smoldering me and making me squirm as he hesitates. I glide my finger over the strap of my costume and drag it off my shoulder, slowly undressing for him. His eyes spark with silver and he licks his lips as I expose my boobs and push away my hair.

"You're asking to be devoured, vixen," he mutters,

leaning down to get in my face. "Tell me to fuck off and stop."

I narrow my gaze at him and press my lips into a line, refusing to listen to his command once again. "No."

I never knew how good it would feel to not fear someone for disobeying. Knox hums deep in his throat, the sexy sound reverberating through my very being. I rub my thighs together, my body going wild with my anticipation. I never get to do things I truly want. Most of the affection I've gotten in my life was bought and easily disregarded. It was about pleasing men as quickly as possible and hoping for the best. I've fed them and once in a while gave someone a blow job. They've never touched me beyond my boobs and haven't fucked me. I've always been good about giving them everything they need without them taking too much. Or maybe it had been Alexander protecting me all along, stopping assholes from trying to get more. I don't like to think about it, but maybe it's why things hurt me so deeply that he now put me at hostile, vile vampires' mercy...

I shove the thought away, hoping that Knox doesn't stop because my mind wanders. Everything in my past doesn't deserve my head space, and I grab Knox's hips and pull him closer to me, needing to distract myself with him and only him. I want something to think about to hold on to forever just in case this doesn't last. And I'd be lying if I believed otherwise. Nothing good ever lasts.

Knox groans and grabs my hands, once again stopping me from trying to unzip his pants to give him something he desires. He kisses me hard and rough, his mouth battling for control but only because he wants to lead. He wants to be the one who kisses me and not me kissing him.

He tangles his fingers into my hair, tilting my head back. "Hayley, you need to push me away now—"

"No," I say, my voice breathy. "You can't make me obey."

Knox play-growls and fingers my costume, yanking it down and tugging it off me completely. I gasp as he grins and glides his tongue over his lips, drinking me in like I'm the best thing he's ever seen in his existence. The fire of his gaze lights my body aglow, and I grab the blankets in anticipation as he lowers himself to the floor at the edge of the bed.

"I need you to speak up with me, Hayley. It's important to me that you know I will not want to stop, but I will always do so if you ask." He kisses my knee, still staring into my gaze. "I want to know what you like and crave and want more of. Do not think about me. Just you."

It's hard for me to even grasp the concept. I don't

even know what I like really. "I—I don't know. I'm not used to this. I—" I snap my mouth shut and swallow. Admitting it out loud angers me more than it should. My thoughts automatically want to go to a dark place, when I just want to feel what it's like to be free.

Knox kisses my other knee, adjusting my body a bit more with his cool fingers, drawing them down the inside of my legs and to my thighs. "Just let me take care of you. We'll find out together."

Knox draws his tongue to the apex of my legs and moans as he kisses the smooth skin of my body. I arch up and clutch his head, the sensation of his tongue sending explosions through me. He peeks up at me from between my legs like he needs to see my face.

"This feels so good," I say, moaning. Saying it out loud sends butterflies through my stomach. "Don't stop."

His eyes flash silver with my words, and he clutches my thighs, keeping my legs spread as he licks the seam of my body until he stops at my clit and rolls his tongue over it, the soft pressure sending my back arching. I close my eyes and lose myself to the pleasure he ignites inside of me. His mouth feels so incredible, and I can barely think. My mouth refuses to do anything other than moan, and I gasp as he slides a finger inside me. I've only ever masturbated by rubbing my clit with my finger. This takes my body to a new level, the pressure slight and exhilarating.

"You're so fucking tight," he murmurs, flicking his tongue while teasing me with his finger, touching me in a way that my body tenses and it feels as if I'm about to explode.

I grab his hair and brace myself, squirming and panting, knowing that I'm going to orgasm. The edges of my vision shadow at the building intensity until I arch forward completely, squeezing his head with my thighs and scratching my fingers into his shoulders. My muscles pulse, my toes curling, and I can't even gasp a breath as I tremble.

Knox slows, the click of his fangs sounding in my ear. He sinks his fangs into my thigh, only increasing the pleasure, and I scream out as his bite triggers a second orgasm, one stronger and so mind-blowing that all I can do is clutch onto Knox as he sucks his bite mark, satiating his hunger and desire.

He doesn't drink for long, pushing up to his feet. Kicking out of his boots, he tugs his shirt over his head, showing off the most intricate tattoo I've ever seen. Blue lines twist and tangle, forming a vine that travels up his side to bloom a strange flower over his chest. I can't stop from sitting up and pulling him closer to trace my fingers over the design from his chest and to where it disappears into his pants.

I map his hard muscles, bowing forward to the V of his hips as I take the initiative to unbuckle his belt. This time, he lets me, playing with my hair as I tug his pants down until he kicks them off. I stroke my finger down his hard cock, bringing his tip to my mouth to taste the pre-cum dripping for me. The mouthwatering flavor sets me off, and I suck him as far as I can into my mouth, deep-throating him. He moans and rocks his hips a little like he can't help himself, whispering my name.

"I want you, Hayley," he murmurs, gathering my hair in his hand. "Will you give me what I want?"

I slide his cock from my mouth and smile at him, the heat of my desire blazing across my chest. I never expected to have my first time be like this—with a sexy man who wants to give me everything I crave. I consider telling him that he's going to be my first, but I press my lips together and nod. It's not important to me. What's important is discovering what it's like to be with someone on a level I truly and unashamedly want. No expectations. No punishment. Nothing that can make me feel less than in this moment. Knox treats me as if I'm on his level and not a donor or blood slave. If anything, he makes me feel as if I'm finally alive and not standing on the ledge of my impending destruction.

"God, you're so fucking beautiful," he says, nudging me back as he climbs onto the bed. "I want to take you over and over again."

"I want that too. I never want to leave." The truth to my words rings in the air, and I grab Knox and kiss, stopping the frown from crossing his face. We both know it's more than me wanting to stay for sex. I want to stay to never have to face Alexander again. But there is nothing I can do.

"It won't be like this forever. I will make you mine," he says, the low growl vibrating against my lips. "You are mine."

"I'm yours," I repeat, arching my back at the sensation of his cock hard against my body.

My breathing quickens, and I clutch onto him as he grabs my legs and stretches them to rest on his shoulders. I bite my lip in anticipation and nerves, my body trembling and hot, my mind just wanting to know what it's like to be this intimate with someone at my choice. This is my decision, and knowing as much gives me the confidence I need to shove my nerves away and just enjoy the act.

Knox aligns his body with mine, pushing his tip inside me. He doesn't rush and watches my expression. The pressure steals my breath, the pain lasting for a moment, but it's not terrible or enough to make me do anything other than moan as he slowly rocks, watching himself as he enters me.

"You're so perfect," he murmurs, spreading my legs to expose my clit to him. Strumming his finger over my sensitive skin, he turns the pressure of his cock into pleasure, and I moan. "I can't believe how lucky I am. How does it feel?"

"Big," I say, squeezing my eyes shut, wishing my brain would've come up with something sexier to say.

He chuckles. "You're so fucking tight. So wet. It's taking everything in me not to just have my way."

I rub my lips together and clutch the blanket. "Show me what you like. I need to know. I want to find out what it's like to really be yours."

Growling with pleasure, my words set him off, and he drops on top of me, keeping one of my legs stretched until I'm doing the splits. I gasp and scratch my nails into his back with his thrust, his hips hitting my body with his powerful desire. My mind whirls as passion takes over, and I bite him, using his shoulder to silence my scream of pleasure and pain and everything raw and wild within me. Tingles flood over my skin, and he finds my mouth and kisses me, slipping his tongue across mine and silencing my mouth as I lose myself to everything he is and everything I had no idea I wanted.

Reaching between us, he takes care to touch me and tease my clit like he needs to ensure I get my fill of pleasure as he drowns in his own. I arch my back as my body explodes, my orgasm turning the ache between my legs into something hot and indescribable.

"Bite me again, Hayley. Bite me as hard as you can. Fuck me up. I like it," he says, his voice deep and growling. "I want your marks all over me."

His words unleash something dark and feral within my soul, and I scratch my nails harder into his back at the same time I bite him. He thrusts faster inside me, turning my mind to mush, and I bite him again, not releasing until his blood fills my mouth and tingles across my tongue. He grunts with a moan, hitting his body to mine hard enough to bang the headboard into the wall. Slowing down, he grunts as he cums. Knox slides his hands underneath me and lifts me on top, petting my hair and not saying anything as I continue to suck his blood, the flavor as intoxicating as the rest of him as it numbs the ache and pain of our passion while leaving only pleasure behind in its wake.

"You're so sexy. So fucking good. I can't get enough." Knox combs his fingers through my hair, slowing me down. "Wild like I enjoy."

I wipe my mouth on the back of my hand and smile,

blood probably smearing my face. If it does, it doesn't bother him, because he kisses me and tastes my lips, traveling his hands over my body to continue his exploration.

"Let me clean you up," he says, scooping me into his arms. "I want to take care of you. Feed and cuddle with you. I want—"

"What the actual fuck!" Sawyer's voice booms through the air as he stares at us from the doorway. He covers his eyes but doesn't leave, kicking the door closed behind him. "Knox, you fucked her? You fucked her in my bed! Fuck."

I tense at the mixture of surprise, anger, and something strange and unexpected—fear—in his voice. Stiffening, I cling onto Knox, afraid he'll abandon me on the bed to start a fight with Sawyer.

I whimper and bury my face in the crook of Knox's throat. "Please don't fight. I'm sorry. I'm so, so sorry."

Silence fills the air as both Sawyer and Knox hear my words.

"Fuck, Hayley. No. I'm the one who should be sorry. I just—I'm not mad. Maybe jealous, but I knew you liked this fucker. I'm just—this isn't my business. I was caught off guard. I'll come back later. I can wait." Sawyer's soft voice trickles through the air. "I'm sorry," he repeats.

The door slams shut, leaving Knox and me alone

again.

I ease away from him and meet his gaze. "I think we all need to talk."

His jaw tightens and he nods. "If that's what you want. But first, we're not leaving until I show you how much I appreciate you. How lucky I feel to be here."

I bob my head. "I hope that feeling always lasts."

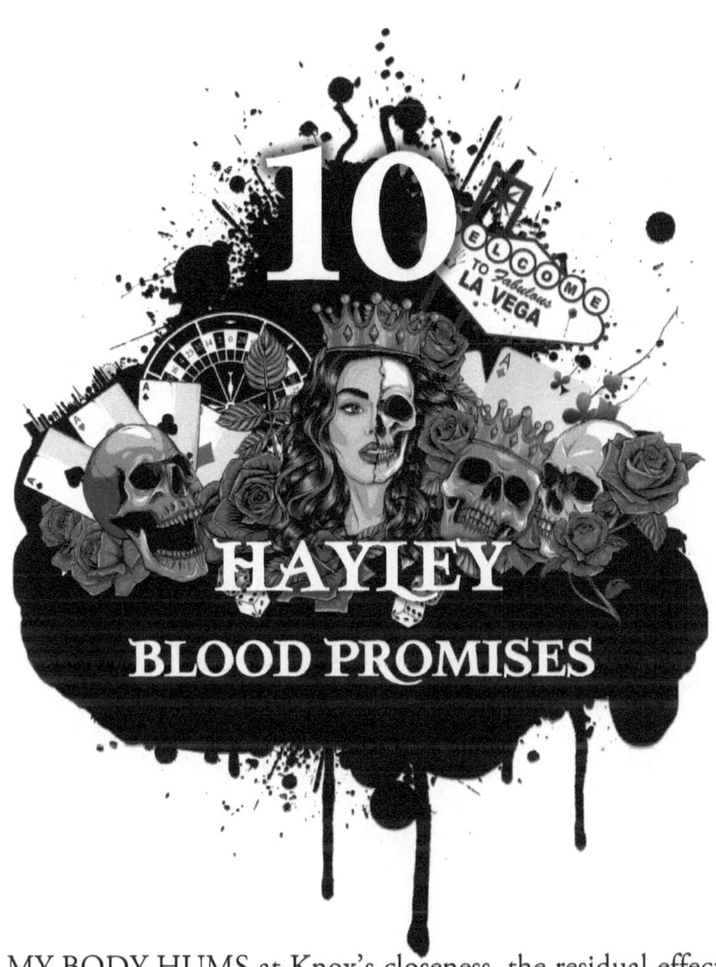

MY BODY HUMS at Knox's closeness, the residual effect of his blood lingering with me even though it's been two hours since I drank from him. I sit on his lap on the edge of Sawyer's bed, now with fresh sheets and all evidence of us having sex gone, though the memory will never leave my mind. Sawyer and Monroe stand together at the desk, filling up a couple glasses of blood and one with water for me.

"I'm going to try not to make this awkward as fuck," Sawyer says, breaking the silence. Turning around, he carries the glass of water along with his own and sits in the chair he brought from the desk. Monroe plops down on another chair from a small sitting area by the window, and I look between the both of them, wondering if I should put some space between me and Knox even if he doesn't want it.

"I don't think anything can make this any more awkward," Knox mutters, finally shifting me off his lap to sit beside me. I think he only does it so that he can see my face. "It was unexpected, and the only thing I'm sorry about is not moving it to my room. You can kick my ass later."

Sawyer tightens his mouth and flicks his gaze to me. "I'll get over it. You're lucky as fuck that I can only smell her still."

I crinkle my nose. "I'm sorry." Cringing, I recoil and cover my mouth, trying to remind myself that I shouldn't apologize. Knox already told me as much in the gentlest way imaginable while we shared a bath and he washed my body and gave me a massage. "I mean, Knox is right. It was unexpected. I—don't know what else to say. I like you

all, and...it's confusing. I know how vampires are, but—"
I close my mouth and shrug, giving up on trying to explain something I don't know if I'll ever be able to. "This is why I wanted to talk to you all."

I drop my gaze to my hands, not even knowing where to start. The three of them don't push me and just sip on their glasses of blood, being far more patient than any vampire I've met. Alexander would've yelled at me by now and Opal would've asked a dozen questions to get me to say what's on my mind. But Sawyer, Knox, and Monroe? They just wait.

I take a sip of water and rest the glass on my knees. "I need to know what we're doing."

It's not exactly what I intended to say, but I guess it's a start. Communicating isn't my strongest skill set, and it's hard for me to articulate my feelings. It's almost painful to do so, watching them glance at each other in silence.

"I mean, what is it you get out of this with me? I want you to be honest. You guys are different, and it excites me but also freaks me out. I'm a donor, and Alexander owns me. Monroe already told me that I have to go back to the Aris Hotel tomorrow, so...I want to know what I need to prepare for. I already never know what to expect, and this drives me crazy." I puff a breath through my nose and bump my shoulder to Knox's arm. "You drive me crazy in a good way but I'm afraid."

Sawyer sets his empty glass of blood on the floor beside him and leans his elbows on his knees, groaning. "We honestly don't fucking know, Hayley. When we were planning to put hooks into Aris and force the fucker there to pay us to keep things civil, we hadn't expected you. We only went to Vampire Nights to case the place."

"And then I saw you and fuck. I was gone." Knox slides his fingers through mine. "I'm nearly fucking certain you hypnotized me."

"Fuck, right?" Monroe asks, flashing his fangs with his brilliant smile. "I thought your ass was joking when you told me about her."

The two of them playfully punch each other, and I can't stop the smile from crossing my face. I flick my attention to Sawyer, but he remains expressionless, his eyes flashing and his thoughts not giving anything away.

I slowly reach out and rest my hand on Sawyer's knee, drawing his attention to mine. Grabbing my wrist, he tugs me to him too fast for Knox to intervene and wraps his arms around my waist until I join him in his chair.

"We don't know what it is about you, Hayley, but all I know is that we're not going to stand by and let Aris keep you. It'll just take some time. We're in the middle of preparing for a hostile seize of the city to get the fucking six heads of the Strip out of here before they destroy our home." Sawyer rests his chin on my shoulder. "The last thing I want is for you to get trapped in the middle of a blood feud. The others on our crew fear you might be our weakness, but I know you're going to be our rise."

"You're going to try to take over La Vega?" I ask, shifting my gaze to each of them.

"It's probably weird to hear because you've always been kept out of things, but things are turning to shit. More and more donors are getting kidnapped and trafficked between hotels when it was in our original agreement after The Divide not to separate them again. The hotel heads are getting careless, and others from outside of La Vega are trying to get their fangs into our city. There was a reason why we didn't incorporate with any of the territories. We had other plans and enough donors to create something we could all be happy with, but power has gotten to a lot of dickheads." Sawyer strokes his thumbs over the sides of my hands, his words sinking in to me.

"I had no idea," I say, pursing my lips. "Is that what you wanted to talk to me about earlier? About Henderson Evada?"

Sawyer nods. "I almost can't believe how we lucked out. It feels like fate brought you to us. We've been trying to figure out who has been behind snatching the donors we protect and picked up the asshole today attempting it. He's not the first, but he's the first to spill who his boss is with his guts."

"You should've seen it, little bird. The fucker won't ever try that bullshit again." Monroe wags his eyebrows at me. "Neither will anyone who sees our warning. I think it was Walcott's best work yet. Tatum had him add a dick on his cheek in your honor, too."

I laugh in exasperation and whip my hair back and forth, letting it pelt Sawyer in the face. "Why that in my honor?"

Sawyer growls at him and smacks him in the shoulder. "You better not fucking answer."

My brows peak on my forehead. Now I have to know. Pressing my hand over Sawyer's mouth, I say, "Yes, you fucking better. Why did she have a damn cock tattooed on that guy in my honor?"

Sawyer groans against my hand, glowering at Monroe.

"Relax, Sawyer. Hayley is fucking chill." Grinning at me, Monroe grabs my hand. "The bastard got a dick tattooed in your honor because Tatum has deemed you the queen of our cocks. Which is fucking true, little bird. Especially now. This—" He waves his hand between me and Knox. "This makes me want to bow down to your grace.

I'm desperate to earn my place and dip my dick in that glorious pussy that makes my mouth water ever since you teased me over the damn banana."

I tip my head back and laugh, his dramatics balancing out Sawyer's intensity. Knox chuckles and steals me back from Sawyer, spinning me away. I squeal at the quick movements and lock my legs around him before he tosses me onto the bed.

"Do I even want to know?" Knox asks, smiling against the crook of my neck.

Monroe play-growls. "She climbed me like a damn tree, teased me with some thigh muffs, and then practically deep-throated a banana all in the matter of seconds. It was fucking awesome and infuriating." He snaps his fangs at me. "I bet she tastes as amazing as her blood."

"Better," Knox murmurs, smirking at me.

"Goddamn it! Hayley, I'm desperate. Just—let me take you back to my room." Monroe hops from his seat and tries to lunge at me, but Sawyer cuts him off and knocks him onto his back.

"Later, okay? Right before I have to go back, so maybe you won't follow through with it." My smile falters with my comment. I intended it to be playful, but three pairs of serious eyes land on me, and I can't stop from flinching. "I mean, I know Sawyer wants to know more about Henderson. You easily distract me, and I'd rather get it out of the way."

Sawyer dips his chin, nodding sharply. "She's right. I also think we need to figure shit out." Turning to me, he adds, "I hope you know that we really fucking don't want to take you back, but if we don't, we'll have to accelerate our plan and fight before we're ready. Right now, the alliances between the controlling covens is strong. We're trying to break them. The shit with The Pala is a start. There are ten more we need to crack at that level before going after the six head bastards at the top."

Knox hugs me tighter. "We will make damn sure Aris doesn't do anything stupid."

I gaze at each of them, my emotions going wild. I shouldn't believe them, but I do. They haven't given me a reason not to, but my trust in vampires is thin at best. It should be instinctual to remain guarded. I'm a food source to vampires. Many of them—most of them—think of me as a means of survival and pleasure. What if things change? What if they realize that I'm not worth the risk? I don't even know if I am in the grand scheme of their plans. They want to change how La Vega is run, but if it came down to me or the city? They wouldn't choose me...or would they?

I'm afraid I'll find out.

"So what can I do? I want to help." My comment surprises me because I have no idea what I can even do. I'm a performer. I can barely stand facing Alexander. He'd know immediately if I started asking him questions.

"I want to say nothing, but you're in a position that gets you close to our enemies." Sawyer tightens his jaw.

"You better not fucking be suggesting what I think you're suggesting," Knox snaps, growling under his breath. "She's been through so much shit already."

Throwing his hands up, Sawyer says, "I know, damn it! I just—"

The two of them square off, confronting each other with silent stares. My fear instincts as a human go crazy, and I feel as if they'll start throwing punches at any second. Monroe gets between Knox, who still holds me, and Sawyer.

"All right, you fuckheads. You're scaring our girl. Get your crazy in check and chill. Everything will go to shit before any of us can do anything if we don't figure out whatever this is between us first." He motions to the four of us. Pointing at Knox, he says, "First, you better get your possessiveness in check. No one gives a damn if you saw her, kissed her, or fucked her first. That doesn't give you a right to go all asshole and controlling. I'm going to put this out there right fucking now. Hayley's life and decisions are already in someone else's hands. When she's with us, the only place she can be dominated is in the damn bedroom and only if she wants to be. I don't want to have to tell you fuckers again. I don't care if you're both more powerful than me. I will still fuck you up. We're not a damn coven. We're a crew and a team. It needs to stay that way for all of our sakes."

My mouth falls agape. Whoa. I don't know what to say or how to react.

"And you know what? I brought her here and promised she'd be safe and have a good time. Right now, you two are making me fail." Extending his hands to me, he silently asks for Knox to hand me over. Knox relents, and Monroe sets me on my feet and drapes his arm over my shoulder. "So do whatever the fuck you two need to do to get over your damn personal bullshit, and until then, I'll enjoy this stunning woman, even if it's just to feed her. You two assholes are either too stupid or caught up with yourselves to realize her belly alarm is growling like a goddamn beast, and there is no way she's going back to Aris starving."

I tip my chin and look at my stomach. I've grown so used to living in a state of hunger that I don't pay attention to the noise my body makes. I've learned to ignore it most of the time unless Alexander withholds food from me longer than anticipated.

"Shit, okay. I have an idea that should help us all and keep our girl out of danger," Sawyer says, scrubbing his hands over his scruffy cheeks. "Knox, call Tate and ask her to hook us up with someone from dining. I'll hack into the universal database with Aris's codes."

"What about me?" Monroe asks, rubbing his hand up and down my arm. "Please tell me I get to entertain our girl like I want."

"You fucking wish." Sawyer grins like a cocky bastard with his words. "I need you to take Walcott and go back to The Pala. Grab their transportation vehicle. I'm not wasting time worrying about Aris finding out. Make sure Perry knows he owes us a debt."

"Gladly. I can't wait to see the fear in that bastard's eyes. Did Walcott keep the cane? I want to swing that thing around. Maybe make him choke on it for a bit. Let him know what it's really like to eat Pala's ass." Monroe's eyes flash silver with his words.

I expect a wave of unbidden fear to consume me at the thought of Mr. Pala and his cane, but Sawyer's mind manipulation holds strong, and I smirk at Monroe's crazy-ass idea. "Can you take a picture or something for me? I need to see."

Monroe spins me around, making me laugh, and

pulls me flush against him, kissing me like we've been kissing forever. "Goddamn it, you turn me on so fucking much. I thought my brand of psycho would freak you out, but you love it, don't you? You want me to fuck everyone up."

The thought prods at my very being. I shouldn't enjoy the thought this much, but knowing that at least some vampires are paying for their bullshit gives me hope for the first time ever. Hope for a different future. Hope for change. Hope that this is only the beginning.

"Just the people who deserve it," I say, kissing him again. "I want them all to pay."

"Damn, there are more than we thought." Sawyer sets the stack of printed photos in front of the rest of the Bella Crew. "At least seven who've left positions of power from surrounding territories. We need to reach out to our contacts. We might not be the only ones gearing up to seize control. I bet no one even realizes."

"Think we should get word out? Make some fuckers nervous?" Govan asks, resting his palms on the table across from me.

I wonder if Mya knows any of this. She was having

fun with Govan when Perry kidnapped me. I feel badly that I haven't thought about her or the others much in the last few hours, and now that I do, I wonder how they're dealing. Someone would've had to step up to fill the spot as headliner. Emerald or Topaz, most likely. Mya would break her leg before ever filling the position. I know she purposely remains imperfect for that reason.

"Not yet but soon. We'll start with our allies at Sphere. Their crew can help monitor the entrance on their end." This comes from Knox, finally speaking up after silently watching me cross off every familiar vampire I could remember.

Sawyer acts like the leader of the Bella Crew, but I know Knox has enough power and wealth that the others seem to treat him equally. As for the others, I'm still trying to figure them out. Walcott and Monroe seem to be the face of terror, always taking care of the dirty work, though everyone seems to participate. Then there is Tatum, Govan, and Sullivan. Tatum is basically the gatekeeper to the donors in the Bella. She knows all of them and makes everything run smoothly. Govan and Sullivan seem to be backup and quiet brute force. As for the other ten or so vampires I've seen lurking around? They're complete wildcards. I'm sure there are more. The Bella Crew wouldn't be able to maintain their home here if there weren't a lot of them.

"The Lux Crew can take the other end of the Strip," Sawyer says, nodding at Knox. "We just need some fucking visuals, so it shouldn't cost too much."

"Cost?" The second the word escapes my mouth, I regret it only because everyone looks at me. I should be used to it, but for the first time in a while, I haven't been under the scrutiny of hungry vampires. They're more focused on what needs to be done.

"Blood, little bird. We have the largest donor populace outside of the head fuckers." Monroe materializes beside me, startling me at his sudden arrival. "We have a system. Crews are more willing to help when you have something to offer. Otherwise they're just as fucking useless as the Strip dwellers."

My mouth forms an O.

"We don't give them actual donors," Sawyer says, making a point to ensure I know Monroe means just gen. pop. blood. "Never will, either. They don't belong to us. This is their home as much as it is ours."

If only it could be my home too. I had no idea there were donors on the strip that didn't have to worry about dying by a vampire's fangs. I always thought that every donor in the world was claimed, and it's strange to know otherwise.

My emotions get the best of me, and I bow my head and stare at my half-eaten plate of pasta. Knox brought me way too much that if I even tried to eat another bite, I'd waste everything I've already eaten.

Sawyer rests his hands on my shoulder, massaging my tense muscles like he senses what goes through my head. "It has always worked out," he adds. "That's how we know it'll work out across the Strip."

"I can barely grasp the idea," I admit.

"That'll change soon. Promise." Monroe leans over and gets in my face, stealing my attention. "Now, come on, little bird. I have to get you home. The limo is waiting outside, and I don't know how long it'll take Perry to get over his shock of me forcing him to suck on the cane. A picture wasn't going to do this justice, and I figured since he had to drop you off that I'd take advantage."

My heart sinks into my stomach at his words. "I have to ride with him?" My voice quakes with my question. Fuck.

"Don't worry. You won't be alone. I'm riding with you," Monroe says, helping me to my feet.

"And we'll meet you there," Knox adds, offering me a smile.

Sawyer stands in front of me and surprises me by biting his arm. "I'm making you a blood promise, Hayley."

He touches my cheek. "And with this promise of our blood, we'll protect you in mind, body, and blood. Now don't look away. I'm going to ensure Aris can't manipulate you, no matter how hard he tries. We might not be able to break his control of you completely, but your thoughts will at least be safe from him."

If only the same would go for the rest of me.

ALEXANDER STARES at me with his fake, show-worthy smile as I hang above him on my hoop. The crowd cheers from below, licking the blood-rain from their lips like they truly think it has spilled from me. At least this time, I was prepared. Opal showed me how to properly cut myself without damaging one of my arteries to have a repeat of me nearly passing out from blood loss.

She also rigged my ring to send blood squirting from it to trick the audience. I'm not even sure Alexander knows. If he did, he'd probably insist on things being authentic despite what it does to my physical state since his blood heals me in seconds.

"All right, you fuckers! Who wants to help my baby doll Ruby with her final act? I'll need one hungry motherfucker to lick her clean." Alexander winks at me, his wicked smile displaying his sharp fangs. "You can even steal a bite. You'll be her first."

What? I freeze, my body stiffening. This wasn't part of the rehearsal, and he's once again throwing me off. After finding out what happened at The Pala, Opal told me she would make sure no one gets within reach of me. I haven't talked to Alexander yet like he purposely keeps avoiding me as a way to fuck with my mind.

"I hear she'd like to be bitten on her fucking incredible tits, that naughty ass, or her supple, smooth thighs," he adds, pretending to bounce my boobs in his hands from his spot below.

My nerves bunch in my stomach, and I tighten my grip on the hoop. This fucker. He's humiliating me and putting it into the audience's heads that they have the right to fuck with me later. If they think I like it, they'll push me and hassle me if they see me on the floor. That's one of the perks of Vampire Nights. We're not hidden and untouchable. He will put me on display in the damn birdcage again. I know it.

Dramatically searching the crowd, Alexander waves his finger over the front row tables of cheering and hollering men. The spotlight roves over them, and the sticky gen. pop. blood glistens under its glow. My jaw hurts from clenching my teeth, my smile never waning as Alexander hops from the stage and shakes his hips while waving his hands, pretending to struggle picking an eager guest.

He stops and taps his index finger to his chin. "Baby doll, I'm not sure anyone wants to help clean you up tonight."

A man climbs onto the table in the second row. "I'll fucking give you a damn blow job for a taste of her!"

Alexander's eyebrows peak on his forehead, and he rests his hand to his chest. "My, oh, my. Doesn't that sound...unappealing. Whoever gets that fucker out of my sight can lick this beautiful bombshell's toes."

Growls and snarls rip through the air as a dozen vampires lunge at the guy. I squeeze my eyes shut, trying my best not to react to the fight. The douche vampire must've expected something to come from his attempt to bribe Alexander, because he manages to dodge out of the way and stab another guy trying to rip his jacket off. The second the douche escapes through the exit, the vampires don't bother chasing him. If they leave, security will not allow them back in.

Alexander shakes his head with a growl. "Despicable. Don't you fuckers know my baby doll is worth far more than a subpar blowie? At least bend over and spread your fucking cheeks wide open for me."

God, please. Don't let anyone think he's being serious. Alexander doesn't need to be bribed with sexual acts. He has his collection of men and women, vampires and donors that he enjoys without strings or stipulations. Opal even fucks him, which is why the performers are off-limits. That's one line she won't let him cross.

Tipping his head back, Alexander laughs. "See, I knew you all were smarter than that." Strutting along the edge of the stage, he finally stops in front of a man, sitting in his seat and leaning his elbow on the table. "I mean, look at this fucker. He's not falling over himself for the chance. I like that. High standards. Power. He doesn't rush to beg because he doesn't give a flying fuck, which means my baby doll needs to change his mind."

The vampire lifts his gaze to mine, his eyes lighting silver with his scrutiny.

"What do you say, Mr. Baker? Would you like to

help Ruby clean off?" Alexander asks, rubbing his hands together. "Just look at her. She's dying to get that blood off. To feel your mouth."

Mr. Baker extends his fangs, finally reacting, and he stands from his seat. Howling in fake excitement, Alexander pats the guy on the back and shoves him toward the stage. The two of them climb up together, and I force myself to wave and blow Mr. Baker a kiss.

Jasper and Pearl roll out the plush, satin-covered bed, causing the crowd to go even wilder. Mr. Baker bites his lip, looking from the bed to me, and he adjusts his cock in his pants, clearly getting a boner just thinking about putting on a twisted show for the live audience.

My hoop hums, the tether unreeling to send me lower toward the stage. Heaving a few breaths, I try to get my pounding heart in control. I feel sick the closer and closer I get to Mr. Baker below me. His gaze devours me, and Alexander chuckles and bumps him with his shoulder, getting him to act like he's squeezing my boobs and pretending to lick the blood coating my skin.

My mind whirls. I don't want to do this. I can't pretend that I enjoy this kind of bullshit any longer. It was one thing to suck it up to protect myself from Alexander's twisted punishment, but now? The toughest of the Bella Crew promised to protect me. They promised that they would be here. But where are they? Would they risk intervening this time in front of everyone?

Fuck. Fuck. Fuck.

"Brace yourself, little bird. You're going to have to choose to fall instead of fly." Monroe's voice hums into my ear from the hidden com device attached to my headpiece. Only Opal has ever used it, but it's rare. Monroe must have hacked into it or something.

And brace myself to fall?

I don't get even a second more to think about it before the wire tethering my hoop snaps, and I scream, freefalling the thirty feet to the stage. I can't do anything as I land on top of Mr. Baker, his surprise stopping him from catching me. A shock of electricity pops overhead next, and the huge spotlight crashes to the stage next to Alexander, sending smoke billowing through the air.

The sparks set the satin on the bed aflame, and the crowd hums in commotion as the audience gets to their feet and heads in the direction of the doors. Vampires might be tough, but they're not stupid, and no one wants to spend hours healing from getting burned alive.

"Shit, Ruby," Opal says, materializing beside me. "Are you hurt?"

Before Mr. Baker has a chance to even try to bite me, Opal yanks me off him and hugs me to her. The world blurs as she relocates me out of harm's way as the stage crew puts out the flames and ensures the audience gets out safely. I'm so in shock that it takes Opal setting me on my feet to realize that my ankle hurts like a bitch. I intake a sharp breath and shift my weight to my other foot.

"Fuck, Hayley! Are you okay?" Mya runs from the dressing room and throws her arms around me. "That looked scary as shit! You were so lucky you landed on that asshole."

A deep, guttural growl reverberates through my bones. "That asshole was a potential ally and now needs something to make up for this disastrous show."

Pearl and Jasper stride in our direction. "We can handle it, Master Aris. He was cute, so you know I'll show him a good time." Pearl offers a seductive smile.

"You fucking better," Alexander snaps. "Take one of your sisters with you and don't disappoint me." Turning to Jasper, he flashes his fangs. "Rush ahead and ensure the suite is ready for entertainment."

Jasper nods and spins, running away without a second thought. Opal turns her attention to Alexander, and they share a few whispered words before she lifts Pearl into her arms and the two of them disappear, leaving me with Alexander.

I wobble, my legs aching and the pain getting to me

the longer he stares at me in sizzling silence. I don't know what to say, so I just try my best not to react under his scrutiny. This is the first time I've been alone with him since before getting taken to The Pala.

"Come on, Hayley. We're going to my office to get you fixed up. I can't have you limping around here and looking like easy prey." Alexander growls with his words, his face refusing to soften. "There are a few things we need to go over as well."

Shit. Shit. Shit.

Alexander grabs my wrist and yanks me with him. I cry out as his quick movements force me to put pressure on my ankle. I fall to my knees, tears burning my eyes, but he doesn't bother picking me up and carrying me like Opal would. Instead, he drops my arm hard, slamming it to the hard floor and locks his fingers to my wig, yanking it to drag me. The pins holding it in place rip at my natural hair, and I flail, trying to hook my fingers to his arm to lessen the pain.

My hip skids across the tile, heating up, and then the floor turns to carpet, and the rough texture burns me. I can't stop the sob from escaping my mouth as pain consumes me. Alexander manhandles me as a way to show me my place beneath him, but this is worse than usual. I don't know exactly what goes on in his mind, but I don't think

I've done anything wrong to deserve this.

Alexander drags me all the way to his private back-stage office, where he hides out when he's not in the mood to deal with the staff or needs somewhere private to truly punish us for something he feels we've done wrong. I've only been in here once before three years ago when I fucked up and kissed someone on stage who was one of the backrow assholes. It was when I first started headlining after the star of our show aged out and didn't know any better. I learned real quickly after that the expectations Alexander never thinks to share and just insists we know.

That's the problem with him. I never know if something I do is wrong until it's too late. I think he does it this way because the not-knowing and fear makes us less likely to push boundaries, which is true.

Until now.

"Why are you doing this?" I ask, landing with my back on the floor. "What have I done wrong?"

Alexander slams his door shut and hits the electronic palm pad to lock it. "Are you that stupid, Hayley? Maybe I should knock some sense into you."

"Wait, please—"

Alexander rips me from the ground, not giving me a chance to beg for his mercy and forgiveness. I land with my stomach on his lap, and he yanks down the bloody bottoms of my costume and whacks me so hard on the ass that I see stars. I tense, my muscles clenching, trying to brace myself for his next hit, but nothing prepares for the paddle he swipes from his desk, the sharp metal studs intended to make me bleed.

Agony swells from my ass cheek, burning over my skin with the force of his punishment, the humiliation of him treating me like this just as bad as the act itself. I gasp and cry, trying to stifle my sobs. I can barely think straight, his beating of my body worse than anything he's ever done. This is worse than getting struck with Mr. Pala's cane.

I'm afraid this might be it. He might've become fed up with me and no longer thinks I'm worth the trouble to keep around.

"Alexander, please," I whisper, managing to find my voice. "Please. I'm sorry for anything I've done wrong. Forgive me. Tell me what I can do to make things better."

Alexander sighs and stops paddling me. He flips me over, causing me to wince, and without even having to see my ass, I know it's raw and bleeding, his strength damaging me worse than if a donor had done such a thing.

He hugs me with tears shining in his eyes. "My baby doll. I didn't want to have to do this. You've always been such a good girl."

My lip quivers, my body wanting nothing more than to breakdown and cry harder. He's so twisted, and there is nothing I can do about it. He claims he didn't want to have to punish me, and I can't even call him out. He'll do worse. I know it. I can feel it deep in my bones.

"I wish I knew what has gotten into you, Hayley. You haven't been trying your best. You've ruined more than one show in the last few weeks. Not to mention, I heard you didn't do a great job at The Pala. I've heard rumors that you were a disgrace and cried instead of being the tough, sexy woman I've raised you to be." He purses his lips and searches my eyes. "There have also been whispers among the staff that you've been seen hanging around those Bella Crew assholes by the pool. I'd expect that from the others—I know they're good looking and bad boys are irresistible—but you have standards, my baby doll. I'd hate to see you fall as your mother had. It's why I'm so tough on you."

His words stun me, stealing away my ability to think. He's lost his mind. We've never had this sort of discussion. None of the other performers face this kind of bullshit, and I'm not the only heir of a former performer. Emerald is too, except her mom still lives here and has retired and was allowed to accept a union with one of the donor cooks to have children.

"I wouldn't, Alexander. I know her mistakes. Please, you have to trust me. I'm not like her. I live for you and this show. There is nothing going on with me. I was hanging out with Mya by the pool and then was taken when I was going back to my room. Maybe one of the staff mistook Perry for one of the Bella Crew? He acted like he was kidnapping me." I shift on his lap, wishing he'd stop forcing me to put some much pressure on my injuries. It stops me from getting my tears under control.

His face softens at my explanation. "I suppose that could've been the case, but it doesn't explain why you underperformed at The Pala. Our contract with that hotel is important. I should be hearing nothing but praise."

I break, my hurt shifting into anger as I think about Mr. Pala and his cane. It takes everything in me not to scream that he's out of his damn mind. If I had known what the hell was happening, I could've been better prepared. Instead, I was just taken and dropped off somewhere unfamiliar and basically told to spread my legs and give the men a good time.

"Of course I fucking cried," I snap, digging my nails into the palms of my hands. "Mr. Pala humiliated me. He hit me with his cane. The guests there wanted him to fuck me with it. They wanted to hear me scream and beg. He said that it was my job to please the crowd. I—couldn't do that."

Alexander groans and shakes his head. "Of course you could've, baby doll. You're the best actress I know. I wouldn't have negotiated a contract like that had I thought otherwise. You know what you're doing and how to please. I'm sure Mr. Pala wouldn't have gotten rough with you had you behaved. You know how it is. Assholes have the need to flex their power. It's your fault if you thought you could test a stranger."

I heave a few breaths, my stomach twisting. "Are you kidding me? You know I wa—am a virgin."

His eyes flash silver and he glowers. I try not to react at my almost admission of no longer being a virgin. "Why do you think I had you do the private show with the Grey Coven?"

Rage consumes me, and I swing my hand out and slap Alexander across the face. He roars and shoves me off him, sending me crashing to the floor. I try to scramble away, but he lunges at me, using vampire speed and grabs me by the wig, yanking the pins out and pulling it off.

"I should fucking cut your hand off, you ungrateful little bitch," he says, snarling with the words. Pulling a dagger from inside his jacket, he aims it at me, focusing on my arms. But he doesn't try to sever my limb. He grabs my real hair and yanks it above me so tightly that I clutch my head. Swinging the blade quickly, he nearly nicks my fingers as he chops through my locks and lets them spill around me. "You're so fucking lucky you need them to perform."

I cry and hit the floor, his cutting my hair also releasing me from his grip. I automatically clutch my scalp, feeling the uneven, chopping pieces left. "Alexander, please. I'm sorry. I didn't mean to. It was a reflex. I'm just—the Greys fucked me up. They tormented me and killed my friend. I hate thinking that you arranged it for them to have sex with me. I know you're not that horrible kind of a man. I know you wouldn't put us with a coven if you knew they'd hurt us. Right?" I sniffle, my eyes blurring, my mouth speaking softly, hoping he buys my act. I know better than to argue with him and his fucked up reasoning. Instead, I need to appeal with his need to pretend to care about me.

I'm still in shock over him cutting my hair, but it's the only thing I can lose. I should be thankful it wasn't my hand. It still hurts me on a deep level.

Releasing a rasping breath, he sets me on my feet and clutches my hands. My ankle throbs, but not as bad as my ass, and I try my best to keep my shit together when all I want to do is cry. I knew it was too good to be true, thinking that the Bella Crew could possibly protect me. I don't even think anyone has access to this section of the hotel beside Alexander.

"Oh, my sweet baby doll. You're so right. I had expected the Greys to treat you like the prize you are and not try to take things without permission. My heart aches for Quartz, and I'm terribly sorry I wasn't there to save you. If I could go back and change things, I would." He strokes my wet cheek, smearing my tears. "Will you forgive me for my poor judgment? I had no idea that you felt so strongly about that. If it would make you more comfortable, I can arrange one of my closest allies to help you with your virginity. I think you could really enjoy him, and then your days at The Pala won't be so bad."

I don't even know how to react to his words. He's dead serious, and now I worry he will stand by and watch the act of his ally thinking they're doing me a favor. I'm too scared to disagree with him. I'd rather wait it out instead of telling him to fuck off and have him beat me until he kills me.

"Can I meet him first? I just—everyone else got to choose, you know? You've been so adamant about what I do that I desire to have the best." My stomach twists and turns at my comment, the idea shadowing the edges of my vision.

"That might be a lovely affair. Perhaps I can arrange a

contract with him as well." Alexander notices me shaking on my feet. "I'll have to discuss it with Opal. She's a bit upset that I gave her no warning about the negotiations with Pala."

Of course she was. I don't say as much. I can't.

"If you could be my perfect baby doll and—" A siren goes off, ringing through the air. Someone hit the stun alarm, which sends all vampires to their knees if they're not used to it.

Alexander drops to the floor, covering his ears for a minute. I've never seen him affected like this before, and I can't help staring at him in surprise.

"Hayley, tell us where you are. We can't find you." Monroe's voice hums in my ear. "We thought you'd be with the other dancers. Mya said you were taken."

I open and close my mouth, afraid to make a sound.

Alexander composes himself and gets back to his feet. He rushes to get to his computer and taps the digital keyboard on the desk, bringing up a glowing projection on the wall. He glowers from the indecipherable stream of words, symbols, and numbers on the wall and to me.

Flying at me, he slams my back into the door and flashes his fangs. "This is the Bella Crew's doing."

I rub my lips together, trying to think of something, anything to say, but no words come out.

Alexander flares his nostrils and searches my face. "You know it's them, don't you? Is this because of you? You've been lying to me this whole damn time."

"What, no," I say, my voice rasping with my nerves. "I don't know what's happening."

He roars and slaps me across the face, sending me sprawling to the floor. "You're lying to me! I know it. I've known you all your life. I helped make you, and I can break you and destroy you all the same. I will do so before I ever let some asshole Strip dwellers think they can come in here and ruin my business."

I hold my arms up protectively. "Please, I swear. I don't know anything. Please. You have to believe me." I say a silent prayer to the universe. "What do I have to do to prove it? Please, Master Aris. Please." I use his title, hoping that it helps him see I'm serious. At this point, I'll do anything. He's hurt me so damn much already that I won't put it past him tearing me to pieces. I can't handle another moment of pain. Of this agony.

I knew I was stupid for thinking things could possibly be different, and that I could even think I was worth saving over the damn donor population. And why would Sawyer, Knox, and Monroe destroy their chance to change La Vega for me? I barely know them. I'm just a donor who likes all three of them. Maybe the idea of sharing me became too much already.

I just—fuck. The only way I can ever keep from drowning in this goddamn brutal world is to act as if my end is inevitable. There aren't psycho sweethearts intended to save me. All I can do is save myself by being Alexander's good girl who lets his guests drink their fill of my blood while also sucking their cocks and ensuring they always come back to the Aris Hotel for more. And now, I know I'm going to have to train myself to exist without hope. I'm not equal to vampires. I was born a donor. I was born a blood slave. And now that I've satisfied those expectations, I will have to spread my legs and accept the life of being alive solely for a man's pleasure.

Maybe it would be better just to die. I don't know how much more I can take. Alexander made it so I can never be tough. He smashed me into a million pieces early on and molded me into his perfect baby doll, so that's how I'll live and die.

Alexander's deafening silence digs deep into my very being as he studies me, keeping his gaze trained on mine. I don't try to speak or beg again. I know there is nothing more I can say. I just have to accept that he controls me. If he deems me useless, then that's it.

Releasing me, he drops me to the floor with a thud. I whimper, covering my mouth with my hand, trying to suppress my painful cries. Alexander strides to his desk and leans over, staring at his glowing projection screen. He clicks a few buttons and brings up surveillance of the hotel, tapping each of the individual feeds until he pulls up one from where the stage caught fire.

I catch sight of a figure blurring around the place, and Alexander follows along with the feeds, watching as the cameras turn off, not giving us a clear view of the vampire sneaking around. It takes hitting the dressing room for me to finally see Sawyer, peeking his head in and glowering.

"There's our asshole," Alexander says, growling deep in his throat. "He's coming for you, baby doll."

I try not to react. "Please, I swear. I don't know anything."

Alexander clicks off the feed and materializes in front of me. I cower in fear, staring at the dagger glittering in his hand. He points it at me, baring his fangs. He doesn't believe me. He's going to end my life right now to protect his business.

Snatching me by my short, choppy hair, Alexander twists the ruined strands around his fist and pulls me from the floor. I screech in pain, unable to silence my mouth, and he holds the dagger to my throat.

"I want you to listen to me very carefully, Hayley. You belong to me and only me. The only reason you aren't dead is because I don't want to get in another fight with Opal, nor do I want to waste an investment I've been growing and nurturing into someone invaluable for twenty-six years. But you need to prove to me that you're worth all the trouble. I want answers. You will find them for me." Alexander traces my throat with the blade but doesn't cut me. "I'll give you a week to give me something, anything, to work with in keeping the lowlifes in control. You will find out what exactly the Bella Crew plans, because I know they're not here for wealth and power."

"I—I don't understand," I say, struggling to find my footing with my throbbing ankle. "You want me to get you information? How?"

"Figure it out. I'll be fucking watching, and they're smart, so don't fuck it up. They'll know if I let your leash loose. You must do it as if I don't know. If you don't get me what I want, I promise you, baby doll. You'll wish you were dead. You'll beg for it. If you think your stay at The Pala was bad, wait until I rent you out to every hotel on the Strip."

I don't know how to respond or even if I should.

He doesn't wait.

Opening the office door, he lets it bang against the wall and disappears. I fall to my side and curl in on myself, my whole body twisting in agony.

"Fuck, Hayley," Sawyer says, releasing a growl.

He roars and punches the wall.

But I can't do anything. I can't find my voice. All I can do is sob.

12

SAWYER

CUT A DICK

"GET BACK. MAKE some room." I cradle Hayley's bloody and bruised body against me as I relocate her from Aris's hidden office. That shit wasn't on the map, nor were there any video feeds leading up to it. If I wasn't scared for Hayley and her condition, I would hunt the bastard down and murder him. I will murder him the second I get a chance. Screw La Vega. I need a war. I need blood to spill.

But I also need to get it together. I wish someone would beat the shit out of me, too. I failed to protect Hayley like I promised. We had managed to intervene with the show, but Opal grabbed Hayley too fast for me to follow and then security came. We weren't expecting to set a damn fire, and it's a shame that more of the place didn't burn along with the fucker who thought he could sink his fangs into my girl.

"What the fuck. Where was she? How did this happen?" Monroe throws a pile of clothes off the unmade bed.

"Don't be stupid. You know how. I fucked up." I flare my nostrils, wishing I could beat my own ass. "Knox! Knox, get your ass in here now!" I don't know where he is, but I know he'll hear me. The fucker has better hearing than anyone. "I couldn't get past the security network fast enough."

And I'm fucking pissed. I was five minutes too slow to figure out how to change the shock alarm to a pitch that would drop Aris to the ground. Five fucking minutes. It should've given me the time I needed to find Hayley, but that damn hidden office was nearly impossible to find. I could hear her screams through the com device I planted on her to monitor her safety. I could hear every damn thing the bastard did to her. And seeing her like this? Aris will pay.

"Oh, fuck. Fuck! Hayley, Jesus." Knox flies across the small hotel room we've taken over as part of our agreement to remain civil here as long as we get free use of the amenities. "What happened?"

Damn it. These assholes need to stop asking. They have eyes. They can fucking see our girl was attacked.

I ignore him with a groan. "Monroe, bring up the feeds. Look through every last one until you get a visual on Aris. He's a dead man." I carefully set Hayley on her side, ensuring she doesn't put pressure on her bloody and bruised ass. The fucker beat her well beyond submission with a studded paddle. He gave her a black eye and cut her long hair. I growl as I search over her small frame, trying to assess what else he did during what felt like the longest minutes of my life.

"I'll get some towels," Knox says, disappearing into the bathroom. "Hurry and try to give her blood."

"She wouldn't open her mouth on the way here. Something's wrong." I bite my wrist and hold it in front of Hayley's mouth, trying for the second time. "Hey, let me give you some blood. Can you drink? Please, I need you to open up."

Hayley doesn't respond, staring blankly like she

doesn't hear me. It twists my insides, and I fear Aris might've hurt her far beyond the point of healing with my blood. I don't actually know how much a donor can be hurt and then healed. I've never tried and there is no way I'd test it out.

"How hard did he fucking hit her?" Knox reappears beside me and lays a towel in front of Hayley and eases her onto it. He pulls out his com device and uses the light to shine it in her eyes. I watch as her pupils shrink, reacting. It's better than nothing. Her heartbeat is all over the place and she's sweating despite it being cool.

"I don't know. Sounded like a slap to her face. I couldn't get a visual. He was gone before I found her." I offer my arm once again, spilling blood on the towel as I try to get her to react to the bite on my wrist. Her jaw remains clenched so hard that I worry about her teeth. "She was hysterical and reactive when I got there, but the second I picked her up, she shut down. It was like a switch had flipped."

"Okay, I don't think he fucked her head up. I think she's in shock." Knox grabs a pillow and gently adjusts her clammy, cool body by elevating her feet. "Our blood will heal her physically, but she's traumatized. I don't have that kind of experience to help her." Knox rubs his fingers through her hair. We each have our skills, and Knox knows donor medicine to an extent. I'm the tech junkie, and Monroe specializes in combat, weaponry, and torture.

I clench my hands into fists, trying not to think about what this trauma Hayley experienced means for her. She was already struggling before. We've been extra cautious with how we treat her, but this? What if she can never recover? I snap my attention away from her before I lose my shit. "Monroe, do you have a damn visual yet?"

"I'm working on it as fast as I can," he mutters, tapping the screen of his com device. He groans under his breath, his finger blurring as he tackles checking through over a hundred different feeds. There are cameras everywhere.

"Yo, Sawyer. Get on her level. Don't tower over her." Knox keeps himself hunched over and carefully rolls Hayley onto her back despite my growling protest to keep her off her ass. Biting his arm, he dribbles blood over her mouth, using his finger to try to part her clenched jaw.

"I don't want to force her," he murmurs, stroking his fingers through her jaggedly cut hair. It shouldn't make me feel better that she doesn't react to his blood either, but it does. It's not just me. "Try to talk to her. See if you can connect with her mentally. But be gentle. Do not force your way into her mind."

A part of me fears looking into her glassy, blank eyes.

What if I'm not gentle enough? What if I hurt her? I keep my growl in check and drop to my knees, resting my chin on the bed. I graze my fingers over her jaw and tilt her head in my direction, finally meeting her gaze.

"Hayley, can you hear me?" I ask, lowering my voice to a whisper. "If you can hear me, just listen to my voice. I want you to try to use your senses. Start with things you see. Think about five things. Could be anything." I touch my nose. "Even if it's just the features of my face."

Her mouth twitches with a tremble, and the most amazing and terrifying thing happens. Her mind opens to me and she floods me with a hurricane of emotions that leave me breathless. I almost lose my concentration and break her eye contact under the intensity and pain that rattles me to my core. The last few times I've connected with her mentally, it was pure bliss, just feeling her trust in me. But now? All I feel is the damage and destruction Aris inflicted on her. She drowns in her fear.

"There you go. That's perfect," I whisper, my voice turning hoarse. I've never felt anything like this. Not with her or anyone. The suffering she experiences shouldn't be able to keep me on my knees. How she even manages to force a small smirk on her face is beyond me.

"Keep going, Sawyer. It's working." Knox rubs his hand over her cheek, whispering in her ear as I work on sending her my strength.

"Now I want you to try to feel four things around you. I don't care what. The bed. Your palms. Knox's fingers. My thumb. Whatever. Just focus on the sensation. I know you're in pain and scared as fuck, but please try."

Her eyes remain glued on mine, caught in my stare, and she groans as her hand reaches up and touches my cheek. I cover her clammy fingers, letting her press the weight of her hand into my skin. I savor it. Crave more. Her touch does something wild to my insides, and I project how her touch lights me up in the best way.

Again, she intakes another deep breath, her heartbeat still fast but no longer erratic.

"Good girl," Knox murmurs, letting her rub her head to his hand.

"You're doing great, Hayley. I want you to focus on three things you can hear. Anything. The sound of my voice. Of Knox's. The hum of the heater. Your own breath. Just listen and notice them."

Her breathing slows, and she remains looking at me, but her focus lingers elsewhere. Knox continues to whisper, and I offer her a smile.

"Beautiful, Hayley. This is what I'm talking about. I want you to breathe deep and concentrate on two things you smell. Hopefully Knox showered for you or I'll smack him." I chuckle, listening to Knox grumble.

Hayley's jaw unclenches with her smile, her eyes shining. "He smells so good."

My heart nearly explodes at hearing her voice and the lightness of her words.

"So do you," she adds, playing with the strands of my hair curling around my ears.

I grin. "Fucking perfect, Hayley. I'm proud of you. I know this was hard as fuck. I know I failed you after I made you a blood promise. And I'm sorry. I hope you'll do one more thing for me, okay? This one is important." I bite my wrist and let my blood pool for a second. "I want you to taste my blood. Let it coat your tongue and fill you up. Let me heal you, okay?"

Parting her lips, she slackens her jaw and quietly waits for me to press my bleeding bite mark to her lips. Her mouth molds over my skin, sending tingles buzzing over my body. The sensation gives me a damn boner as she sucks softly at first and then latches on and moans with a long drag of my blood.

"Damn, my turn. She's going to drain you," Knox murmurs, running his fingers over Hayley's back and silently checking her injuries.

"I'd be happy to let her." I smile, my fangs protruding from beneath my top lip.

Hayley hums under her breath and eases away, only to have Knox silently offer her his bite mark next. He lies next to Hayley and rolls her on top, so they face each other and she can stare into his eyes, enjoying their closeness.

I suppress my sudden jealousy, knowing that they have a connection on a more intimate level, but I know she's not ready for me. I'm not even sure if I'm ready for her. I want to prove myself worthy of her attention, and so far? I haven't.

"Hayley?" I ask, drawing my fingers over her sticky shoulder, still coated in blood from the performance. "Can I clean you off a bit to make sure you're healing? If not, maybe you'll let Knox?"

Hayley eases her mouth away from Knox's arm and cranes her neck, resting her ear to his chest. Her vibrant blue eyes flick over my face in consideration. "I'm feeling so much better. Can I just take a shower?"

"Of course. I'll get it running and find something else for you to wear." I hold out my hand and help her ease off the bed. "I'll have Govan bring some food or something."

Hayley tests the strength of her legs, rolling and moving her ankle. Relief escapes her with her sigh, and she puts weight down on her sprained ankle, hurt from her fall. I didn't want to have Monroe drop her from the height he had, but we needed the distraction, and I knew we could heal her. It was one of the hardest choices, and I hope she'll forgive us when I'm brave enough to admit as much. But right now? I just want to take care of her on the level she needs.

I guide her to the small bathroom with a standing shower and turn on the water for her. Steam fills the air, and I hesitate, nervous to leave her but wanting to give her privacy. Her gaze flicks toward the mirror, and I wish I could cover it. She reaches for the short strands of her hair, her mouth trembling as she takes in her appearance.

"It's okay. It's just hair," she whispers to herself so softly. She doesn't realize I can hear her, and I don't want to comment and agree with her. Because while she's right about it just being hair, it doesn't diminish the abuse Aris put her through. "It could've been worse."

I steel myself. It takes everything in me not to react and engulf her in my arms. She's more guarded than before, and I'll wait for her to show me she wants my affection without forcing it on her.

"I'll be right outside, okay? Just call if you need anything," I say, unfolding a towel to hang on the glass of the shower.

She turns and throws her arms around me, hugging me tightly, and I puff a breath and kiss her, thanking the universe that she gives me another chance to make up for my failures. I wait until she's ready to let me go, kissing her softly on the top of her head. She pulls away and drops her top without waiting for me to disappear, and I have to force myself to leave her and shut the door.

Even covered in blood, with red-rimmed eyes, a pouty mouth, and getting her hair hacked off, she's still the most beautiful woman I've ever seen.

I rest my back to the door, tensing at the sound of Hayley bursting into sobs. But she doesn't call out to me to come back.

Monroe punches the wall of the suite, leaving a fist-sized crater. His fangs extend, his eyes silver with his anger. Knox flexes his muscles, his body rippling with the same deadly desire I have.

"Where is he?" I ask, my chest puffing as I try to keep in control. I don't want Hayley to hear us.

"The coward left with that asshole from the show—Baker." Monroe spins around and slams his fist into the wall again. "Opal has security searching the hotel for Hayley. She cornered me and asked if I knew what happened. She's freaking out."

"I don't want to send her back out there," I say, hunching over and resting my palms on the desk. "Aris is up to something. I heard him demand Hayley to find out what we're doing. If she doesn't, he's going to fucking rent her out to the entire Strip."

Knox roars, his voice echoing through the room. He punches the wall mirror, shattering it to pieces. "I'm calling Walcott. We need to arrange another attack here. Full force this time. I want this hotel fucking down."

I stare at the two of them, my thoughts at war as I try to figure out what to do. The two of them will cut my dick off if I disagree with them, but I don't know if we're ready for that kind of blood feud. But right now? I fucking need to cut a dick on Hayley's behalf. If I don't maim or kill some asshole soon, I'll explode. I'll try to take on every damn bastard who works for Aris myself.

"We can call in the other Strip crews. See if we can get a couple who want to make some fucking noise," Knox adds, scrubbing his hand to the back of his neck.

I nod my head. "Something. We can work this bullshit in. Maybe they can do it for us, and we can still move forward."

No one gets the chance to agree with me, because a shock alarm blares, sending my head spinning. I clutch the wall and brace myself. We've all purposely exposed ourselves to every damn alarm on the Strip to keep us desensitized, and I'm fucking glad for it.

A thud sounds on the hotel door, and it shudders on the hinges. I slide my dagger from beneath my jacket and get ready to take out every last damn security personnel who thinks they could even stand a chance against me.

Rushing to the bathroom, Knox slips inside with Hayley, locking himself in with her. Monroe prepares beside me, waiting for the door to fling open. They'll regret it. I can't fucking wait for them to come in here.

Growls sound out on the other side of the door, and someone screams in pain. I glance to Monroe, wondering what the fuck is going on. Silence settles in the hallway outside the door. My chest heaves, and I clench my jaw in anticipation. What the fuck?

A light tap knocks on the door. "Mr. Noble? May I please come in?" Shit. Opal's voice trickles through the door. "I'm alone and unarmed. I'm also aware that you have Hayley, so please open up. I don't want to fight. I just want to see if she's okay."

"Opal?" Hayley's soft voice whispers from beside me.

And damn it. There is no way I can tell Hayley to get back into the bathroom and let me handle this. It's written all over her shower-damp face that she wants to see the second in line to the Aris Hotel.

If I tighten my jaw even more, I might break my back teeth. Glancing at Hayley, I ask, "Is it okay to let her in? I won't if you ask me not to."

Hayley frowns with my words. "She's my caretaker.

She didn't know Alexander would act this way."

"Fucking right, I didn't," Opal's voice echoes through the wood, and the doorknob turns down as she opens it. She had the capability all along and asked for permission as a courtesy. She tucks away the device she used to pop open the extra door lock and stands with her arms at her sides. She claims she's unarmed, but I'm sure she has something hidden on her. We both know she's a smart and powerful woman. She wouldn't carry the Aris Coven name if she wasn't.

I don't even have the chance to brace myself as Hayley rushes past me and jumps into Opal's arms. Knox quietly growls under his breath, watching our girl hug the woman that lets Aris get away with far too much bullshit. Monroe whacks him and gets him to stop. Hayley obviously has an attachment to this woman regardless of our feelings and there is no way in hell that I will try to take that from her.

"God, my gem. I was so scared." Opal touches Hayley's damp hair, her eyes darting to mine as she realizes Hayley's tresses have been cut. "Fuck. Did Alex do this to you?"

Hayley starts bawling, her pain and anguish flooding from her as she struggles to speak. Opal lifts her up and carries her into our room, letting the door shut behind the two of them. Knox and Monroe look to me for guidance, but I have no fucking clue what to do. Opal cries with Hayley like the two of them share the pain.

"I'm so sorry, Hayley. He knew better. He broke our agreement." Opal strokes her hand down the length of Hayley's back, smoothing her hand over the towel. "I knew the fucker did something when he left without saying anything to me."

"He hurt me so bad," Hayley cries, sounding child-like in Opal's arms. This is the kind of bond I've seen between parents and children—never between a vampire and a donor—and I don't even know what to make of it.

"I'm so sorry," Opal whispers again. "I'll take care of things, okay? I just want you to go back to your room and stay with the others. They're worried about you too."

"No." The word escapes my mouth before I have a chance to think about what I'm saying.

Opal whips her attention to me. "Excuse me? Hayley is mine. You will not come in here and try to take her from me."

Like fucking hell is she going to stop me.

Hayley shifts on her bare feet and holds out her hand, raising her palm at me. She turns to Opal next and touches her cheek. It's the only thing that stops me from snatching Hayley away.

"Please, don't fight." Hayley peeks over at me. "I know you all are worried about me, but I trust Opal with my life. If you try to take me...I can't go. Alexander will try to destroy you. Everyone knows I belong to this hotel, and he made it clear that he'll destroy me."

"He fucking beat the shit out of you. I don't care if he tries to start a war. We're not weak," Knox says, his voice booming.

Hayley startles, and Opal wraps her arm around her protectively. "Knox, please. Alexander wants to use me against you. You can use that, can't you?"

I groan and shake my head, wishing Hayley would stop talking in front of Opal. She isn't our ally. She's not even our friend. The only thing she is to me in this moment is an obstacle to get past.

"Not here, Hayley," I murmur, trying to keep from scaring her.

She purses her lips. "We can trust her."

Monroe shakes his head with a grimace. He steps closer a foot, ignoring the subtle hiss coming from Opal. Hayley might trust Opal, but for all we know, she is playing the good guy to balance out the bad guy that Aris is. It's easy enough to manipulate humans, and the rest of our crew will riot if they even suspected we gave anything away to an enemy coven.

"They can't, Hayley," Opal says, flicking her gaze to mine. "They never will, but it doesn't matter. It's time for them to get their shit and leave. We hadn't had these problems until they showed up, and I'm not losing any more of my gems. Whatever bullshit they're up to, we're not going to be a part of."

Hayley knits her brows together. "Opal, please."

Shaking her head, Opal says, "You need to tell them. They're here because they have their eyes on you. Make them go."

That's only partly true. We have been planning this seize for a while, but Hayley makes us want to fight harder.

Hayley shakes her head. "No. I can't. I need them. Alexander said—"

"I will deal with him," Opal snaps.

"Opal—"

Opal covers Hayley's mouth, cutting off her words. "Hayley, my answer is final."

Hayley yanks away from her, and I tense. Scrambling back, she closes the space to us, whipping her head back and forth. I expect Opal to react and try to grab her, but she remains firm in her spot, managing to keep her cool with Hayley's disobedience.

"No," Hayley says again. "I'm not making them go.

Alexander will sell me to the Strip if he thinks I can't get information from them."

Knox spins Hayley toward him and kisses her. "You need to stop. We'll handle it, okay? No more talking. She can't be involved."

Opal heaves a few breaths, looking from Hayley and to the rest of us. "I don't know what kind of bullshit this is, but I'm not going to stand for it. I will handle Alex, and we're going to get this shit sorted out, okay? Trust me, my gem."

Hayley remains silent. Shock washes through me. She's made it obvious in her decision. Hayley's choosing us. She trusts Opal, but she trusts us more.

Glowering at me, Opal flashes her fangs. "Don't even consider leaving this hotel with Hayley. Do you understand? You can stay for now, but don't think for a second I'll ever let her go. Understand?"

I remain tight-lipped.

Without another word, Opal vanishes, leaving me staring at the open door.

"Call the other crews," I say to Monroe. "We need to be ready for a war in case."

I just hope things don't have to go that far.

AS MUCH AS Sawyer, Monroe, and Knox wanted to keep me hidden in their hotel room, they thought it best to get out. Staying there would mean we were trapped when Alexander decides to show his evil face again. It would also be easier to just take them out. The last thing I want is them getting hurt on my behalf.

I don't have to see Opal or any of the security to know she monitors us. It feels as if everyone watches our every movement, trying to listen in on our conversations.

"Walcott is in the lobby," Monroe says to Sawyer, keeping his face expressionless.

"Go meet him," Sawyer says, strolling up behind me to look over my shoulder as I slide the hangers along my wardrobe, trying to figure out what to wear that isn't an over-sized man's shirt. It'll draw too much attention, and could cause more problems for me if the regulars think I'm open for this kind of thing. "Knox, you should go too. I'll bring Hayley down in a minute. I want to talk to her."

I swallow and tip my head back, staring at the bottom of his chin as he keeps his eyes trained away. I think I have an idea what he wants to talk about, but I'm nervous. I have no idea what the fuck is going to happen. I want to leave with them so badly. I would give anything to step outside this hotel again. The safety I felt at the Bella was incomparable, and it makes me sick to my stomach that I may never feel that way again.

"You got it, man," Knox says, waving a silver dagger.

The two of them disappear together, leaving us alone in my suite. Sawyer fidgets behind me, glancing at his com device for what I think could be the thousandth time since I asked them to bring me here to change, and it makes him nervous. Again, he probably feels trapped.

I finally decide to wear a shorts-style, one-piece jumper, covered in sequins. It covers everything on me from my thighs to my collar, only showing off my legs and arms.

"Can you help me with the back?" I tug Sawyer's big shirt over my head and drop it to the floor in front of me.

He intakes a soft breath, the heat of his gaze devouring me in the mirror hanging on the closet wall in front of me. Goosebumps prickle over my skin at the sensation of his body hardening against mine from behind. He gulps and nods, struggling between keeping my eye contact in the mirror and looking down as I stand completely naked.

I bend down and accidentally—okay, not accidentally—bump my ass against him as I step into my one-piece costume. He grunts at the sensation and reaches to steady me with his big hand on my hip. He feels enormous against me, his hard-on pitching a tent in his pants that he doesn't even try to hide.

"So, you were a virgin," he says, his voice remaining even.

I tense and slowly rise to my feet and lift my hideously uneven hair, some of the strands only three inches in length now. "Is that what you wanted to talk to me about? You heard everything between Alexander and me, didn't you?" I try not to frown, replaying the horrible punishment in my mind. Even though Sawyer helped ease the pain with my permission, it still gets to me like Alexander permanently branded my very soul so forgetting would be impossible.

Sawyer clears his throat and shakes his head, quickly and effortlessly busying himself by fastening my snaps in place. "No, but I just—I'm sorry. It's none of my business. Forget I asked."

I spin around and smile at his sudden nerves. I'm glad he brought it up, because it helps distract me from all of the other bullshit going on. "No, I'm not forgetting. I think you have earned the right to know the truth. You're risking a lot by staying here."

His lips disappear into a thin line, and he studies me, trying to tell if I'm serious or not.

"I mean, unless you really don't want to know." I grab his hand and slide my fingers through his. "You can just tell me what you had planned to say."

"It doesn't matter to me. I was just surprised." He puffs a breath of air through his lips. "That sounds bad. I don't know how to explain it without sounding like a dick."

I don't know if it's the fact that we're alone or that he saved me from one of the worst moments of my life, but I feel closer to him and want him to stop being afraid of asking me questions. It probably helps that he's been in my head. Opal once told me that some vampires who excel in mind manipulation can even feel a donor's emotions. I'm certain Sawyer is one of them. "You don't sound like a dick. You sound nervous and curious."

He licks his lips and holds my gaze. "I can't help wanting to know everything about you yet I also don't want to push you."

"Sometimes I need to be pushed. I'm...it's hard to remember that I can speak my mind with you. I like it." I trace my fingers up his chest, memorizing his solid pec. "And so you know, I was a virgin in a sense that I've never had sex with another person before Knox. I'm experienced in other things, though. I know what I'm doing when it comes to pleasing someone."

"Does Knox know?" he asks, flicking his gaze past me.

I shrug. "I didn't tell him because it wasn't important. I don't really have expectations in regards to anything. I was just glad that..." I let my words trail off. Bringing up Alexander and how he used to treat me isn't what I want to think about. I knew I'd eventually have sex, and I'm glad I got to pick who I wanted to experience it with. It was exciting and amazing knowing it was completely a decision I had a choice in. I lift and drop my shoulders again, offering him a smile.

Bending forward, Sawyer surprises me with a sensual kiss, taking his time to gather his thoughts while distracting himself with my mouth. I stretch on my tiptoes, balancing by holding his shoulders. Like an explosion booms between us, I let Sawyer lift me up and kiss me harder. I hook my legs around him, kissing him deeper, gliding my tongue over his. He groans and cups me by my ass, keeping me flush against him. I love his need for a distraction, and I hadn't realized how badly I needed one too.

I break from his lips and kiss my way to his jaw, sucking and licking his skin, enjoying the sweetness that reminds me how incredible it felt sucking the blood from his arm as he healed me. Drinking vampire blood isn't exactly my thing. I do so to keep my body free from scars and also to help myself when I'm injured. And right now, it's really fucking strange that I'm thinking about doing it again without having the need.

"You're so hot," Sawyer murmurs, clicking his fangs in my ear. "So intoxicating. I love being close to you."

He's as turned on as I am, though I'm certain his could be triggered by more than just my closeness. He's probably hungry, and I know that a vampire can be triggered from blood hunger to blood lust, and I'm teasing a dangerous line thinking about offering my throat to him.

But I want to. I want to just use him to forget everything and to push away my thoughts about my life before he and the Bella Crew came rushing in with weapons blazing. I want to remember that tiny moment of what freedom felt like when I was at the Bella. I want something to savor and to hold onto as we're forced to face the shitshow of a reality I'm not so sure I can truly survive.

"You want a taste?" I whisper, exploring the planes of his taut muscular back. It's so broad that it could take me all night to memorize every inch of it.

"Hayley," he murmurs, kissing my throat. His tongue caresses my skin, and he sucks the skin of my neck hard enough to leave a hickey. "I shouldn't. I'm already taking things too far."

"Too far? Not to me. I like this and don't want to stop. I give you permission to bite me and drink. You're hungry." I tilt my neck to the side, exposing more of my throat. "You've taken such good care of me. I want to do the same for you. Please, let me."

He groans, scratching his fangs along my skin, teasing me without biting. "I don't want you to feel like you need to exchange things with me. I'll never ask for anything in return. My protection doesn't have strings attached. I expect nothing from you."

I can't stop the smile stretching across my face. My cheeks hurt in a good way, and I can't remember ever smiling this big except by force during one of my perfor-mances. "That's why I'm offering. I know you don't. So let me give you this. I don't have much to offer, and it bothers me. At least let me do this."

Humming deep in his throat, he brings his lips back to mine as he kisses me with explosive passion that makes me gasp against his mouth. I comb my fingers through his hair and bend my neck again, this time guiding his face to my throat.

The world jerks around me, and I laugh at Sawyer suddenly relocating me back into the room. He sits in one of the plush chairs, letting me straddle him with my knees outside his. The sides of my legs press into the arms of the chair, and I use my strength to haul myself as close as I can get to him until I feel the length of his boner between my legs.

"Bite me," I whisper, loving that despite the low tone of my voice the words still come with an unexpected command.

Brushing his fingers into my hair, Sawyer repositions my head and kisses my throat. I moan at the sensation of his fangs piercing my skin and can't help myself from reaching between us to rub his hard-on.

He shifts beneath me, his desire running as hot as mine. I want him now more than I realized, but a part of me fears putting us in a vulnerable position in a moment we need our guards up.

Breaking away from his bite, Sawyer licks the blood from his lips and kisses me again. He sinks his fangs into his tongue enough to send his blood flooding into my mouth. Tingles burst through my body, and I can't stop from turning our kiss into a full-blown battle to suck his tongue, feeling as his blood eases the slight ache of his bite until it disappears altogether.

"You're an amazing kisser," I say, easing away as he slows down. "I want to do it all night."

"I'm about to figure out how to get past Opal just to make it happen for you." His gruff mention of Opal snaps me back into reality. "She's going to cause problems."

Oh. Not only does he bring me back to reality, he unintentionally slaps me with it. I don't know what I was expecting from Opal. She raised me. She's been my caretaker while Alexander has been my master all my life. I don't know why I expected things to just be magically okay between her and the Bella Crew.

"She's protective of me," I murmur, sighing and resting my head to his shoulder. "She's doing what she thinks is best."

"For her and the Aris. Not for you, Hayley." Sawyer draws his fingers up and down my spine, his affection the most incredible thing in the world. I never want him to stop, but I know that nothing good can ever last. The fact that he moves his hand to scrub his chin proves it. "We need to make some decisions and soon. There is no way I'm leaving you here. She can only do so much to protect you, and it's not enough."

I twist my mouth to the side, unsure of what he's getting at without assuming. "So what are you saying? What do you suggest? I can't let you hurt her. Without her, the other performers—my family—won't survive. Can't you form an alliance with her? It would help. You could tell her about your plans and—"

"No." Sawyer's sharp word interrupts me, and his eyes blaze silver. "She belongs to the Aris Coven, Hayley. I know it doesn't feel like it to you, but she is our enemy. She has to be. My crew will not stand by and hope for the best. There is a war coming, and if it comes down to it, she will fight against us. Against you."

I drop my gaze and hang my head. "Okay."

Touching my chin, he nudges me to look at him. "No, it's not okay. I know you love her and look to her as your caretaker, and it really fucking sucks that you're in this position. It kills me that I know you're only agreeing because while you care about Opal, you hate Alexander more. He's been abusing you for your whole damn life. I wish it didn't have to be a decision you have to make either, but it is what it is. I need you to think long and hard about it. Do you want us to get you out of here? If we do, you're never coming back."

"And if I stay?" I can't help asking.

I want to leave. I want so badly to run away with the Bella Crew and never have to think about Vampire Nights, performances, Alexander, or risking my life every damn second just by existing. But what about Mya? The other performers? I've only been with the Bella Crew once outside of this hotel, and what if it turns out to be worse? He's talking about a war. About Blood Feuds.

"I can't promise to be able to protect you like I thought I could." He slumps his shoulders in defeat. "Aris is more cunning than I realized. I can't keep asking my crew to endanger themselves for my selfish obsession with you. I'm not always a good man, Hayley, and the fact that I will ruin everything for you without a second thought...please. Come with me. Come with us."

I think about his words, letting them swirl through my mind. I've never felt so conflicted in my life. He's not asking me to sacrifice myself to change the future. He's telling me that he will sacrifice the future for me.

I sigh a long breath and kiss him again, just wanting to feel his closeness. "Ask me using mind manipulation," I finally say, meeting his beautiful sky eyes. "Pull it out of me. I need to know what I truly want."

Sawyer furrows his brows. "Hayley, I ca—"

"You can. Please." I comb my fingers through his hair. "I want to know what my heart really wants. I need to see if it aligns with my thoughts."

Closing his eyes, he cuts me off from his gaze and slackens his jaw, a dozen expressions twisting over his features. He thinks quietly to himself, and I stroke my fingers over his cheekbones until he finally opens his eyes to look at me.

"I'm afraid," he admits, resting his head back. "What if it's not what I want to hear? I want you to go. It's taking everything in me not to just kidnap you."

"There is always that," I muse, trying to lighten the mood.

He chuckles and shakes his head. "Now you're tempting me, but really, Hayley. It needs to be your choice. It's what me, Knox, and Monroe agreed on."

I blow out a breath. "So ask me." Clutching his face, I lean in and capture his eyes like I can force him to prod into my head.

He reacts, locking his gaze to mine. My body relaxes as he opens my mind, connecting with me on a level that might be as intimate as sex. I don't feel like he's controlling me, but I do feel more open and less guarded.

"Hayley, I want you to speak freely, okay?" he asks, his eyes now steel-colored with his power.

"Okay," I respond, my mouth and brain feel a bit of a disconnection as the answer automatically comes from me.

Leaning closer, he ensures to fill my world with him and only him. "I need you to make a decision. Tell me, do you want to stay or do you want to go with us?"

I lick my lips, my stomach fluttering. "I want—"

The door to the suite flies open, jerking Sawyer's gaze from mine, cutting off the pull of his mind manipulation to get answers from me. He growls and hops up, clutching me in his arms. I whip around and catch sight of Garnet in the doorway.

"Hayley," she says, tears streaking down her made up face. "Help me."

I frown. "What's wrong?"

Garnet waves her hand, drawing my gaze to a knife. "Hayley, please. Help me."

My eyes widen. "I don't under—"

My words turn into a scream as Garnet jerks the knife across her throat, sending blood spilling down her pure-white costume. She drops to her knees and falls flat on her stomach.

"Hayley?" another voice says from the hallway. Mya

steps into the doorway, not even reacting to Garnet bleeding on the floor.

I spot the knife in her hand.

"Hayley, please," she says, her voice monotonous.

"No!" I shout. "Mya, no!"

UNEXPECTED ALLY

MYA SWIPES THE blade with a scream. I shriek, my whole body going numb. A figure materializes behind her so fast that it takes my mind a second to catch up. Monroe protects Mya's throat with his arm, taking a deep cut to his forearm from his wrist to his elbow. He swears with a growl and snatches the blade from her grip.

"Get her! The fucker manipulated her mind. You need to break it, Sawyer." Monroe carries Mya into the room.

She flails, kicking and screaming, the high-pitch of her voice ringing in my ears. My eyes blur with uncontrollable tears, and I freeze in my spot, trying to grasp what the hell is happening. Knox touches my cheek, getting me to look at him. I throw my arms around him and break down, unable to control the grief swelling inside me as I realize that Garnet slit her own throat and Mya nearly did the same.

"Hayley, look at me," Knox says, guiding my head back until I peer into his sapphire blue eyes. "I'm sorry about your friend. We had no idea that Aris had gotten into their heads. Something must've triggered their manipulation. They could've been walking around for who knows how long like a bomb on a timer, waiting for something to set it off."

I grimace at his words, trying to figure out what any of that means. "He manipulated them to kill themselves? I don't understand. Why would he? They bring him money. He—" I yell in anger, letting my voice fill the room.

"Mya, don't fight." Sawyer's voice snaps through the air, stealing my attention. "I won't hurt you."

I shift in Knox's arms, summoning the courage to

stare at my best friend now hanging placidly in Sawyer's arms. Her arms hang by her side. Gripping one arm across her back and clasping her face with the other, Sawyer leans in so close that only an inch of space remains between their mouths.

"You're going to feel some pressure while I connect to your mind on an uncomfortable level. It will hurt a bit, and I'm sorry." Sawyer keeps his voice low as if he speaks to a frightened child. His hulking body towers over her, and seeing her look so fragile twists my stomach.

"Hayley, please," Mya says, keeping her eyes locked on Sawyer's as she talks to me—but she sounds weird. Almost like a recording and like she's not really there.

Sawyer growls under his breath, his fangs extending. Mya releases a tiny whimper, her body turning completely limp as he focuses on her with his silver eyes. Tears stream down her face. I clutch onto Knox, using him to support me. I can barely stay still watching this. Her features twist with her pain.

Fuck. I don't know if I can handle this. It's one thing to be on the receiving end of mind manipulation when it involves protecting someone, but this is different.

"Mya, you will forget whatever Alexander Aris put in your head. You are the only one in control of your mind." Sawyer leans so close that their noses touch. "Do you understand? You will not be controlled by Alexander."

Mya heaves a few breaths, her body reacting to the mind manipulation. A wail rips from her mouth, her pain smacking the air from my lungs. Sawyer clutches her tighter, refusing to let her go. I cover my ears, the sound unbearable. I hate this. I hate everything about Sawyer digging into her mind, but it's worth it. I would rather her survive this and not die because of something Alexander did. She's my best friend, and it's bad enough that she's dealing with this alongside me.

"Hayley, hey. Hey. Concentrate on me," Knox says, twisting me back to him to steal my attention from the madness unfolding. "He's almost done."

I turn and let Knox help me cover my ears, his big palms hiding mine as he gently presses down. I study the blue color of his eyes and wonder what it looks like in real sunlight. I don't know why I even think about it. I haven't been in direct sunlight, and only UV lights.

What am I even thinking about? Such a thing would be impossible. He can never go out in the sun, and I'm pretty sure that neither can I.

A vicious snarl startles me, and Knox snatches me, lifting me off my feet. I stare in shock as Opal shoves Monroe, sending him tripping over Garnet's body. Flashing her fangs, she yells in anger and tries to launch at Sawyer and Mya. Her eyes shine silver as she grabs the back of Mya's costume.

"If you pull her away, I might accidentally damage her brain," Sawyer says, his deep voice rumbling with his words. "I'm trying to help her."

"You killed one of my gems." Opal yanks a dagger from a hidden sheath. "I'll take your heart. Now release her!"

Monroe intervenes and tackles Opal, knocking her into the wall. The two of them flash their fangs, the scary-ass growls of their voices igniting a spark of panic inside my chest.

"Opal, please don't," I say, my voice shaking as I find my words. "This wasn't them. They're trying to help. Alexander did something to them. He got into their minds. Garnet surprised us."

"I'm so sorry, Ms. Aris," Monroe says, using Opal's formal title. "I couldn't get here fast enough for her." He points at Garnet's body, taking a second to snatch the blanket from my bed to drape over her body, blocking my view of my fallen friend.

Opal stands frozen, her whole body rigid with her devastation and anger. Her eyes rove over the blanket covering Garnet and to Mya, hanging limply in Sawyer's arms. A dozen emotions cross her gorgeous face, and tears sparkle in her eyes.

I slowly ease away from Knox, forcing him to let me go, despite knowing he doesn't want to take his hands off me. "Opal, they're telling the truth. Alexander did this. He's punishing me."

Opal doesn't respond to me and silently strolls to where Garnet's body hides under the blanket. She lowers herself to the floor and rests on her knees, heaving a few shallow breaths as she gets the nerve to pull the blanket down. My lip trembles and tears fill my eyes, seeing the blank stare and blood all over Garnet. Her sisters will be devastated. They've been here since I was a teen and were part of the show before I was. They do everything together. I can't believe this happened.

"Are you certain it was Alex?" Opal asks, her voice stern and sharp with her words. "It could've been one of you setting this up. Alexander knows how much these girls mean to me. We have an agreement."

I shuffle my way closer to her and kneel by her side, wrapping my arm around her. "You don't really believe I'd let them do this. Have you ever seen one of the Bella Crew members hurt a donor? They wouldn't. This was Alexander getting back at me."

Closing her eyes, Opal bows her head, whispering something that sounds like a plea under her breath. I hug her close, listening as Sawyer commands Mya to fall asleep and to forget he was ever in her mind.

Sawyer locks his hands to the back of his head. "This is why we want to take Hayley from here. What he had done to her...it was irredeemable and inexcusable. What he's done to your performers is just as bad."

"We had a deal. I can't believe it." Opal purses her lips and blinks the tears from her eyes.

It takes her a long moment of silence to gather her nerve and strength to get back to her feet. Reaching down, she grabs my hand and helps me to stand. I know that Sawyer told me that I'd have to choose between leaving and being under his protection or staying and risking my life. I had made up my mind in the matter and was going to go. As much as Opal cares about me and has been here all my life, she has never truly protected me like the Bella Crew. Her alliance lies with Alexander and has forever. They have eternity when my life could end in a couple years, months, or days even. I could die in an hour. That's how vulnerable and small my life is in comparison to an immortal. With the Bella Crew, it doesn't feel that way.

"This is why you need to let us take Hayley. She wants to go, and we can protect her." Sawyer steps closer and takes my hand, tugging me away from Opal. "I think you care enough about her to let her go. Don't leave her to the fate of your coven brother."

Opal hisses and rakes her fingers through her hair, her emotions going wild. "You don't understand. She needs me. You think you can take care of her but there is more to it. You have no idea what—" A chime rings through the air, cutting off Opal's argument. Her eyes shift around the room, and she looks more frazzled than I've ever seen her. Tugging her com device from her pocket, she glances at the screen and then to me. "My answer is still no. Hayley isn't just a performer to me. I will fix this. Alexander needs me to make this work, and I will remind him. The show won't go on otherwise. My gems will not perform. That's a promise."

Sawyer, Knox, and Monroe all growl. My heart sinks into my stomach. I thought that perhaps after Opal saw what Alexander had done that she'd trust the Bella Crew to keep me safe. I thought that this could lead to a possible truce between them. Now? They're more angry than ever.

"Ms. Aris, please reconsider," Sawyer says, tightening his jaw. "Let Hayley go. He will kill her. You didn't see what he put her through."

She squeezes her eyes shut and darts to grab onto Mya. "He won't. I will protect her. Now don't make me fight you. These girls will get hurt being in the middle. Just let us go."

I whip my head back and forth. "I'm not staying, Opal."

"Hayley," she argues, clenching her fingers into fists. "This isn't up for discussion. You don't even know who you're truly dealing with. The Bella Crew murders people. They're vile and disgusting monsters. You think they'll treat you any differently? You won't—"

"You're a fucking hypocrite," Monroe snaps, growling with his words. "You're far worse than anything we could ever be. We—"

Swinging Mya by her arm, Opal throws her in our direction. No one has a chance to react or fight as Mya awakens from her haze and crashes into me. A strong hand locks onto my ankle and another on my wrist. I screech in pain as Opal and Sawyer both refuse to let go of me, stretching my body between them.

"You're going to hurt her," Knox says, unsheathing a dagger. "Just—fuck! Drop her now!"

"No!" Opal hooks her fingers to my other leg and pulls harder, using all of her vampire strength.

I wail in pain, feeling as if my body will rip in half. Sawyer gives in and releases me, his growl reverberating through my bones. Throwing a knife, Opal strikes Sawyer in the chest and drags me to her. She abandons Mya and darts away with me, running at vampire speed. I scream and try to fight against her as the world blurs. She turns and heads into one of the corner suites. Sawyer calls for Monroe and Knox to split up and head to the lobby. I tilt my head back and stretch my arms, reaching for Sawyer. He's too far away though.

Opal races to slam her hand on one of the palm pads of the suites, and the door unlocks and swings open. I hadn't realized it, but the sun hangs low in the sky. I rarely ever pay attention to the world outside the tinted windows. I've already lost track of time with my lack of schedule the last couple of days, and now I feel disoriented. Fearful even. Opal slams and locks the door and charges toward the door leading to a balcony. She's going to take me outside. She's willing to risk sun exposure to keep me away from the Bella Crew.

Oh-fucking-no.

"Opal, please. Don't do this. You're going to get burned." I dig my nails into her arm, trying to get her to let me go.

Opal sets me on my feet and spins around, searching the room for something I'm unsure of. "You're worth the risk. I know you don't understand it now, but I'm thinking about what is best for you. I know you think you like those guys. I know they've treated you unlike any man has treated you in your life. If you were any of the other dancers, I wouldn't fight so hard. You're special. I made your mom a promise all those years ago to look after you, and that's what I've been trying to do."

Anger rushes through me at her words. Opal snatches the duvet from the king-sized bed and wraps it around her. Grabbing a pillow next, she strips the case off of it and adjusts it over her head. She's creating sun-protection gear.

A loud bang knocks on the door, shaking the thick wood. Opal hisses under her breath and runs to the balcony door, hitting her palm on it to get it to unlock. If it were another guest, it would remain locked until sundown to stop anyone from trying to use the sunlight against a vampire—because I guess that has happened in the past between vampires and donor companions—and it freaks me out that Opal lets the light in.

I squint and shield my eyes, the light as intense as what I'm used to smiling through on stage. Opal stands just out of the way of the streak of sunlight and rubs her hands together. The second she shifts toward the door, testing out her sun protection gear, I break away from her and run toward the exit leading into the hallway. I don't make it far. Opal materializes in front of me, stopping me from unlocking the door.

Lifting me up, she forces me to hug her with my

whole body. If she wasn't rushing toward the balcony, I'd try to fight her, but her quick movements trick me into holding on tight. Light engulfs us, blinding me as my eyes try to adjust, and I hear Sawyer yell and the door smashes to the wall.

I scream and try to fight Opal. All she does is tighten her arms around me and swings her leg over the balcony. My chest clenches at the sight of the drop toward the street. We're at least twenty stories up, maybe more. She's going to jump. I know she's going to. My mind whirls with fear, and my eyes blur with tears. I'm not usually afraid of heights or risking falling, but this is too much. Opal is being careless. She can survive splattering on the ground, but I fucking can't.

"Opal, please," I beg, squeezing her as tightly as I can. "I'm scared."

"Don't be. I'll keep you safe, my gem. I'll do better from now on. You'll see." Opal balances on the ledge, and I jerk my attention to see Sawyer's figure within the room and just out of the sun's rays.

"Sawyer, please! Help me!" I reach around Opal and lock my hand to the bar, trying to hold on and stop Opal from jumping.

"Trust me, Hayley. Now brace yourself. It's going to be a quick drop." Opal counts to three under her breath.

Sawyer charges from the room, braving the sun with-out anything to protect him with, and I call out his name again. I expect Sawyer to snatch me in time. I expect Opal to lose her nerve and to just give me up. What I should've expected was that Opal would jump before Sawyer could reach us.

He hollers, shouting my name, but his voice gets lost on the wind, My stomach jumps to my throat. I can't scream or fight or even breathe as I wait for the ground to shatter every bone in my body. This isn't how I imagined my life to end. I thought I'd die by Alexander's hand or by some other cruel vampire's fangs. This seems far worse. I trusted Opal. I never expected that she'd be the one to kill me.

The world jerks to a stop after a few seconds, and Opal swings me up and onto another balcony. I drop to my knees, my whole body screaming with anxiety, and I dry-heave. The quick fall fucked with my insides, feeling as if my organs have been rearranged. Opal flips onto the balcony and slaps her burned hand to another palm pad.

"What the fuck?" a man growls, hollering at the beam of light cutting across the backs of his naked legs as he kneels next to a bed and sucks on one of the room service donor's dicks. I knew that some offered extra services dur-ing feedings for bigger stipends, but it throws me off that it's the vampire sucking the donor's cock.

But then I see the bleeding bite marks on his thighs. Shit.

Opal slams the balcony door closed and ignores the vampire cussing at the burns on his legs. He doesn't bother to get off the floor and turns back to his donor, seeing we're not a threat and only a mere inconvenience to his end of the night meal.

Dragging me with her, she pulls me toward the door. She tightens her grip on my wrist, keeping me by her side as she glances at the video feeds on her com device. I pretend like I'm going to wait by her side while she figures it out, but I shift on my feet and get ready to fight. I don't have a weapon, but I can try to slow her down with my teeth and nails. I can use the fact that she really doesn't want to hurt me against her.

"Opal, please think about what you're doing," I say, trying to distract her. "You're running with me, but it's pointless. The Bella Crew will get me. Am I really worth risking your life for? I love you. You've taken care of me and taught me how to survive with very little, but I can't stay. It kills me that you can't see how badly it hurts for me to exist in this hotel anymore."

"Hayley, I know it's hard. I know you're unhappy. I also know it will pass," she says, taking a breath and cracking open the hotel room door.

"When I'm dead." I tense, preparing to fight against her.

She flicks her attention to the hallway and then to me. "Alexander won't kill you."

Fury rushes through me, sending heat through my body. I clench my jaw, my mind and body aligning to get me through this. Shadows edge my vision, and the second Opal tries to grab my waist, I swing my hand out and slap her as hard as I can.

"Help!" I scream as loudly as I can, projecting my voice in hopes that one of the Bella Crew members in the hotel hears me. "Sawyer!"

Opal growls and spins me, rushing into the hallway. A gunshot pops, the noise startling me. I whip my attention in the direction of the noise and catch sight of Monroe and Knox standing at the end of the hallway, armed with more than just knives. How did they find me? I don't even fucking care.

"Ms. Aris, put Hayley down." Sawyer's voice booms from the opposite direction. "There isn't another balcony you can jump onto in a safe distance without risking Hayley's life. I know you don't want her hurt."

"You're making a grave mistake, Mr. Noble," Opal says, keeping her voice low. "Alexander has returned and he seems to have brought in a new security staff. I will allow you to leave now if you agree to forget about Hayley. She doesn't belong to you."

"I don't think you realize that we don't fucking care," Monroe says, aiming his gun. He shoots at the ceiling, breaking one of the lights.

Opal intakes a breath but doesn't comment. "You won't hurt me. I know you won't. Hayley will never forgive you."

I purse my lips and shake my head. "Then you don't know me. I don't want you dead, Opal, but I can't stay. I'll die. I won't put my life beneath yours. You're not my master. You're not even my damn protector. You promised to take care of me, yet you can't. Why can't you see that you're not enough? My mom would want you to do this. Letting me go is protecting me. It's the only way I'll ever have a chance to live."

A soft sob escapes Opal's mouth, and her lips tremble. "I don't want to lose you. They could hurt you. They don't know how to take care of you."

"I can take care of myself," I say, managing to ease out of her arms.

Reluctantly, she lets me go. "Hayley..."

Grabbing her face, I stare into her eyes. "Opal, I'm not a child anymore. You need to accept that this is the only way things can be. I will die here. Alexander made me that promise. And if I don't die right away, he will make it so I beg for it. Please. You can better care for the others if I'm gone."

Sawyer, Knox, and Monroe slowly make their way closer. I wave my hand at them, silently asking them to give me a second more. Opal searches my eyes like she might find the answers she needs to see in my gaze. And I hope she does. I hope she can believe the truth to my words. I hope she finally realizes that it's more than about the show and being her gem. About some old promise she made a long time ago. For once in my life, I need her to see that it should be for me and only me. I no longer need her as my keeper and caretaker. I need her to set me free.

Opal leans in and presses a kiss to my forehead. "I hate to let you go. I want to be here for you."

"You can," I say, stepping back until I bump into Sawyer's hulking body. "You will. Letting me go with them ensures it."

Opal rubs her lips together. "There is something I need to tell you before I can let you go."

I frown and tilt my head. "What?"

The shock alarms suddenly go off along with the lights. Voices boom from every which way, and I cover my ears, trying to figure out what's going on.

"Quick, in the room. I'll call them off and distract Alexander," Opal yells, motioning Sawyer, Knox, and Monroe to take me into the room with the vampire and blood donor. "Wait ten minutes and take the elevator. Everyone will expect you in the stairwell."

Without waiting for us to respond, Opal disappears.

Monroe pulls out his com device and growls into it. "Get fucking ready. This might be war."

15

HAYLEY

SHOWSTOPPERS

"STAY CLOSE. KILL anyone who tries to get in our way. Do not break formation." Monroe adjusts my arm across his chest. He nudges me with his head. "Hold on as fucking tight as you can. Act like you're trying to choke me or squeeze the life out of me. Show me how strong those sexy legs are."

I rest my chin to the crook of his neck and do as he says, using my thigh muscles as I would use them to keep myself in place on one of the performance bars that stretch from the floor to the ceiling on stage. I grip both arms around him, riding on his back so he keeps his arms free and his view clear. He clutches a dagger in one hand and a gun in the other. Guns are illegal, especially within the hotels, but the Bella Crew use them because while they don't kill vampires, they can injure them and give them an advantage by keeping some space between them.

"We got the lobby covered. Apparently Opal managed to distract Alexander. I see the two of them fighting behind the lobby counter." Sawyer towers behind me, sandwiching me to Monroe, and Knox hangs by my side, tense and ready to fight. He studies his com device, viewing the feeds to direct us.

"You sure about the elevator?" Monroe asks, keeping a donor pace. "What if she's setting us up."

"Doesn't matter. All of the stairwells are blocked." Sawyer hangs his com device over Monroe's shoulder to show him a view of the security personnel. And damn. They're armed with guns too.

"Damn," Knox says from beside us. "I know those fuckers. They're part of the Wy Crew. He must've offered them something good to take on a job." The Wy Crew?

I've never heard of them before. From what I can see on the video feed, they look as wild as some of those vampires that are a part of the Bella Crew. UV tats, piercings, and all scowls and fangs. Leather and weapons.

"Shit." Sawyer hides the view of his com device again, studying it closer. "We can handle them. They'll realize that whatever Aris offered isn't worth it. We'll fucking go to their hotel and fuck shit up if we have to."

"Let's just get the fuck out of here first." Knox rushes ahead and races the distance to the elevators to slam his hand to the button.

The guys stay close together and out of the way of all the elevators in this tower of the hotel. Any of them can open and have asshole vampires charge out. I take long, deep breaths, trying to settle my nerves. I hate not being able to see behind the doors. I know Sawyer can see the elevators on the com devices, but they can stop and pick people up at any moment and on any floor.

I startle at the ding of the elevator behind us and tense as the door slides open. We're greeted with only our reflections in the shiny walls. The guys don't waste time and rush on hitting the button for the lobby. Fuck, there are a lot of floors. At least we get to skip at least thirty since this particular elevator only goes to the top floors.

"All right. Get ready. There is one security guard outside, but he's paying attention to the casino floor, making sure only staying guests have access to the elevators. Don't run. Let's try to blend in. I don't want to draw attention too early." Sawyer hugs me for a moment from behind, resting his muscular chest to my back. "Five. Four. Three. Two."

The elevator door slides open with a ding, and I bury my face into Monroe's neck, hiding the best I can. Instead of the bright colored wigs I'd usually wear, I chose a black one that hopefully looks more natural to fit in. Sawyer stole the personal blood donor's uniform from the guy in the hotel room to help disguise me better, making me blend in as a staff member instead of one of Alexander's dolls.

The loud chimes of slot machines whistle and ring through the air. For being this early in the evening with the sun still out, there are a surprisingly large amount of guests roaming the floor. I don't know if it's because they never left for the day or what, but something about it makes me nervous.

"All right, Walcott and Govan have the crew in place. They're watching our backs." Sawyer keeps his voice low.

My heart raps against my ribcage, spotting one of the usual security guards watching over the floor. He only pays attention to those who enter the elevator lobby and not those who exit, but all it would take is one look for him to see us. Hopefully he'll know better than to try and intervene.

Without pausing, Monroe strides forward, keeping his head up. Knox falls in closer, keeping an eye on the surroundings. I hold my breath and tense as we pass the security guard and enter the casino. It takes everything not to peer behind me to look at him. I refuse to look at all and squeeze my eyes shut, listening to the sounds of the vampire's around us and of the music and murmurs.

"Alexander! Get back here! I'm not done." Opal's voice screeches through the casino.

"Fuck," Sawyer mutters under his breath. "Go right. Keep to the slots. We'll go through instead of around. It seems they're taking their fight elsewhere."

A growl hums over the ringing of the slot machine music, and I risk giving myself an anxiety attack by peeking around. The commotion between Opal and Alexander draws everyone's attention from the casino as they watch their drama unfold. I should thank my good luck for the distraction. I thought that the universe might have been against me, but maybe it is finally realizing that it doesn't have to be a bitch all the time. Maybe it's okay to give me something I want after denying me basically everything I've wanted all my life.

"Alex! If you don't stop and talk to me, I will cancel the show indefinitely!" Opal shouts, her voice humming with a growl.

The hairs on my arms rise, and I stiffen, expecting for Alexander to snarl and attack her. It wouldn't be the first time. He's hit her at least a handful of times over the years. Sometimes she fights back. Sometimes she doesn't. She has always been one to pick her battles instead of constantly going for all-out war with her coven brother.

"If the show doesn't go on, then you don't need your precious gems anymore." Alexander's voice booms through the casino.

Monroe doesn't stop, and I crane my neck, unable to control my curiosity. I want to see what happens. He's threatening the performers. Fuck. I can't stand the thought of him trying to hurt them all because of me. I nearly ask Monroe to put me down and to let me go. I almost lose my nerve to even go with them.

But then a scream rips through the air, and I catch sight of Alexander snatching one of the blood servers off his feet and bending his neck. Stretching the man's neck, Alexander sinks his teeth into the man's throat so hard that blood squirts everywhere. The guy's scream cuts off as Alexander breaks his neck and drops him to the floor.

"Do you see this? This is what will happen to your

gems." Alexander swipes his hand over his mouth. "But they won't be killed. I'll just put them on a fucking tap and have the guests pay for a drink. That will be the new attraction."

Opal hisses and shakes her head. "You'll have to kill me first, brother. We had a fucking deal. They're mine. I will do with them as I please and until you fucking get your shit in control and stop making everything about you, then I'm stopping the show."

"You are not!" Alexander yells. He snarls and roars, yanking his com device from his jacket. "I will put you in your damn place, Opal. You will regret ever confronting me over something so petty."

Opal rushes him, shoving him back. He hits a slot machine and dodges out of the way, spinning her around. Grabbing a fistful of her hair, he yanks her head to the side and bites her on the throat as he would a donor.

Guests gasp at the sight.

Alexander finally realizes that the whole casino watches and that he isn't on some plane above them all like he pretends, and it's enough to make him shout into his com device and snap his fangs at some of the donor staff.

"Everyone out of my casino!" Alexander yells, grabbing a glass of blood from one of the guests and shattering it on the floor. "Get the fuck out! We're closing for an hour."

I blink my eyes, clutching onto Monroe while keeping my gaze trained on Alexander. Dozens of people flood around us, trying to escape before Alexander attacks them. Being in the casino is more of a privilege according to Alexander. It's somewhere to be that isn't on the Strip.

Sawyer swears under his breath again as the two of them blur in a fight and donors screech and run. Security floods the casino floor and starts ushering guests out. It's not the first time for this to happen. The security knows when something happens that can jeopardize business that it's their duty to get the guests out.

"Time to fucking fly," Monroe says, racing forward.

Too many people get up and rush toward the exit. It's impossible to get out as quickly as we need. The crowd swarms the entrance and guards take visual checks of everyone, ensuring no one takes advantage of the situation and tries to leave with one of the donor staff members.

"Clear a path. I don't fucking care who you hurt. We're getting out of here," Monroe mutters, calling into his com device.

Walcott's voice echoes through the line. "You got it. Incoming."

The world blurs as Monroe suddenly relocates me, backing against a wall and out of the way of the anxious and annoyed crowd as the fighting persists between Opal and Alexander. I stretch my neck, keeping my eyes trained on them. A part of me fears that he'll kill her. If that happens, the performers will be dead. He will murder them in a rage.

Gunfire pops through the air, and vampires scream and push harder against each other, trying to exit the casino. Sawyer and Knox stand in front of me and Monroe protectively. I dig my fingers into Monroe's shoulders, my body trembling at the gunfire and madness within the sea of angry vampires.

It's enough to draw Alexander's attention away from Opal. Swinging her fist, she punches him in the jaw and knocks his feet out from under him.

"Fuck, we can take him out. We can do it now." Sawyer mutters the words, watching as Opal overpowers Alexander.

"I'll redirect the crew." Monroe snaps a command into his com device, demanding that all available guys hit Alexander hard.

I gasp a breath, watching as some of the Bella Crew members push through the crowd and race to Alexander and Opal at vampire speed. I can't believe it's happening. I can't believe they're going to try and take him out now.

"Get Hayley out of here. I'll catch up." Monroe

hands me over to Knox, and I just grip him in silence.

I don't think I could speak if I wanted to. I can't even truly think anything apart from Alexander's death. I never imagined it would come.

Alexander snarls and spins, flashing his fangs as bullets rip through his pristine suit and ravage his chest. He doesn't go down like I expect. He takes round after round, clenching his jaw and fighting through the pain. Opal cowers and scrambles out of the way, disappearing within the slot machines to protect herself.

"Is that all you have, you fuckers?" Alexander shouts, raising his hands into the air like the cruel, psychotic bastard he is.

"Fuck, he's strong," Knox says, tightening his arms around me.

The crowd thins and Knox pushes through. We're only a dozen feet from the shaded entrance vampires refuse to move away from because of the last rays of the setting sun. A fan blows my wig all over the place, and I clutch it with my hand, keeping it in place because I was in too much of a rush to pin it.

Alexander's booming yell cuts through the casino, and I whip my attention away from the door and back to him. I suck in a breath, my stomach heaving. He swings a severed head above him and chucks it at the wall above us.

Blood splatters and peppers over us.

"I'll destroy all of you fuckers!" Alexander shouts. "Just test me. You better take my head and scatter my remains, because this will be a war you can't win."

"You fucker!" Sawyer shouts, jumping from the crowd and toward Alexander. The two of them blur in a fight, punching and stabbing and biting each other.

My eyes can't even keep up with the madness of it all, but fear clenches my chest. Alexander looks invincible in this moment. No matter how many guys try to attack him, he just keeps going.

"Hayley!" he shouts, his booming voice sending panic crashing through me. "I will kill everyone you ever loved if you don't call them back. I know this is your doing!"

"Ignore him. He's lying." Knox adjusts me in his arms.

But what if he's not?

"My guests, no one leaves! Take the heads of everyone by the doors. Serve me well and I'll give you access to all my dolls!" Alexander shouts the words, slashing his knife across Sawyer's chest in the process.

My eyes widen at his words, and several of the vampires fighting to get out hesitate. Whipping around, a guy at the front punches another guy, sending him back. The mad dash to leave turns into a scary-ass fight, and Knox has no choice but to fall back and get out of the way as someone loses an arm.

"We'll take another way," he says, his breath heaving.

"If you catch my Ruby, you can have a night with her as well!" Alexander adds, his breath heaving as Sawyer punches him in the gut.

Knox growls and aims his gun, firing at a vampire who rushes from the fight. It draws more attention, and I clench my jaw, my heart going wild with fear. What the actual fuck?

"Stay back!" Opal's voice rings through the air. "Don't touch her!" She materializes from her place near one of the slot machines and punches her fist through a vampire's back, sending his heart out through his crushed sternum.

Three guys fly at her, getting her away, and a fourth one steps in front of Knox, blocking his way. "Come on, Knox. Give her here. You have plenty of your own damn donors. Let her be mine. We'll call an alliance if you give her to the Wy Crew."

Oh fuck.

"There is nowhere for you to run. Make it easy or we'll cut your dick off." Another grumbly voice mutters from behind.

I screech and swing my hand, slapping a dirty guy

across his face as he tries to sneak up on Knox. "Get back!"

Sawyer's yells cut over the pounding in my head, but I can't look at him.

The shock alarms kick on, shrilling through the casino, dropping the guys around us to their knees. Knox wobbles on his feet but manages to hop over a guy trying to grab him. I whip my attention around the casino, and my heart drops into my stomach, threatening to spill across the floor.

Alexander pins Sawyer down with his hand shoved into his chest. The edges of my vision shadow, and I gasp and release a scream.

"Get her out!" Sawyer yells, grinding his teeth.

Knox hesitates for a second, but Sawyer yells again, gripping his hand around Alexander's wrist, stopping him from removing his heart.

"My doll! Hayley! I don't want a fucking war with the Bella Crew, but if you leave, there will be one." Alexander flashes his fangs and tries to twist his hand, making Sawyer holler. "It won't be just this one asshole. It'll be all of them. Their donors. I will get the leaders of the Strip to agree with me that they're too much of a threat. We will destroy them. And when we do, I'll bring you back and you will wish for your death. But it won't come. I won't give you that luxury."

I whimper, my whole body turning cold with his words. "Knox, please. Let me down."

"Fuck that." My voice kicks him into action and the world blurs.

"Knox! Stop! Put me down! I don't want to go with you anymore!" I slap him across the face, my whole body aching with the action. I don't want to fight him, but I'm afraid he's lost himself in his need to possess me that he can't actually hear the truth of Alexander's threat. "I don't want to go! I don't want to risk it!"

"I'll protect you, Hayley," he argues, darting between slot machines.

"No! You don't get it! Put me down. This is my choice. I'm not going to be the reason he destroys every-thing. You won't force that guilt on me." I whack him again, flailing and struggling to escape his grip. "We'll find another way. Just please. Don't treat me like your posses-sion. Let me make my own decision."

The world suddenly stops, and I find myself on my feet. Knox flashes his fangs with his anger, his silver eyes solid with his rage and hunger. His annoyance that I just asked him to let me go.

"Alexander, you win," I say, heaving a breath. "You fucking win. Just don't do this. Let everyone go."

A soft hum reverberates through my bones, and Alexander drags Sawyer along, his hand still in his chest cavity. "That's my good girl. Finally using your disobedience for something I can agree with."

Knox growls from behind me, remaining close without touching me. Two figures blur through the casino, and I spot Opal shoving Monroe in our direction. She tightens her mouth, refusing to look at me. Another strange man materializes on her other side and he holds the backs of two other Bella Crew members. One last strange vampire tosses Walcott and Govan to the floor, and I try to figure out what the fuck is going on and who these guys are.

"Thank you, brothers," Alexander says, smirking at the two strange guys. "Thank you, my sister. I understand how difficult things have been, but I think this arrangement will work best for all of us as long as you can get your gem to agree."

I tighten my jaw. His brothers? I had no idea that Alexander had coven brothers. I've never seen them around. And Opal? I try to grab her attention again, but she trains her eyes on Alexander.

"She will. She will understand her place as long as you keep to the agreement. I will not stand for another disagreement." Opal smooths out her dress and finally turns her attention to me. Our eyes meet, and silver flickers like streaks of lightning across her gaze.

My mouth refuses to open, my body shutting down and turning compliant. I'm afraid that if I speak up, one of these vampires will hurt me.

"Go on. I'd like to get things back in order and back to business, so our brothers can return to their homes," Alexander says, narrowing his eyes at me.

Opal steps forward and tries to take my hand, but I cross my arms. "Hayley, I was wrong to think that it would be better if you left with the Bella Crew, and I'm sorry for my poor judgment. You belong to us, and it is pivotal to our hotel that the show goes on. You understand, right? But I know you're unhappy, so you're no longer headlining."

I frown. "What do you mean?"

"We've decided that you've outgrown your role as one of the gems. You will now take the Strip by storm. As long as you agree, Alexander doesn't feel the need to slaughter anyone. He is willing to make an arrangement." Opal licks her lips and swallows. A frown breaks her expression, and I realize I'm not going to like what she says. "We've decided that the best way to get back into a good business place is to hold an auction and rent you out as a performer across the strip. Everyone will be included to ensure all vampires are able to participate and hopefully ease the tension. We don't want a war."

My head whirls with her words. An auction? They want to put me up for auction like I'm a damn piece of property? Fuck.

"No," Sawyer mutters, his growl whipping me in the chest.

"If you don't, we'll have to figure out new means of power and wealth. Do you know what that will mean for my gems?" Opal asks, her lips trembling. "I don't think they'll survive that, but I know you can."

But can I? I don't think I can.

"Agree, Hayley. It's the only way anyone is leaving here alive. If you don't, Opal will also have to find herself some new performers, because these ones have already been ruined by the circumstances. Make your decision. You have five seconds." Alexander squeezes Sawyer's heart again. "Four. Three."

"Wait, okay. If this is what it takes, then I'll do it. But I need a minute with them. Please, they won't leave me so easily. Just let me talk to them." I wring my hands together and risk stepping closer to Sawyer.

Alexander relents and slowly slides his hand free, leaving Sawyer's heart intact. I gasp and rush to him, ignoring the growls echoing around me. I hug him and press my face to his neck, praying with everything in me that he sees reason. That he realizes there is no way I'm giving up, but I also can't let him do this.

"Take the deal. Don't fight here. Please. I can't be the reason you die." I breathe against his ear. "Please." Tilting my head back, I look at Knox and Monroe. "I want to stay. Just let me stay."

"I hate this, Hayley. It goes against every one of my instincts to leave you with these monsters," Sawyer whispers in my ear. "We will figure this out. There is no way I'm letting any other fucking hotel get their hands on our girl."

I crash my mouth to his, only to have two strong hands yank me away. The world blurs as Opal races away with me.

The last thing I see is the Bella Crew disappearing from the casino. The elevator door slides shut, cutting me off from the world again.

Fuck. This is the end for me. I know it.

If Sawyer, Knox, and Monroe can't buy me at auction, my life is over.

"THIS IS BULLSHIT. Fucking bullshit," I mutter, slapping my palms on the long table. "Even if we pooled our resources, there is no way we'll have enough. We'll be broke, and everything will go to shit."

Monroe stabs his knife into the old Las Vegas map, one of the few still around. Most every hotel on the Strip has been remodeled and all back-world evidence destroyed to ensure donors forget there was ever such a place where humans ruled and vampires—well, we were far and few and hid in the shadows.

I push away the thought of my mortal life. I had never expected to transform with the first wave of the Vampire Uprising. I was a medical professional and practically killing myself in the ER. It's been too long that I can't remember much. I just know I was attacked. When I transformed, I ran. I ended up in this very hotel before half the name was demolished along with the city's name.

"I'll call in every damn debt that we're owed," Monroe says, yanking out his knife to pierce it in again. "We'll manage."

Sawyer picks up the table and flips it over, sending everything flying into the air. "We need to have a backup plan. I'll destroy every bastard who thinks they can even put in a bid for our girl."

The click-clack of heels sounds from the elevator, and I ignore Tatum strolling in our direction with Walcott. She leans into him, whispering too lowly for my super hearing to pick up. I ignore them the same as they ignore me. We might be a crew, but we all have our own self-interests to look after. Until the leaders of La Vega allow for any vampires to officially blood bond as a coven, we're basically living by a set of rules with none of the perks that come with a position of power. We fought hard to keep this hotel, and if we pool all our wealth, property, and donations from the donors who cohabitate the place with us, we would risk ending up in the shadows on the La Vega Strip. My brain says to chill out and think things through. Something deeper, wilder, begs me to just say fuck it all for Hayley.

"You guys still trying to figure out how to get the Queen of Cock?" Tatum asks, pursing her lips.

She cares as much as anyone about a donor, but she's more of a "think bigger" woman. I don't even have to be able to read her mind to know that she'll intervene if we risk our current blood supply just for Hayley. My rationale knows it's selfish, but I'm fucking obsessed with her, and even before I got to slide my cock between her pouty lips and fuck her like a damn starving vampire.

"Don't even think about touching my shit," Walcott mutters, scrubbing his hand over his face tattoo. He was fucking crazy to do something so elaborate. UV ink doesn't heal as it would were we human. It stings, and would annoy the shit out of me on my face. Having it inked on my chest and side reminds me that I'm not truly invincible, but it also helps keep me stronger.

"Your shit's fine. We're figuring out another damn

way. There is no way that what we have could cover more than a day." Monroe throws his knife, stabbing Walcott in the chest. "So shut the fuck up and help me determine who we can work with to get close to any competition on the Strip. We have Pala handled. I think we only need to worry about Ri, Astor, and possibly the Etia."

I'm sure there are others he missed, but those assholes at those towers will purposefully screw with us as leading covens. We need allies and fast. I'll do whatever it takes to secure some arrangements.

"All right, bastards. I think we should hit up the Bay and Lux. I know you don't want to hear this shit, but you can probably negotiate her safety while she's in their care. No fucking, kissing, manhandling, whatever, but let them have her blood for that time." Walcott tenses, steeling himself toward our growls. Even the thought of someone else sinking their fangs into Hayley makes me want to join Sawyer on a dick cutting spree.

"He has a point," Tatum says, shifting to stand in front of Walcott. I glower at her and wait until she gives me some dumbass reason why I should listen. "Hayley is used to feeding assholes. It wouldn't be as traumatic as her ending up with a fucker who will spend the day raping and draining her over and over again. That would kill me. You guys need to get over your fucking possession and consider a compromise for the best possible outcome."

I grumble and kick the table, sending it skidding across the tiles. "I fucking hate when you're right, Tate. It makes me want to trash your cock collection and make it rain severed dicks across the Strip."

"I still don't like it," Monroe mutters, flipping another knife in his hand. The guy carries enough weapons to arm at least ten people at all times.

"You don't have to like it, but you can live with it. I bet you a fucking dick tattoo on your ass that Hayley would agree with me." Tatum traces the air, drawing an invisible cock with her finger.

Monroe shakes his head and glares. "The bet doesn't work when you already have one, Tate. Maybe if it was a third tit or something."

Sawyer whacks Monroe. Straightening his back, he stands tall, towering over all of us. "No bets. Just get ahold of your damn contacts. Take Knox with you and cut a deal. I'll handle everything here."

I sigh and crack my knuckles, trying to keep my cool. I know it's the right thing to do, but another part of me still wants to selfishly figure out a way to get Hayley and keep her as ours.

"Load up, Knox." Monroe hands me a gun. "There is a price for entry to get within reach of these mother fuckers."

I groan. "How many fangs?"

He shrugs. "Ten to be safe. Maybe a head."

Fucking great. Really fucking great.

"Son of a bitch!" Monroe shouts and yanks the head of the snarling vampire back, shoving the barrel of his gun into his mouth. A bullet will only slow him down unless he shoots enough to blow his head off, but that's not what we want...yet. "If you bite me again, I'll take both damn fangs."

The vampire struggles, gnashing his teeth against the barrel. He couldn't speak if he wanted to with the gun shoved so far in his mouth that I wonder how often he deep throats one of the other ten assholes of this piece of shit group too powerless to even call a crew. It's not that I care, but it's annoying as fuck that he doesn't choke yet, continuing to fight.

"Damn it. I need help," Monroe says, trying to hook his pliers to one of the bastard's fangs. "This shithead isn't giving up. He's about to swallow my gun."

Yanking fangs, severing limbs, and chopping off heads isn't really my thing, and I usually leave it up to

Monroe and Sawyer unless I have to. I know Monroe is fucking twisted, getting kicks out of putting dickholes in their places and taking out his anger on anyone who he thinks deserves a good ass kicking.

I sigh and snatch the pliers from him, letting him grip the guy's head while I pull. I yank his right incisor out, ensuring I get the whole damn thing, root and all, and dangle the two-inch long bloody fang in front of Monroe.

"You know what? Fuck it. Take both. He's pissing me off, and I think it's the last one we'll need." Monroe jerks the vampire's head back again, pressing his thumb into the guy's gum to force his remaining fang to click and extend fully. "He looks like a rip and spitter anyway. Look at the pattern of those blood stains. Such a fucking waste."

I don't look, keeping my gaze trained on his other fang. "Hold him tight."

"Take a couple extra while you're at it. Force him to be civilized or maybe turn him into a gummy." Monroe chuckles at his own joke. The last thing I want to think about is him gumming a cock.

"You're a psycho ass," I mutter, gripping the man's other fang. He bucks and tries to break free, but I'm too quick, yanking out his other incisor.

Monroe slides his gun from the prick's mouth and whacks him hard on the head with it. We vanish from his shadowed shelter outside of the Ri and only slow down at the sight of the bald watchman at the door.

Monroe shakes the bag of fangs. "Let us in, asshole. I'm looking for Mesquite. Tell him some bastards from Bella want to make an arrangement."

Flicking his gaze from the empty street and to Monroe, the fucker lifts an eyebrow but doesn't respond.

I groan at the guy's mistake.

Yanking a short sword from a holster on his shoulder, Monroe stabs the guy in the throat, surprising him. The bastard doesn't even get a chance to open his mouth to try to scream as Monroe severs his head, dropping his body to the floor.

"Damn it. You think Ri will speak to us now?" I ask, kicking the guard's body in the gut.

Laughing, Monroe swings the dripping head back and forth. "Guaranteed."

I sigh and follow him inside the tall tower, lit up with neon lights. The casino chimes, but the place is nearly dead. Only a couple vampires sit at slots, and a man in nothing but a speedo strolls around, carrying a tray of blood to offer guests. I don't know why this crew bothers. It's nearly impossible to bring in vampires when the blood is watered down, the machines never pay, and the only benefit is getting out of the daylight. But this time of night? The guests here must have credit. It might be the only hotel still willing to give it.

Monroe releases a wolf-whistle. "Hey, Mesquite! Come fucking accept this damn gift I brought you!"

I straighten my back and peer around the casino, but no one comes rushing to greet us.

"Yo! Don't make me pick another. You only have three assholes here. I doubt they'd even put up a fight." Monroe races and stands behind a guy smacking buttons on a machine.

I shake my head, twisting my lips to the side. "Really?"

He shrugs. "If Mesquite doesn't show his ugly mug in three, two—"

A figure blurs from the back of the casino, flying in our direction. I tense and unsheathe a dagger from a hidden holster in my leather jacket. Monroe and the guy blur in a fight, and I tap my fingers on the top of one of the machines.

It takes thirty seconds for Monroe to pin the short, buff vampire. He aims a knife at the guy's heart and flashes his fangs.

"Give me one good reason I shouldn't cut your heart out and take control of this hotel?" Monroe narrows his eyes, glaring at Mesquite.

"Because the plumbing is shit, the top ten levels are trash, and I have twenty male donors and no females. But you know what? You can have this bullshit." Mesquite grins with his words. "I'll give you a rub and tug just to take it."

Monroe breaks his glower and the two of them laugh and wrestle until Monroe helps Mesquite to his feet. I haven't dealt with the guy much that I can remember of from the last century, but he's right about this hotel being garbage. It's worse than ours and still the same as the day it was taken over.

"Stop trying to seduce me, you asshole. Have you forgotten we share a blood bond? I don't care if we're on different crews now." Monroe whacks the guy upside the head. "Plus, my cock has been claimed."

"Finally giving in to the ass, huh?" Mesquite hollers a laugh at Monroe's expression. With the female population down, and desperation for fun with something else that isn't a damn hand, many male vampires have decided pleasure is pleasure. Hell, if you find a donor that doesn't cut his hair, it's easy to pretend, according to Walcott.

"Fuck no. Fifty years or a hundred, this horny bastard dies and falls limp at just the thought no matter how much I reason with the big guy." Monroe cups his groin and shakes his junk through his pants.

Mesquite laughs harder, flashing his fangs with his smile. "Give it two hundred."

"Don't need to. I found my snake tamer. She's fucking sexy as sin, talented, and will be my perfect little princess if we can manage to fucking put Aris in his damn place." Monroe fists his hands, growling deep in his throat at the thought of the bastard.

Mesquite flicks his gaze to mine and back to his blood cousin twice removed. I knew Monroe had a relative on the Strip, but I hadn't realized it was a crew head. Like with legitimate covens, crews don't have members with blood bonds. It keeps power more even and stops bloodlines from dominating. Like donors were divided and separated from each other, so were vampires who were blood related in the back-world. All of my relatives were massacred in the first year of the Vampire Uprising after I was turned by a patient that I killed in defense, so it's never really bothered me.

"You better not be fucking talking about Ruby Aris, you dickwad," Mesquite says, flaring his nostrils. "I got an invitation an hour ago about an auction."

Rage rushes through me at the thought. "Yeah, that's her. Bella has an unofficial claim."

"We don't want to have to go on a damn murdering spree or start a blood feud, but any asshole who tries to bid will fucking get their dicks whacked off with my bluntest blade." Monroe glowers at Mesquite. "Unless they make a deal."

"What kind of deal? I might be interested in an arrangement. You know how this shithole needs something good to bring people in. The starting bid is reasonable enough that I bargained with some Strip dwellers to go all in for a five-year access to our facility, including gen. pop. blood." He motions toward the donor in the speedo.

"Manage to claim a day of the week and agree to only blood, and you'll get to keep your damn head and ten percent of our gen. pop. pool through blood bags once a month." Monroe tugs out the small bag of fangs we collected and opens it. "You'll also get guaranteed protection while she's on site."

"Access to her blood is good for one. That's not going to bring my hotel guests." Mesquite rubs his hand over his clean shaven face. "Throw in visual entertainment like what she does at Vampire Nights, and I'll agree."

"I could just fucking cut your head off now," Monroe mutters, tightening his jaw.

I step between them. "We'll take the deal if you agree to back us up and spread around the fucking warning about trying to put in a bid."

He nods his head. "I'm always looking for a damn

good reason to fight."

A ring chimes through the air as all three of our com devices go off. The sound of another two from the casino drags my attention away from Mesquite and Monroe, and I watch two men pull out their old-ass phones from the back-world, still managing to be connected to the City Notification System.

I tap on the screen, my anger getting the best of me. It's a reminder about the Vampire Nights auction with an adjustment in the time. The auction has been moved from next week and to tomorrow. Shit.

"We gotta go, Monroe. We're running out of time," I say, trying to suppress my anger. "We still have five other crews to negotiate with."

Another chime rings through the air.

I snarl at the change of date once more. Swinging my fist, I smash it into the side of a slot machine. "He's a fucking dead man."

Staring at the notification, I can't stop the wave of hopelessness crashing through me. Aris changed the auction time to start in ten minutes. Doors will lock in nine.

He's forced our hand with a damn war.

We're out of time.

AUCTION

I STAND IN front of the mirror, still wearing the gross uniform of the personal donor that I stole. It's been maybe two days, could be three, since Alexander locked me in this room on the eleventh floor. I've never been in this area of the hotel with the basic rooms with a queen bed and a bathroom. I'm lucky he even gave me something to eat.

Touching my hair, I play with the uneven strands, wishing that I was given a pair of scissors to fix the style as best as I can. But scissors can hurt me or others, and Alexander isn't going to let shit go down. He even took the hangers, bed sheets, and everything that wasn't screwed down. The window doesn't open with only a small vent allowing fresh air in, but it's not like I'd do anything. There isn't a balcony or soft thing to land on. I don't have a death wish yet, but after tonight? God, I hope the universe shows me mercy. I'm scared. More scared than I've ever been in my damn life.

A soft knock taps on the door, but I don't turn away from my reflection to open it because it's locked from the outside. I'm guessing this floor is intended to be used as some sort of prison or something. I had no idea that Alexander kept donors in this hall. I'm not the only one a prisoner. I guess there has to be a way to control any reluctant donors other than murdering them. Vampires like to protect their food sources and all, though Alexander is growing more and more careless. According to the Bella Crew, he's not the only one either.

"Hayley, it's me. Opal asked me to come help you get ready. The performers are putting on a show for our guests, so we have about thirty minutes." Mya's voice trickles through the heavy door, and the bolt slides open as if whoever monitors me opens the lock. Swinging the door open, Mya peeks in and ignores the vampire guard looming behind her, trying to get a look at me.

I still don't speak or move and wait for her to shut the door completely. The second the vampire is cut off from us, I spin and rush my best friend, throwing my arms around her. Tears well in my eyes, stinging my cold cheeks as they spill. Shuddering a breath, Mya cries quietly on my shoulder, squeezing me tightly.

"Are you okay?" she whispers, keeping her voice low.

I shake my head. There is no point in lying. I'm far from being okay. This is the worst I've ever felt, like I'm waiting for my execution but instead of dying, the executioner fails over and over again, leaving me in a state of agony and despair.

Mya's lip trembles. "I hate this. If Alexander would allow me to take your place, I would. I'd do anything for you, Hayley. You don't deserve this. I just wish I understood why he's changed so much. He used to be good to us."

To her and the others. He wasn't always good to me. It's not the first time he's gone crazy over something out of my control, but this is the worst. He usually cools off and moves on. Something must be happening outside of the hotel and is only heated by the conflict with the Bella Crew, making him explode like a raging lunatic And not the good kind.

"I wish I knew too," I murmur, tugging her with me to the bathroom. I turn on the shower, filling the room with the sound of running water, hoping it's enough to stifle the sound of our voices. "Something is going on. There were men here that were a part of the Aris Coven."

"What? They have more brothers?" Mya asks, furrowing her brows.

I shrug, because like her, I didn't know about them either. "I think he's flexing his power more because of them. And the Bella Crew. There was a new guy at the last show as well. I wonder if things are getting fucked up because of it. I just hope that the Bella Crew comes through for me."

Mya eases away and looks me in the eyes. "Govan said that he's not sure how they're going to manage. They don't have enough wealth or power to truly compete. He thinks that they'll start a war and Alexander will just decide to kill us all. He wants me to leave with him."

I blink a few times, trying to process what she says. I knew that it would be tough for the Bella Crew to compete with the Strip leaders, but I also know that they won't just give up on me. They consider me theirs, and not in the same way Alexander and Opal do. It's hard to explain, but it feels different. Better.

I blow out a breath and lick my lips. "I think you should."

She cocks her head with a frown. "What? Really? Alexander will fucking make things worse if I do."

"He'll make it worse regardless. We can't know for certain that he'll keep his word. Opal is tough, but she will bow to him as her leader. She always does." I hug her tighter. "The last thing I want is for you to be hurt or worse."

"I'm scared. I don't even know what I would do if I go. Govan's fun and all, but his friends scare the shit out of me." Mya puffs a breath of air through her lips.

"They're not so bad." I smile sadly, thinking about the day I spent at the Bella. There was so much I never got to do or see, and I crave to run away now and find out what it's really like to be tagged a possession of the Bella Crew.

"Yeah, because you grip onto three of their cocks," she teases. "Which is as crazy as me running away with one of them. My family could be hurt."

"Tell him to take them too." I lock my gaze to hers. "Use the auction to your advantage, Mya. I mean it. There is no getting out of this for me, but if I know you and your kin are safe, it makes me feel better. It'll make this all worth it in the end to me. You're my best friend forever, and I want you to do this."

She squeezes her eyes shut, sending tears dripping from the corners of her lashes. "I love you, Hayley. I know things are going to work out."

I wish I felt the same way, but I need to be realistic. Hope will only destroy me. I can't pray and wish for the best when I'm staring down at a room of savage, barbaric vampires who think that because I'm a donor and they feed on me that they can do whatever the hell they want. Many lost their civility and never gained it back. They're just good at acting the part until they flash their fangs and tear out your throat.

A beep chimes through the room. "You have fifteen fucking minutes, donors. You better be ready. I'll fuck you up before I end up on Aris's shit list." The voice booms through the air from a speaker against the wall.

I cringe and shake my head, my eyes burning with more tears. Fifteen minutes. I have fifteen minutes to find the strength I need to get through this.

"I brought you some things that Opal wanted you to have," Mya finally says after another moment passes. "I know it sucks, and I don't want to be the one to help you get ready for this nightmare, but it was the only way I could get time with you. Opal is busy with the performers, and there was no way I was going to let someone else take my place."

I release a shaky breath and nod. "I'm glad you're here despite it. I was afraid I'd never get to see you again."

Mya gasps a sob, trying to compose herself. Sliding the small bag off her shoulder, she sets it on the marble counter of the wide sink. I try not to react to the skimpy bikini she pulls from the bag, basically all strings, leaving nothing to the imagination. Beneath it lays a wig bag, and Mya carefully unties it and shows me my favorite turquoise wig. I touch the soft strands of fake hair, shining in the light from above.

"Alexander told Opal that if you don't put in an effort to look your best, he'd force you to go on stage completely naked." Mya grimaces with her twisted words. "He's a fucking asshole."

I sigh. "Might as well be naked," I mutter. "That way I'm not sparkling like a damn gift for them to tear into."

Mya blinks her watery gaze again. "I hate this. I fucking really hate this."

I let her help me adjust the wig onto my hair, not bothering to pin it in place. "Just remember what I said. Go. Get out of here. I need you to make this stupid forced sacrifice worth it."

"All right, my gem. I need you to listen to me." Opal stands beside me, motioning for me to get into the golden cage that will be lowered to the damn stage, turning the auction into a true spectacle. "I know you're going to want to fight. I know you'll want to disobey and do whatever you can to make it look like they can't control you, but it would be a mistake."

I flick my attention to her. "You don't have to tell me to be a good girl. I already know that the grossest fuckers want someone they can put in their place. I'll stand there and shut up."

Tears glass over Opal's eyes, and she helps me climb into the cage. "I am truly sorry for all of this, you know."

"Sure," I say, refusing to accept her apology. She tried to help me and then just gave up. I thought I could count on her. I thought she was better than her brother. But she's not. And I'm so angry because of it.

"Hayley," she whispers, touching my cheek.

I tighten my mouth without responding.

"You're doing the right thing. I want you to know that." Pinching my chin, Opal swipes a blush-colored lipstick across my lips. "I know it doesn't feel like it, but complying means people won't unnecessarily die. Your friends will have better lives because of it."

"Until the next headliner does something to fuck things up," I mutter under my breath, rubbing my lips together to smooth the makeup.

Opal pouts her bottom lip and sighs. "No one is quite like you, so I promise that all this bullshit with Alex ends here."

Her words prod at something deep inside me, and I open my mouth to ask her what the fuck she's talking about, but music blares through the air. Quickly shutting the cage door, she ensures the wires are secure and hits the button to send me gliding forward and off the rafter. The cage rattles as I hang in the air, and I wonder how much movement it could withstand before crashing down. Maybe I can swing it hard enough to snap the wire and free fall on top of Alexander, who stands below, blabbing to the crowd. I can't hear anything past the pounding in my head, and the spotlight steals my vision, making it impossible to see beyond the bright-white light.

"Settle down, you fuckers!" Alexander shouts, his voice booming through the world through the giant speakers on each side of the stage. "It's time for the main event! If you have never laid your eyes on my most precious baby doll, then you're in for a treat. If you have, well, get fucking ready to bid. You won't want to miss your chance at claiming a contract with the most exquisite donor in all of La Vega!"

Whistles and catcalls fill the air, roaring over the music with the standing crowd. With their reaction, I'd have thought someone just nailed the perfect performance for this kind of standing ovation.

My nerves twist inside me, tightening my chest and bunching my stomach. I don't smile. I don't pose. There is no fucking way I'm going to give my best performance to the men who want a piece of my blood, body, and mind.

Alexander moans deep in his throat and waves his hand as the cage bounces with a stop, hanging three feet in the air. I keep my gaze down, using my fake eyelashes like shields to protect me with.

My hair hangs around my face and over the tiny triangles covering my boobs. I clutch the side wires of the swing, and ignore everything around me.

"Delectable, isn't she?" Alexander asks, flicking open the door on my cage. "Come on, my doll. These gentlemen want a better look at you and your amazing assets."

I tighten my jaw and keep my stare at the bottom of the cage. It takes everything in me to stand up and let Alexander help me out.

He hooks his fingers around my waist and spins me in a circle, trying to make me react with a smile. Other times, the quick movements would work and I'd screech and giggle, but now? My body shuts down. My brain has cut the line, and I can't get myself to do anything.

"Aw, my baby doll. Don't look so sad." Alexander speaks into his glittery microphone. Setting me on my feet, he pushes the long strands of turquoise hair to my back, giving the audience a better view of the glittery strings making up my costume. "You see, gentleman, Ruby is afraid no one will bid for her. Why don't we show her that's not true? Let's show her that you sexy devils are all here just for her."

The spotlight drifts away from us and over the crowd. For the first time, I can't stop myself from looking up. I want so desperately to see the faces of the Bella Crew that I'll risk meeting someone else's gaze.

"See, baby doll? They love you. Now why don't you give them a smile?" Alexander slides his arm around my back and leans in. Whispering, he adds, "You better fucking do it or I'll let one of them come up here for a closer look."

I force my mouth to smile, showing off my teeth. A part of my being dies, and I try to concentrate on each individual voice chanting my name, creating the discordant melody of my impending doom.

"Get her naked! I want to see her tits!" a man yells, rushing toward the edge of the crowd.

Whistling through his fingers, another guy joins him. "Bend her over. I want to see that tight pussy and ass."

My body chills, my head spinning.

"Open your mouth, Ruby! I need to see if I can fit it all in." The gruff voice laughs with his comment.

"Small mouths aren't something a jaw dislocation can't fix," another says.

A figure waves his arms over his head. "Come on, Aris! Give us what we want! I want to see my new blood bitch."

Nails dig into my shoulder as Alexander yanks me to him. "You heard the gentleman, Ruby. Let's show them what they're paying for."

Be a good a girl. Don't do anything stupid. He'll destroy you. The thoughts spin through my mind, and I tremble in fear. Alexander spins me around and rips at the strap of my top, sending crystal beads flinging across the stage.

A roar sounds through the crowd, Sawyer's voice whipping at my insides. He's here. He made it.

"Someone's anxious, baby doll. Come on, now. Turn around. Please the gentleman." Alexander forces me to spin and grabs my wig, exposing my boobs. The crowd cheers and Alexander grabs for my waistband next.

Something dark snaps inside me.

I lose my fucking shit.

TWISTING, I SURPRISE Alexander by launching at him. It's like my body acts without my mind's consent. I collide into him and hug him with my whole body. I scratch my nails into the back of his neck and bite his throat, using my body as a weapon.

I thought I could handle this. I thought I could close

myself off from the savage world around me for the sake of my survival, but I can't. I can't just let him auction me off like this to men who will make me want to die but force me to live. I'd rather fight and get killed trying to save myself than just accept my fate.

Alexander snarls and tries knocking me away, but a gunshot blasts through the air. He grunts as it hits his shoulder, coming from somewhere in the crowd. A strange vampire tries to snatch me away, managing to sink his fangs into my shoulder. I screech in pain, releasing Alexander from my bite. His blood stains my face, the taste lingering on my tongue.

Unsheathing a dagger, he throws it with perfect accuracy at the fucker who bit me, dropping him to his knees as blood spills from the wound on his neck. Alexander grabs my waist and forces me away, no longer in shock by my attack. He throws me onto the stage and kicks me in the stomach, sending me rolling over and over again until I crash into the legs of one of the security guards.

"Fuck yeah! I love them wild! I'll give you twenty percent of my barely mature donors!" a man shouts from the crowd. "All healthy and ready to be trained."

I gasp, trying to suck air into my lungs. Alexander ignores the man, striding across the stage to me. I swing out and try to get the security guard to move, but he doesn't budge. Flashing his fangs with his fury, Alexander bends down and snatches me by my ankles, spinning me so quickly that all I can do is brace myself to smash into a wall. He drops me to the floor and kicks me again, knocking me to my stomach.

The crowd goes wild, a mixture of laughter and growls filling the air. The security guards manage to stop the fights quickly, but an occasional gunshot rings through the air. I try to find my will to get up. I summon everything in me to continue to fight. But I'm disoriented, my head spinning with dizziness.

Alexander clicks his tongue and steps on my back, squeezing the air from my lungs. "Ruby, baby doll. What do you think you're doing? You know I don't like hurting you."

I sniffle, trying to remain calm. He thinks he can break me, but I'm already broken. I'm damaged goods. All he will do now is light a fire in my soul. Instead of burning, I'll explode. I'll blow up and take him out with me.

"Now, be a good doll and get up slowly. Everyone's anxious." Alexander flips me onto my back with his foot and extends his hand to me. "Let's just get this over with. You'll be happy. These gentlemen plan to let you take good care of them. I know how much you like it."

I blink, trying not to react. I'll not only take care of

them. I'll fucking cut their dicks off in their sleep. I'll be a good little girl, obedient, and on my knees, pretending to please, but they're not the only savages. I will wait for my chance and strike. All of these fuckers will regret even showing up today.

But I must take care of Alexander first.

Letting him lift me to my feet, I stand for only a second and wait for him to bring his microphone to his mouth. I jerk my hand out and try to snatch the knife from his belt. He catches my wrist and looks at me. I do the only thing I can think of and swing my leg up, kicking him as hard as I can in the balls. The force of my leg sends him into the air a few inches, and he howls in pain. The crowd cheers and shouts, the whole room enjoying me humiliating Alexander in front of La Vega's toughest assholes.

I don't wait for him to react.

Dashing away, I run toward the side of the stage. If I can get at least a dozen feet between us, maybe Sawyer can reach me from his spot in the crowd. I know Alexander wouldn't have let the Bella Crew come in here armed and unescorted by security. They're probably as far away as they possibly can be.

"Hayley!" Alexander hollers, breaking his role as emcee and auctioneer, turning into the monster he truly is.

"You fucking ungrateful donor. You're going to beg me for mercy."

I swivel, shading my eyes to peer at the restless crowd, more fights breaking out across the room. A light beams over the audience, and I realize that one of the stage technicians purposefully shines the spotlight where the Bella Crew fights a few of the security guards and steals their weapons.

"Sawyer!" I shout, taking a few steps back to put some distance between me and the four-foot drop that leads to the crowd. "Sawyer!"

This might be the stupidest idea I've ever had, but I can hear Alexander growl as he rushes in my direction. The cage falls, blocking his path for a second, and I run as fast as I can and take a flying leap toward the audience. I know there are monsters in the audience. I know one of them could try to kill me, bite me, kidnap me, or worse, but at least I'd have a better chance because I'd be closer to the Bella Crew. If I can get to them—

A heavy body collides into mine, sending me crashing on top of one of the tables. I catch a whiff of Alexander's bitter cologne as he smashes me to the table. Vampires crowd around us, and dozens of hands touch every part of my body, trying to just get even a feel of my skin. I scream and struggle, squeezing my legs shut, trying to stop them from trying to grope me. Someone slides their hand between my body and Alexander's heavy weight, grazing their cold fingers over my nipple.

Shrieking, the hand goes limp and warm blood drips down my side. I twist, trying to get a view of what's happening, and I see a vampire clutching the bleeding stump of his severed hand. Alexander swings his short sword around, getting the audience to back away or risk losing their limbs. Ripping me off the table, Alexander yanks my wig off and tangles his fingers into my hair. He drags me from the table and carries me back to the stage.

Throwing me to the floor, he stomps on my back so hard that the worst pain I've felt in my life consumes me. The wave of agony steals my vision, and as hard as I try to get to my feet, I can't. I can barely breathe.

I pass out. For how long? I have no idea.

Nails bite into my skin, making me bleed. I lie on my back under a bright spotlight that haloes Alexander. He heaves a breath, extending his fangs completely. If he were to sink them into my neck, it would be a kill bite. I know it. I can see the murder flashing in his eyes.

The lights turn off and the shock alarm blares, dropping the crowd with the noise. It cuts off, leaving utter silence in the air. The crowd stops fighting, and the heavy weight of their stares penetrates into me.

"I've decided to put a stop to the auction," Alexander says, his voice booming through the speaker. "All vampires are allowed to submit a bid of any amount over one percent of your donor population, and I will draw out six assholes to split the rest of Ruby's contract. If one of you kills her, that's on you."

I try to get my eyes to focus. I try to pull my thoughts together. But I can't do anything as Alexander straightens himself up and towers over me.

"You may do so now. Until everyone has a chance to submit a claim for the lottery, I will punish this donor for ruining our event. Take as little or as much time as you need, and enjoy the rest of the show. The Aris Hotel appreciates its guests and those who love Ruby as much as I do."

The crowd murmurs in uncertainty, but Alexander ignores everyone. Clapping his hands, he summons one of the stagehands, who brings out a chair for him to sit in. Shoving his fingers under me, he jostles my body, and I scream again. I think my back might be broken. Every inch of me blazes with pain that I can't be certain.

Alexander sets me across his lap, ignoring my screech of pain. I black out again, but the relief of nothingness doesn't last long. Monroe yells directions at someone— maybe Knox, maybe someone else—and his voice gives me something to focus on as Alexander whacks his paddle hard to my ass. The studs shoot pain down my legs and to my toes, and I scream louder, my voice filling the air.

"I never wanted to do this to you, my baby doll. This is your fault. All you had to do is behave like a good girl for daddy, and I wouldn't have had to resort to this kind of punishment. Your actions have consequences, and you'll never learn if you don't have to face them." Alexander's sharp voice snaps over me at the same time he hits me with his studded paddle again even harder.

What the fuck? What did he say? I can't think. It's too much. I just want to black out again. For the first time, I'm not afraid to die. I just want this misery to be over. I want him to just hurry up and finish my life off. He once said he made me and he can destroy me. So why doesn't he?

"Kill me," I say, my voice a whisper. "Just kill me."

"And waste a future heir? I don't think so. Once your contracts expire after you're nice and broken and malleable, I plan to continue the bloodline. You will carry an heir like your mother had." Alexander whacks me again, knocking his words from my mind, not giving me a chance to process. "I will get what I want in the end."

"Enough!" Opal's shout cuts over the pounding in my ears.

The world flies around me, and I fall to the stage and off Alexander's lap. My vision crowds with shadows, and I squint, watching as two forms blur around me. It takes Opal squatting beside me and pouring her blood into my mouth to bring my senses and concentration back to me. Alexander growls and heaves, panting on his knees with a knife protruding from his stomach.

Opal pets my cheek, combing my choppy strands away from my face. "Hayley, I'm so sorry. I'm a coward. I should've fought harder for you. I should've never let it get so far."

I open and close my mouth, but she doesn't let me speak, filling me up with her blood. I finally get my mouth to cooperate, and I suck her arm, feeling the tingling sensation of her blood blooming in my stomach. The pain in my body lessens the longer I drink, and I blink my eyes clearing the tears from my vision.

"I'm done with the Aris Coven. You're mine, as well as the other gems, and I'm taking you away from La Vega. I have an ally in a territory who doesn't allow for the mistreatment of donors but especially women." Opal scoops me up and cradles me in her arms. "We're packing up now."

Her words shock the hell out of me, and I think about what she just said. She has an ally in another area?

She's cutting ties with her coven? We're leaving La Vega? Whoa. My heart and mind go to war, and all I can think about is how I want to leave but I don't want to leave Sawyer, Monroe, or Knox. But if it's this life I have to live? I need to do something for me. I can't stay.

"Can you stand?" Opal asks, spinning around to face Alexander. She doesn't wait for me to respond and sets me on my feet and shields me protectively.

"Dear sister, I see that you've healed her. How nice of you. I do love extending the punishment. Only half of the vampires have entered the lottery." Alexander straightens his sparkly tuxedo jacket and leers, showing off his fangs. "Now give her back and I'll forget what I just heard."

Opal growls and clutches her dagger. "Run, Hayley. Head backstage. The others are waiting."

I hesitate for a moment, gripping onto the back of her dress.

"Hayley, go!" she shouts. "Go now!"

I summon my nerve and spin, rushing toward the billowing curtain over the back wall. A man in one of the Aris Hotel staff uniforms waves at me, motioning for me to hurry. My feet slap on the cool stage, and I only glance behind me once to see Alexander and Opal blurring in another fight.

"Hurry, Ms. Aris. There's no—" A hulking figure

materializes behind the vampire staff member and punches his heart out.

I skid to a stop, staring with wide eyes at one of the bastards that Alexander called his coven brother. I scramble away, trying to put space between us. The vampire flashes his fangs and rushes me far too fast for me to comprehend. I trip over a fallen chair and land hard on my back. The guy looms over me, preparing to grab me and hoist me up.

Gunshots ring through the air, and he jerks as his chest is ravaged with bullets. I push on my hands and feet, trying to get back up. He stomps closer again, looking like he's going to tackle and drain me at any second. Maybe he will. Opal can't protect me. I don't even see her.

The man reaches out his arm, bending down to grab me. I stare in shock as another figure swings a blade down so fast that he can't move. His severed arm lands on top of me, and I screech and throw it, smacking him in the face.

"Gotcha, little bird," Monroe says, hooking his arms under mine and dragging me off the floor.

Sawyer spins and swings a long sword, one stolen from security, and gets the snarling Aris brother to get back. He gives up and snatches his arm, carrying it away as Sawyer chases him. I release a small sob, my whole body relaxing under the familiarity of Monroe's embrace.

"I'm sorry I've failed you," he murmurs. "Security was a bitch to get past. I'm going to fucking kill them all though."

I can't speak. I can't find my voice at all. I gasp in breath after breath, wanting nothing more than to beg him to get me out of here.

"Come on, I'm—" Monroe jerks with a holler, and I stare in shock as a blade slices through his throat as someone stabs him in the back of the neck.

His blood spills over me, and I jerk my attention to see the other coven brother of Alexander. Losing his grip on me, Monroe drops me. The asshole catches me and punches Monroe in the face, knocking him off his feet.

"You belong to the Aris Hotel," he mutters, adjusting me in his arms. "My brother is failing to hold up his duties. I cannot let that happen. You will be sold to pay for our losses."

I clench my teeth, anger rushing through me. I know better than to fight, but he hurt Monroe. I can't even see him and if he's okay. Fisting my hand, I clock the vampire in the nose and use my teeth to bite at his neck. I snap down on his ear, and he jerks away, yowling like a feral cat.

I spit flesh and blood onto the floor and whack him again, aiming for his eyes. He spins and throws me, and I tumble across the stage and right between Opal and Alexander. I curl in on myself, screaming, knowing they're both going to try to grab me.

Opal locks her arms around me and drags me to my feet. Her need to save me and to get me away distracts her from the fact that Alexander dodges past her. He growls and punches his fist into her back, making her scream.

Opal's hold loosens on me, and I catch myself in a crouch. I back up only to hit another pair of legs. I tip my head back and stare at an unfamiliar man, one with neatly brushed hair styled with a side part wearing a tie with a ruby-studded pin on the front of the silky black fabric. He growls at me, warning me to stay in my place. The quiet of the room cools my blood. I lick my lips, my whole body trembling. Shifting, I peer around. My heart slides into my stomach. There are more vampires in the room than there were before. Who are all of these guys?

Alexander clears his throat. "Dear sister. I had a feeling you'd go against not only our coven but the entire La Vega Leadership. You are guilty of treason and attempted relaying information to our enemy territories. The word of your alliance proves it."

Opal hisses, only to scream as Alexander squeezes her heart in her chest. Her mouth opens and closes. She can't utter anything more than a cry, and her eyes dart to mine.

She mouths that she's sorry, and I tense.

"Your crimes will be punished by death and all of your assets will be inherited by our coven," Alexander says, his voice booming through the room. "As for those of you plotting to stand against the leadership, you will bow before us and swear your loyalty. If you do not, you will not only be withdrawn from the lottery, but you will not make it from this room alive. We will not stand by and watch you destroy the city we worked decades to bring together. Do you understand? This lottery is a gift, and you will not try to take it for granted."

I intake a sharp breath.

"This was a fucking setup!" a man hollers, rushing toward the stage.

One of the unfamiliar vampires materializes in front of him and severs his head before he makes it within a foot of the stage.

"Say goodbye, dear sister. May you burn in the depths of Hell." Alexander's voice yanks my attention back to him.

Opal's eyes widen, her gaze never breaking from mine. Flashing her fangs, she screams until Alexander rips her heart from her body and smooshes it within his fingers. He drops Opal to the stage floor and chucks her heart away, sending it splattering on the floor. I clutch my chest, my heart seizing. I can't breathe. I can't think. All I can do is stare with burning eyes at Opal's dead body. At the ring of powerful vampires surrounding us.

Wiping his hands on his jacket, Alexander grins at me, his wicked smile stabbing me through my very soul. "Shall we take an intermission and get things cleaned up?" Alexander asks the crowd as if they'll dare respond. He claps his hands and winks at me. "Lovely. Finish entering your names in the lottery. The show must go on."

I CAN'T BELIEVE I'm back in the cage, and this time, there is no getting out. To torture me, Alexander dragged Opal's body and dropped it in front of me, forcing me to look at my dead caretaker's empty eyes.

I'm still in shock.

I can't find the will to do anything but stare at her,

ignoring the rowdy room gathering and taking their seats. My soul weeps, my whole body cold and stiff as if I've died along with Opal, but tears don't stain my cheeks any longer. I'm mostly numb. Hopeless. Utterly and completely defeated. I should've known Alexander would win and this whole thing would be a setup, bringing together La Vega's most powerful vampires. I've never seen the ruling vampires before, but hearing Alexander refer to them as the La Vega Leadership freaks me out. They all have to be older than the Vampire Uprising and just as ruthless. They're the ones who destroyed and rebuilt this city after all.

"And so the show continues..." Alexander dramatically lowers his voice and lets it echo through the speakers. "We have over a hundred entries tonight in the lottery for my beautiful, delectable, and dare I say virginal baby doll, Ruby Vixen."

Murmurs sound through the crowd at his comment.

I close my eyes, pushing the world away the best I can. I'm sure there are a lot of sick motherfuckers here who will want to fuck every hole on my body like their sex slave. The thought roils disgust through me. I will cling on to the thought of severing their dicks when they let their guards down if they even try.

"What? Don't believe me? I can guarantee one place

that has been off-limits in my dear sister's care...if you know what I mean." Alexander chuckles at the crowd's reaction and hums under his breath. "Some of you are going to be lucky, lucky, lucky men. Are you ready to find out?"

The crowd breaks into applause and whistles, stabbing my already bleeding soul with the pain of a thousand fiery daggers. I want so badly to cover my ears and block the world out, but another part of me needs to hear Alexander announce which vampires will surely be my ruin. If they don't break my body, they will break my soul. I'll be a living dead girl with only one desire in life, which will be to find my end.

The crowd settles, and I finally get the nerve to open my eyes, watching as Alexander stands in front of my cage. He shushes the crowd by holding his arms out and lowering his palms toward the stage floor.

"We're going to do this the back-world way. What a blast from the past, am I right?" He chuckles again and others humor him with fake laughter.

If I didn't think he would hurt me again, I'd boo him, hoping the crowd would participate. I want nothing more than to humiliate him again. Bite him. Do whatever I can to make him ache and bleed.

"I'm sure we all want to get out of here and have

some fun for the rest of the night, so I'll be quick. There are six lucky spots on my baby doll's contract. If you fail to uphold the terms for the duration of your time, you will face a penalty of what I see fit, which includes failing to pass her on to her next owner, accidental death, dismemberment, including teeth, and permanent damage to her skin. She is to be show ready at all times to be fair to the vampire who claims her after. If you do not agree, please withdraw your entry if chosen." Alexander motions to a vampire staff member, getting him to bring over a glass bowl of folded pieces of cream-colored paper.

I wring my hands together, my anxiety triggering my heart to erratically beat in a chaotic rhythm. I'm going to be sick. My head hurts and stars pepper my vision. If I don't pass out, I'll throw up. Maybe I'll do both.

Alexander swirls his hands through the paper, laughing like a damn child. He plucks out one of the entries and waves it over his head. "Luck be this beautiful donor tonight," he murmurs, unfolding the paper. Swiveling, he peeks over his shoulder at me and winks as if I'm the one waiting in excited anticipation.

"Well, this was unexpected. What a lucky, lucky girl you are, baby doll. I know how much you enjoy entertaining the weak." Alexander waves the paper in the air. "The first lucky spot on Ruby Vixen's contract goes to Monroe of the Bella Hotel."

My mouth falls open in surprise. "What?" I can't stop my voice from sounding out. I don't believe it. Fate was really with me tonight.

"Mister...Monroe. Please see my coven brother at the side of the stage. You must complete the arrangements, prove you have proper accommodations, and agree to all terms of the contract." Alexander tightens his jaw, his smile disappearing. He shoves his hand into the bowl again and pulls out another slip. Frowning, he stares at the paper for a minute. "The next lucky gentleman is from the marvelous Alibur. I'm thrilled to announce Mr. Clark Alibur. Please proceed to the side stage."

My mind and body shut down at the name of a unfamiliar vampire. I knew it was too much to hope for that Alexander would draw the names of only vampires from the Bella Crew. Calling the next winner, Alexander does an ass shake before me at the vampire's reaction. My head throbs too much that I can't even remember her name, though I heard it.

Two more times, Alexander calls vampires from the crowd, and I ignore the room. The excitement flares and the murmurs drone on and on, growing louder as Alexander pulls the final name.

He hums under his breath and taps his chin. "Uh-oh.

It seems there was an error. Unfortunately, we can't accept this entry. The requirements to participate in the lottery was at minimum one percent and this one's ink is smudged. Because I can't read it, it's only fair that I pick someone who took care in filling out the form. It's a shame too. I know my Ruby was fond of you, Mr. Noble."

A deep growl reverberates through the room, and the spotlight cuts across the crowd and lands on Sawyer. "Are you fucking kidding me? You're lying."

"I'm afraid I'm not." Alexander tosses the crumpled paper over his shoulder. "So, it looks like someone else will be lucky tonight. Congratulations to Richmond of the Mingo Hotel."

"This is bullshit!" Sawyer yells, getting up from his chair. The crowd hums in anticipation, and the rest of Sawyer's crew and even some other guys I've never seen get to their feet. "I won the lottery. You fucking purposely disqualified me."

Alexander raises an eyebrow and claps his hands. "Security! Please escort Mr. Noble out."

A few vampires blur through the room in his direction. Sawyer swings his fist, knocking a man away. Alexander growls and hops from the stage, flashing his fangs. His coven brothers materialize by his sides, and they face the Bella Crew straight on.

Alexander's eyes flash silver. "If you don't leave—"

One of the unfamiliar guys with Sawyer punches Alexander in the face, shutting him up. I stare in shock, watching as Alexander's brother unsheathes a dagger and slices it so fast through the guy's neck that I only realize what happens when his body falls and his head rolls.

"You have five seconds to take your allies and leave. If you do not, I will revoke the day your hotel has already earned through Mr. Monroe." Alexander crosses his arms. "Do I make myself clear?"

Without a word, Sawyer, Knox, and the rest of the Bella Crew disappear.

All feels lost.

"I hope you're happy. You've ruined everything." Alexander leads me down the back hallway and to his secret office backstage.

Security cleared the club faster than I've seen, and Alexander left me hanging in the cage for what felt like days, but I know only hours passed. I'll be here until my contract to the collection of vampires gets approved by the leadership. I don't know what it entails, but I'm assuming it gives everyone a chance to pay their entry fees.

"Opal died because of you. Do you know how deeply it hurt me having to execute her in front of everyone? Had you been obedient, it wouldn't have had to happen." Alexander tugs me, forcing me to walk in front of him. "I can barely stand to look at you. I took exceptional care of you, gave you a home, treated you like family, and how do you repay me? Be thankful this is your punishment. It could've been far worse."

Fury ignites inside me, and I can't stop from turning around to glare at him. "Worse than being passed around the Strip? Treated as a blood slave? A sex slave?" I spit in his face with my anger. "You're a monster! A twisted son-on-a-bitch!"

I brace for him to tear my throat out. I expect him to rip me off my feet and paddle me until I can't walk. But he doesn't react. All he does is wipe his face on his sleeve and release a warning growl.

"Do that again, and I'll disqualify the Bella Crew contract. You should thank me that they even have one, considering their entries weren't actually drawn in the lottery." Slamming his hand into my back, he pushes me into his office.

I stumble forward and catch myself on my hands. "What?" I wish my mouth would've stayed shut. He's lying and baiting me for a reaction. I know it.

"It was rather fun watching Mr. Noble's face when I gave him hope to claim you and stole it away." Alexander chuckles to himself. "It was such sweet satisfaction. It'll haunt him for the rest of eternity, especially after you make your first round and return to them utterly broken. Maybe they'll realize the beauty of a malleable, obedient blood donor."

I tilt my head up and stare at him towering over me. I don't even know what to say.

"But, my doll, this arrangement doesn't come without a price. You might think I'm a monster, but this is a favor I've granted." Bending over, he touches my chin and meets my gaze. "Do you remember our failed arrangement? About you getting information for me? That is still in place. If you do not give me everything I want to know, you will not only end up somewhere far worse, I will kill Mya. Painfully."

My eyes widen at his words. Mya was supposed to leave with Govan.

Leering, Alexander's face sparks with a wicked smile that makes my skin crawl. "Hmm, you look surprised. You should both be grateful that I didn't administer her final donation for attempting to steal donors from me while breaking her contract. It's a shame I had to make an example."

Alexander pulls out his com device and taps the screen. He holds it out for me to see, and I nearly lose my stomach. Chained to the wall, Mya hangs limply with the body of someone at her feet. I can't recognize him, but I think it might be her brother.

I clench my teeth, tears burning my eyes. "I hate you!"

"You won't forever. Once you realize how good you had it here, you'll come groveling back, begging for me to buy back your contract. But unlike your wretched mother, I might grant you some mercy as long as you behave and know your place. I wasn't joking about you producing an heir for my bloodline." Alexander caresses my cheek, his eyes flashing silver. "Maybe two or three. Maybe an army. Forever is a long time."

I scrunch my brows together, confused by his words. What the fuck is he talking about?

I don't get the chance to ask him.

Locking his gaze to mine, he breaks into my head. Pressure explodes behind my eyes, his mind-manipulation feeling as if he cracks my skull open. I can't move or fight or do anything. His eyes turn solid silver, the gleam so reflective that I can see my own face.

Oh no. I thought Sawyer protected my mind, but this feels different.

"You will forget this conversation, Hayley. If you try to tell the Bella Crew about our arrangement, I will not only kill Mya, I will kill all of the performers. And not only that, you will fight against them and take their hearts any way you can. You will feel as if you're burning alive if you don't succeed. Do you understand?"

"Yes." The word comes automatically from my mouth, and my eyes blur with my unshed tears.

"Good." Alexander smiles at me, releasing me from his stare.

Confusion steals my thoughts, and I stare around the room. I expected him to hit me or do something, but all he does is turn his back and grab a few things from his cupboard. My hands tremble in nerves at his silence. I know he doesn't acknowledge me on purpose, trying to get under my skin.

His phone chimes, and he glances at the screen and releases a breath. Whipping around, he flashes his fangs at me. He flies forward and drags me off my feet, swinging me around until my back hits the wall.

"It looks like everyone was approved for the contract. It pains me to send you somewhere you think you enjoy first, but it'll make it that much harder on you when you have to leave. I'll be watching, Hayley. If you so much as put up a fight or if the Bella Crew tries to fuck up the agreement, I'll—" A knock sounds on the door, and Alexander growls, whipping his attention toward it.

"Mr. Aris, the driver is here to collect Ms. Ruby," a husky voice says through the wood, speaking because Alexander doesn't respond. "Do I need to pack her things?"

"No," Alexander snaps. "She will be out in five. Don't let anyone speak to her and take her directly to her transportation. Follow them to ensure she arrives at the Bella. I will not have them trying to fuck with the contract or find a loophole."

A loophole? I glance from the door and back to Alexander, his eyes boring into my face, but I refuse to look at him. I wonder what he's talking about.

Grabbing my hair, he yanks me to my feet and snarls. "Like I said, be a good girl, Hayley. You will regret it otherwise. Now get out of my sight. I can't stand to look at you a moment longer."

He shoves me to the door, and I drop my gaze instead of looking at the guard. I should feel relief in this moment. I'm getting out of here and going to the Bella. But why does something feel so wrong? Why does my life feel like it's over?

"Goodbye, my doll," Alexander says, his voice low. "You better make me proud."

"THIS ASSHOLE." I growl and stab my dagger into the table in the lobby. "Do we have any connections with the others? There has to be something we can do. Buy them off. Threaten them. I'll chop off and choke them with their dicks."

My whole body trembles with my anger, and I clench

and unclench my fists, trying to get my muscles to relax. We should've seen the setup from a mile away. I want to kick myself for not being smart about things. I was just so concerned about Hayley that I didn't think about much else.

"Walcott is pulling up with her. You need to get your shit together, Monny." Tatum pats my back and leans forward, looking into my eyes. "I'm sure she's scared out of her mind and will just need you to be strong."

Sawyer sighs and knocks his fist to the table. "Let us handle everything for a while. I'll make some calls. Collect on some debts. Your job is to get Hayley settled, make sure she's okay after all that bullshit, and ensure she knows that we're going to fucking take care of everything."

I crack my jaw, loosening the pressure of my teeth grinding together. "Maybe Knox should take her today. I'm not sure how good I'll be at any of that. I just want to destroy the fucking city."

"No, Monroe. I'm just as pissed as you. Hayley needs your kind of psycho today. You will help her. Me? I'll just want to fuck her pain away." Knox puffs out a breath.

Knox, Sawyer, and I agreed that it might be overwhelming for Hayley today, so only I'm supposed to hang out with her for a while. She has this ingrained nature to serve and please, and with all of us, she might spread herself too thin before she can handle the change in her life. It doesn't help that she lost her caretaker. Opal was motherly, and her connection to the vampire was strong enough that she struggled over leaving.

And then there is also her friend.

Govan had asked us permission to bring Mya to the Bella, and we agreed. It's not like we could deny him after all the bullshit he puts up with us. Sawyer thought it would help ease Hayley's stress if her friend was here. If only shit didn't go down. Govan was lucky he even made it out with his head. But the fucker shouldn't have tried to bring Mya's family too.

The sound of the entrance beeping steals my attention from Knox and Sawyer, and I straighten my back, steel myself for what I'm sure might be the poutiest face and saddest eyes I will ever see. I might be tough and won't hesitate to take some asshole's head, but when it comes to tears? I'm scared as fuck.

"Fuckers, we're home," Walcott calls, his voice bellowing through the air.

I race toward the glass doors, trying to keep my shit together. I swear Walcott better have not said anything stupid. I'll kick his fucking ass. I didn't even want him to pick her up, but Aris made it clear that it had to be someone else. His silent threat included Sawyer and Knox, and shit's bad enough.

I spot Hayley strolling through the door as Walcott holds it open for her. She keeps her eyes trained on the ground, looking completely lost and defeated. My chest tightens, and another wave of anger crashes through me. I hate Aris. I hate the leadership. I fucking hate the damn universe.

Walcott doesn't linger, vanishing to join the others. I swallow my nerves and stride forward at a human pace as to not startle Hayley. It takes everything in me not to scoop her up and rush to my room before finding out the state of her mental health. What she went through? It was fucked up. As fucked up as The Divide.

"Little bird, welcome home," I say, keeping my voice soft.

Hayley snaps her gaze from the floor and surprises me, throwing herself toward me. I release a breath and engulf her in a hug, burying my face into the crook of her neck. She sniffles and the warmth of her tears soaks through my cotton shirt. I don't know what to say or if I should say anything at all. I know she struggles to speak before spoken to, but damn it. I just want to cuddle the hell out of her.

"Can I take you to my room? I have a meal ready and waiting." I stroke my fingers up and down her spine, taking care not to shower her with promises she might not believe.

I can't read her mind, but with how vulnerable she looked on stage, I could tell that her hope died in front of the audience. She might not be receptive to any of my words until I can show her proof. Because I will fix this. I'll kill anyone who even thinks of putting their hands, fangs, mouths, dicks, whatever within reach of my beautiful woman.

Hayley sniffles again and eases away from me. "Alexander wouldn't let me bring anything."

It dawns on me that she's empty handed. I hadn't even noticed that she wears Walcott's jacket. I was too focused on her arrival, which might've been a good thing. But now? I want it off her. Call me jealous. I can't help it.

I suppress the urge to offer my jacket instead and say, "I'll get you taken care of. As soon as we get you fed and settled, we'll pick out a room and fill it with anything you need."

Her brows scrunch together. "My own room?" Fear lines her voice, and she sucks her bottom lip between her teeth.

"We thought you would like your own space," I murmur, flicking my eyes from hers to the sidewalk outside. It remains empty this close to sunrise.

"Oh," she whispers. "Okay." Nodding, she tries to soften her features, but she can't hide her frown.

"Unless you want to stay the day with me? I don't mind. I love your company." I smile and caress my knuckles to her cheek.

She nods quickly, her eyes lighting up with my words. I can't stop the smile from crossing my face. Hugging her close, I brush my lips to hers and relocate us to the elevator. Hayley practically attacks my mouth with hers, sliding her hands into my hair and ensuring I don't pull away from her. Not that I'd want to. Her lips taste fucking amazing and the warmth of her body even better.

I rush us blindly down the hall until we reach my room, and it takes everything in me to set her on her feet. "I'll go grab some clothes for you to choose from. One of the elderly men volunteered to make your meal, so we couldn't fuck it up. I hope you like pasta."

Hayley grabs my hand, stopping me in my tracks. "Don't leave. Please. I don't want to be alone. I just—I don't know."

I hug her again and lift her off her feet, kicking my door closed. Strolling across the room, I set her on my bed. Just seeing her there staring up at me gives me a massive boner. I inwardly groan, silently yelling at my cock to chill the fuck out. Just because Hayley's on my bed, staring up at me with her gorgeous eyes, and refusing to let go of my hands doesn't mean anything. She needs comfort and not pleasure.

Stupid cock. It clearly doesn't believe me, and my nuts clench as Hayley pulls me closer, silently inviting me to sit on my bed with her. And goddamn it. She shifts closer, her face finally lighting with a smile. Knox said he couldn't be here for her because he'd just fuck her pain away. Fucking shit. She leans in and kisses me, looking like that's the only thing she wants. How can I deny her?

Must. Resist. Must-fucking-resist.

I clear my throat and ease away, putting space between us. "Hayley, I fucking want you so badly. You have no idea. But—"

She cuts me off with a kiss, pushing me onto my back. Climbing on top of me, she peers down and rests her hands to my chest. And damn. She puts all her weight on me, trying to keep me down. My body goes wild, and I play-growl, my eyes wandering from hers to her cleavage peeking out from Walcott's jacket.

Grabbing the zipper, she starts to slide it down, and I snatch her by the wrist. If she does it, it'll be hard as fuck for me turn back. I crave her on every level. I want to do everything she asks of me, which is weird as hell. I prefer total control and being responsible for her every need. But like before, I know I haven't earned the right to her sub-mission. I can't just flip her off and have my way no mat-ter if she allows me.

"Hayley, you've been through a lot," I manage to say. "I don't know if this is a good idea."

My balls ache at my words. Who is this fucking nice guy? My body hates him. My cock is about to riot and promise a damn eternal boner for the bullshit coming from my mouth.

Hayley sits silently on top of me, tightening her knees at my sides, squeezing me. "Do you not want me?"

Fuck me. She's mistaking my need to make sure she's okay with rejection.

"Fuck yeah, I do. I want to whip it out and let you ride the hell out of me. It's killing me not giving in. My cock throbs. I just...I don't want to fuck this up. I want to make sure you're okay without sneaking my desire into things. You've been through a lot. I—" I snap my mouth shut, watching her body stiffen.

"Stop treating me like a broken doll. I know I've been through a lot. I know this whole situation is fucked up. I just—I want you to treat me how you would if you didn't win me in a lottery." She digs her nails into my shirt. "Treat me like I ran away with you."

Her words unleash something dark and wild within

me. I hesitate for only a second, staring into her eyes, seeing the truth to her words. I was wrong about what she needed. I thought she needed to be coddled and taken care of. I thought she needed me to threaten the world. But what she needs is to be in control. She needs me to let her make her own decisions instead of trying to do things that I think she needs.

I flare my nostrils, my fangs clicking, drawing her attention to my mouth. "Are you sure? I need to hear you say it."

She narrows her eyes, bunches my shirt in her fingers, and leans in, getting into my face. "Fuck me. Fuck me how I want. Fuck me how you want."

A rumbly moan escapes my mouth, and I flip her off me and onto the bed. She snatches my shirt, tugging it up and over my head in a race to get me naked. I tear the zipper on Walcott's jacket, growling and throwing the worn fabric at the wall.

"He's not getting that shit back. You're mine, Hayley. He's not even getting a second alone with even your scent." I kiss her, molding my lips to her and gliding my tongue into her mouth.

She moans and maps my chest with her fingers, rubbing her thumb over the barbells piercing my nipples. Breaking away from my mouth, she drags her tongue down my throat, unleashing a wild side I want to devour. She tilts her head, drinking in the sight of my body and flicks her tongue over each of my piercings, making me moan. She fucking loves them.

"Your skin tastes so good," she murmurs, sliding lower as she touches my belt buckle. "I want to suck your cock."

Holy shit. Goddamn. I want that too.

"Is that so?" I ask, grinning at her while she slides my belt off.

She hums in agreement.

"I'm taking what I want then, too," I mutter, stroking my hand over her tit, rubbing my fingers over her tight nipples.

Hayley gasps as I knock her on her back and strip her out of the torn costume. My cock drips at the sight of her smooth skin, her body the epitome of perfection. She reaches out her hands to me. I kick out of my pants as I crawl forward and nestle my shoulders right between her legs.

She pulls my hair with her fingers and moans, her back arching as I start slow, teasing her pussy with my tongue, savoring how fucking amazing she tastes and smells. I don't even need her blood if I can bury my face between her legs. I'll survive on giving her pleasure until the end of time, her body enough to satiate me on every level.

Spreading her with two fingers, I expose her clit to me and roll my tongue across the heat of her body, listening to her react. She moans so loud as I pick up speed, using my vampire speed to the silent tune of an upbeat song in my head. She scratches her nails into my shoulders, squirming like crazy. She's so wet and turned on that I want more.

"Give me your cock," she says, her words breathy with her moan. "Let me taste you too."

I ignore her, working my tongue harder and faster until she tenses with an orgasm that splashes pussy juice across my face. And hell fucking yeah. I want to bathe in it. In her. I never want to leave this damn room.

Sitting up, I stroke the length of my shaft, watching her eyes trail down my body. She teases me by opening her legs and stretches her arms out to invite me closer. I lean in to kiss her, craving for more, wanting to give her a world of pleasure, but the naughty little bird hooks her legs around me, uses her torso strength to fly up, and shoves me back. My back hits the bed, and she beams me a teasing smile. She's proud of herself for getting her way, and how can I resist her as she sways her body until she kneels between my legs. Her small hands lace around my cock, and she licks the top, sucking it into her mouth.

I moan, my lids turning heavy with my desire. She's so goddamn perfect that I can barely stand it. Her tongue twirls, tracing around my girth until she sucks in cool air between her lips and sucks my entire length into her throat. I'm impressed as hell, watching her deep throat me without gagging. She bobs her head, the sensation zinging pleasure to my balls.

"Don't try to make me cum," I say, growling with my moan.

She meets my gaze with a raise of her eyebrow. I don't even have to hear her thoughts to know that she's going to do it anyway, and that there is nothing I can do about it no matter how much I want to please her instead. She deserves to be taken care of. Her pleasure deserves to be above my own.

"Hayley," I groan, combing my fingers through her hair. "Fuck. Your mouth feels incredible. I want to fucking destroy the damn world for you."

Humming again, her voice vibrates over my cock. I pant and close my eyes, losing myself to the pleasure she creates. She bobs her head, working her mouth faster, increasing the pressure of her sucking with her lips. My body aches with desperation as I feel my cock on the verge of exploding.

I tighten my hand even more, stopping her as I cum, grunting at the ecstasy rolling through me. She slowly glides her mouth up and licks her lips, swallowing instead of spitting. And damn. She smiles like she enjoyed it.

"So good," she murmurs, patting my cheek with a smile. Straightening her back, she stretches her arms over her head.

I don't let her get away. Instead, I hook my hand around her waist and pull her to me. She giggles and presses her hand over my heart, her eyes lighting up in a way I've never seen. I could lose myself in their blue depths. I could lose myself to her completely.

"I'm not done with you, little bird. I want more," I mutter, my voice deep and husky, my fangs protruding from beneath my lips.

"Is that so?" she asks, using my own damn words against me.

I growl again and press my fingers into her back. "You're mine. I want to fucking let the world know. I want the universe to see. You're mine and no one is going to get in my way. I will cut off every dick and tongue in this damn city if they even think they can try to touch you. You belong to the Bella no matter what shit documents say."

My chest heaves with my words, my stupid possessiveness getting the best of me. I expect Hayley to react with a frown, but her face lights up even more and she throws her arms around me, kissing me again.

"Tell me more," she says, stroking her fingers along my shaft, already hard and ready for her. "Tell me how you're going to destroy the bastards."

My eyebrows lift, my head cocking to the side. Damn. I hadn't expected her to like it, and now she wants more. Okay. This is proof that she's my damn perfect woman.

I lower her onto her ass and adjust her legs, wanting to watch myself enter her body. She holds her knees, her eyes staring at me rubbing my hand over my length. "I will fucking break every damn finger of any bastard who doesn't have your permission to touch you."

She bites her lips. "That's not enough."

"That's only the beginning." Slowly, I lift her hips, cupping her ass with my hands, and I align our bodies, testing her with my tip, feeling how soaking wet and slippery she is. I don't rush to push into her and just ease in and out, listening to her gasps at the pressure. "I'm going to fucking cut their fingers next starting at the first bend and working my way through all ten of them. They will regret even standing in your space."

"I want them to scream," she says, reaching between

her legs and rubbing her clit, giving me a show.

"That's when I'll cut off their damn tongues." I grip the base of my cock, guiding it in more, letting her body react to mine until it's as if I get sucked into her, the tightness of her pussy stealing my breath.

It's fucking bliss. Her heat warms me up, getting my blood pumping. I rock my hips more, watching her brows pinch together with her pleasure. She moans and pants, rubbing her clit harder and faster like she enjoys getting herself off at the same time.

I groan, picking up pace, sinking in deeper. "I will continue to cut them up inch by inch, taking care to keep them alive through it. And when their bodies are stubs and just hunks of bleeding flesh, I'll throw them to the sun. They'll never have a chance to heal nor will they die. And I will do it to all of them. Just for you."

She moans and nods her head in appreciation, loving how twisted I can be. I bow forward and kiss her, curling her body with the movements. I can't get enough of her. I won't ever get enough.

"You're mine," I repeat, thrusting harder, stealing her breath away. "Bella's. I hope you know that. We will take care of things. And you. You have my promise."

"Good," she whispers, her eyes locking to mine. "That's what I want. This is all that I want."

Our moans fill the air, and I lose myself to everything Hayley is. She's not weak. She's not broken. She's a fucking amazing human and has incomparable strength. She has lived through and survived things no one should have ever had to experience. She deserves everything she wants and desires, and I will come through for her. I'm ready. Fuck the world. She's who is important. I can't explain it, and I don't care. She's mine.

Adjusting her back to the bed, I take over and strum my thumb over her clit, playing her body to the beat of our passion. She arches her back and closes her eyes. Her pussy tightens more, practically gripping me, and I grunt at the sensation of her orgasm. Her body pulses, and it gets me right in the balls. I savor every second of her moaning and grabbing the blankets, so hot and sexy in this moment until I cum.

I bow into her, sliding my arm across her back and flipping her with me as I crash to the bed. She snuggles against my side, kissing my ribs and tracing her finger over my nipple piercing.

"This is how I want life to be," she says, releasing a sigh. "I don't ever want to leave."

I nod my head, my words sticking to my tongue. I want the same, but it's not possible. Not yet. I don't know what tomorrow will bring, but we better fucking figure it out. We have to stick to the terms of the contract or risk not only losing our lives but everything.

"I know, little bird. But don't worry. We will figure it out. Sawyer and Knox are working on calling in favors. We will keep you here, okay?" I rest on my elbow and kiss her gently.

A holler sounds from the hall, pissing me off. How dare someone ruin my moment with Hayley. Flying from the bed, I cross the room and fling my door open, peering into the hall. I spot a donor waving his hands, desperate for attention.

I glance at Hayley sitting on the bed and quickly close the door. "What the fuck?" I ask, not waiting for him to approach me.

"They took my wife!" the man yells, gasping for breath. "You have to help me."

I frown. "What do you mean?"

"Aris! The Aris Hotel came in. They took her. They had a contract." The man covers his face with his hands. "How could you?"

I growl and pull out my com device, tapping the screen. Shit. The fucking bastard Aris. These weren't supposed to be live donations. I worked everything out beforehand.

"Go back to your room. I'll take care of it," I mutter.

Sawyer and Knox materialize at the end of the hall-way, and I shake my head in anger. I don't even have to ask them to know that something changed. Something is fucking wrong.

"Aris filed a complaint with the leadership," Sawyer says before I can ask. "He claims our presence led to him losing business. To stop further bullshit, he demanded he take live donations to ensure he gets the blood. We're not the only ones. They're targeting all hotels not run by covens. They're scared."

I growl. "They better fucking b—"

"Monroe?" Hayley's soft voice calls from behind me.

Turning, I spot her wrapped in only my blankets, her eyes searching over the three of us. "Alexander took donors from here? Because of me?"

I whip my head. "No, he took them because of us, but we'll fucking fix this. His control is up."

"Damn right," Knox says.

Sawyer growls under his breath. "This is what we needed to give other crews a push. They'll realize we've been right all along."

"You remember what I told you?" I ask her, sending blush to her cheeks. I tighten my jaw, trying not to smile at her reaction. "Those fuckers are going to pay."

"I CAN HELP. You have to let me help." I sit on Monroe's lap, running my fingers through his soft hair. "I don't even need much to perform. I'm known for my hoop, but I have experience with sinks, poles, trapezes, and floor routines."

"Absolutely not. We keep our hotel closed for a reason. The last thing we need are more assholes coming in, trying to threaten what we have." Sawyer rests his elbows on his knees, staring at the empty glass of blood he set on the floor.

We all sit together at one of the old roulette tables, away from the rest of the crew. Tatum and Walcott keep looking in our direction from across the empty, quiet casino. A couple others hang around the slots, whispering quietly. I think Monroe, Sawyer, and Knox purposely keep me away from the others, but I don't ask about it. It's not an uncommon thing for vampires to do. And who knows? They could all be upset about what happened to the donors—not *could* be. They *are* pissed off. I just don't know if it involves me.

"You can perform for me anytime," Monroe whispers into my ear, kissing the sensitive skin of my throat. He draws my attention away from the vampires across the casino floor.

Warmth flushes through my body, and both Sawyer and Knox glance at me. Monroe's fingers tighten around me, and I'm nearly certain I catch Knox's lips twitch. Vampires can be super quiet in conversation. One look at Sawyer proves they're talking about me. I consider calling them out, but a part of me fears speaking up. What would I get out of it?

Knox clears his throat, realizing I grow uncomfortable by the quiet attention. "What Sawyer means is that we'll discuss all of our options, but as of now, we want to keep our home safe. Monroe is enough of an asshole already anyway."

I flick my gaze toward the other vampires, pretending to mind their business. "What about the others? Your other crewmembers? I think they should have a say. It might help with the tension."

My mouth dries thinking about the way Govan looked at me from his post as Monroe showed me around to distract me from the commotion and outrage of the donors. It was obvious that he's pissed that I'm here when Mya isn't. But I...my head pounds, causing my eye to twitch.

"Hayley?" Monroe taps his finger on my knee. "Did you hear Sawyer?"

Sawyer and Knox both stare at me. Again, silence falls between us, and I shift on Monroe's lap, trying to remember what we were even talking about.

"Hayley? You okay?" I blink a few times, realizing Knox kneels in front of me. He tilts his head and gets me to look into his eyes. "Does something hurt? You're wincing."

I shudder, pushing the strange feeling rising inside me

away. "No, I'm okay. Sorry. I was just thinking."

His eyes search mine, and he studies me in silence for a minute. I squirm under his intensity. The way he looks at me? I enjoy it more than I should. I can't help running my fingers through my new layered A-line bob. It's still weird getting used to my short strands, but I'm thankful that Tatum found a donor who could fix it.

Monroe plays with the hair on the back of my neck and kisses my skin again. His closeness and affection stir something deep inside me. For being a man who loves fucking people up and instilling fear into the hearts of the toughest vampires, he's sweet. I savor every ounce of attention he gives me. It's not even because we just fucked. There is more to it, and my soul hurts even thinking about how time runs out.

I clear my throat, reach out, and poke Knox's nose. "Stop it. I'm fine. If you continue to stare at me, you might as well just kiss me. At least then I won't question whether you guys are silent because you're talking about me too lowly for me to hear or if you're trying to control your hunger. If that's the case...bite me."

Knox's eyebrows shoot up on his forehead and both Monroe and Sawyer's fangs audibly click as they extend, triggered by my words. They're either really hungry or they loved what I just demanded of Knox. Probably the latter since they've all been sipping on gen. pop. blood. The sure way to tell whether a vampire is hungry or horny is by looking to see if they get what Mya teased as a fangboner.

I laugh, the strange feeling disappearing. "You liked that, didn't you?"

"You little tease," Monroe murmurs, practically purring like a feline as he scratches his fangs gently over my neck, hooking them to the collar of my shirt. I've never worn something so plain in my life, the soft material like a feathery hug around my body. I was a bit surprised Monroe picked out comfort over sexy for me, though he did say I could just wear his sheet.

"What are you waiting for? Give her what she wants." Monroe presses his chest into my back and snatches Knox by his shirt, dragging him closer.

Stopping himself from crashing into me, Knox hugs me, sandwiching me to Monroe. I laugh and bonk my head to Monroe's. Sawyer watches with a soft smile on his face, and I wiggle my fingers, inviting him closer. It's like I have a deep-seated need to include them all. They've risked a lot for me.

Switching spots, Sawyer sits beside us and kisses my temple. It's surreal being in the middle of them as they take turns showering me with affection. I know the crew members don't comprehend how this is possible with a vampire's innate possessiveness—I'm not even sure I understand for that matter—but I'll devour it and fill my very being with everything they are. The universe might have given me a shitty existence, deprived of the emotions I truly craved all my life, but it's sure making up for it. If only it could last. A driver will show up at any minute. What happens to me after...? I can't think about it. I refuse to allow myself to carry any hope. The only thing I can summon is patience and trust. Because I will be back here. Sawyer, Knox, and Monroe aren't perfect, and they don't claim to be, but I know they'll do what they can to keep me safe behind enemy lines, which according to Sawyer, is the rest of the world.

A beep sounds from Sawyer's pocket, but he ignores it, guiding my face until he can kiss my lips. I think about what would happen if I push the three of them and how far they're willing to go to give me what I want. If only I knew what that was in regards to them. Right now, I'm just content existing within their world and the safety of their home.

"Yo, Sawyer!" Walcott shouts, his voice bellowing through the air. "There's a fucker outside with a copy of Hayley's contract. He demands we let him in."

Sawyer rises to his feet, his tall form towering over

me. Cracking his neck, he rolls his shoulders and unsheathes a dagger. Monroe scoops me up with him as he stands, and I'm nearly certain he'll never let me down again. Someone's going to have to pry me away kicking and screaming.

"He's too early." Sawyer strides across the casino and toward the locked doors. "He can wait."

"He claims that the beginning of her contract starts an hour prior to trade off to give time for transportation." Walcott waves a gun around carelessly, making me nervous. He's the type to shoot just to see if he hits anyone or to watch someone bleed.

"That's not in the contract." Monroe glowers, his golden gaze lighting with silver. "I read it twenty fucking times. Start time is the pickup time."

"He says he's going to call the leadership and complain that we're refusing to hand Hayley over." Walcott shakes his head with the words. "You need to fucking take care of him. I'm not dealing with anymore of the authoritative bullshit."

"He's right, Sawyer. We've been through enough today." Tatum twists her lips to the side. "This asshole doesn't want to relent."

My chest tightens as tension grows between everyone. I open and close my mouth, trying to summon my nerve.

I could cry and beg for them to not give in to the impatient bastard, but another part of me fears the repercussions. What if this guy from Alibur decides to punish me the second we're alone? What if he does it just for spite? It was obvious at the auction that the Bella Crew wanted me. I've now turned into a prize others think is fun to fight over only because they can.

"Monroe." My voice hitches, the sound of his name on my lips hoarse. "I think it's better to let him take me." Tears burn my eyes, and panic grows and grows, expanding through my body like it'll burst free and splatter my insides across the floor.

"It's not his time yet. If we give the douche even a few extra minutes, he'll keep trying to take more until he starts showing up in the middle of the day." Sawyer glances at me and turns toward the security feed showing a strangely familiar man out front, standing between two giant beast-like statues under the unlit carport. I haven't seen it in the day, but I'm sure it had once been grand. Now, graffiti covers everything and the windows of the skylight have been shattered.

"He's right," Monroe says, hiding his lips in a thin line. "He's testing us because he can."

But what if it's more?

I can't ignore the fear roiling in my chest. "Please,

can't you compromise? I'm scared. You don't understand. He can hurt me."

Knox reaches to me and squeezes my shoulder. "We won't let hi—"

Sawyer and Monroe growl in unison, flexing and rippling in anger. I tense, spotting Walcott materializing at the door in the security feed, going against Sawyer and letting the vampire from Alibur in.

"What the fuck does he think he's doing? I'm going to fucking kill him." Sawyer strides a few feet before Tatum blocks his way.

She holds her palms up, flashing her fangs. "Sawyer, listen. You heard Hayley. You know tension is high. If she's scared and willing to go early, you need to let her. Monroe might have his name on some fucked up contract, but we don't own donors here and you know it. There is no price when we manage to trade or pick them off the streets. You bought a day of her freedom and not fucking her."

Tatum fists her hands, straightening her back, though Sawyer still towers over her by a foot or more. Monroe sucks in deep breaths, trying to control himself. Knox looks ready to throw punches at anyone in the vicinity of him.

"Aw, well. Look at this gorgeous donor. You're even

prettier than your picture." The smooth voice feels as if it steals the air from the room. Everyone turns toward the older man, at least in his late-forties with graying hair at his temples. It's been a while since I've seen a vampire transformed at his age, and I can't stop from staring until he smiles at me.

My instincts scream, clenching my muscles. It's not because he's threatening me, but he carries the same presence as Alexander and even his coven brothers. His designer suit fits his average frame, and a diamond sparkles on a ring on his finger.

Sawyer steps in his path and blocks his way. He releases a warning growl, wiping the smile from the man's face. "Let it be known that today is the only day we will allow you to pull this arriving early bullshit. You damn well know the contract agreement. If you pull this bullshit again—"

"Settle down. I'm not your enemy. I take pride in my possessions and assure you that this marvelous donor will find great joy being in the care of the Alibur. Our clientele is...different than what you find elsewhere. I know the rules and limitations. I was also warned about the possibility of hostility from you." The man proffers his hand to Sawyer. "I give you my word that Hayley Aris will be well taken care of. Now, if you'd excuse me, I'd like to greet the Alibur's new donor queen performer."

Sawyer growls again, but Tatum snatches the back of his shirt and stops him from trying to intercept the man. He struts closer, only stopping a foot away from me and Monroe. I keep my eyes trained toward the floor, afraid to look at him again. Head down. Don't speak. Obey. The rules I've been following all my life swirl through my mind.

"Beautiful Hayley," the vampire murmurs, leaning in without touching me. "It'll be a great joy having you around."

Darting out his hand, the vampire surprises everyone by snapping a metal collar on my neck. Growls and snarls echo through the quiet lobby. Figures blur closer, more and more Bella Crew members closing around us. Even with the two-dozen or so quiet vampires, the man remains smiling and unfazed.

"What the fuck?" Monroe grabs the metal collar, trying to unlatch it, but it auto-locks in place.

"This is only a precaution. It doesn't harm the donor." Extending his hand, he wiggles his fingers. "Now, if you'll please release her, I'd like to go. Do not make me call Alex."

I blink a few times at the way he says Alexander's name. Only Opal ever called him that nickname. No one on the Strip would dare call him anything other than Aris, Master Aris, or Mr. Aris. Even me thinking his name without his title is inappropriate.

Walcott jabs a small knife into Monroe's shoulder, forcing him to loosen his hold. If Govan didn't intervene, the two of them would've broken into a fight. I clench my jaw, touching my feet to the cool tile. My knees shake, the fear swelling bigger and bigger inside me.

I don't make it a foot toward the vampire before Sawyer stops me. Leaning in, he whispers, "I need you to try to be brave. We will follow this fucker and make sure you get there safe. The Alibur is open to the public, so we won't leave either. Just stay calm. You can do this." It almost sounds like he whispers the words to himself.

I stretch up and kiss him, not caring if the man growls. An electric shock zings across my neck, startling me, and I gasp at the sudden burst of pain.

"Your time is up. Hayley, it's time to go." The vampire snatches my wrist, tugging me away from Sawyer. Lifting me into his arms, he carries me through the entrance and to an idling car, rumbling with a strange noise. The cars I've heard so far on the Strip, including the limo, were silent. Electric powered. But this one? It's from the back-world.

"It's an antique," he says like he can read my mind.

"There aren't many around. I paid a steep price for this one, but not as much as I paid to get you." Opening the driver's side door, he sets me onto the front seat. "I'm Lawrence, by the way. My sister has told me so much about you."

I jerk my attention to look up at him, but the man slams the door and slides behind the wheel of the vehicle. Something is wrong. So incredibly wrong. I reach for the door handle, but it doesn't open.

"Settle down. If you make a scene, you will be very unhappy with the consequences, my heir." Lawrence smirks at me. "I've always known Alex would fail to realize what he had created. When my dear little sister Opal told me, I couldn't believe it. My very own blood sister was a caretaker to a dhampir. If only she was stronger. But don't worry, Hayley. You will never be Ruby Vixen. I won't let my sister's hard work go to waste."

A what? My head spins with his words. I'm so confused. He called Opal his little sister. Blood sister. That means that they were born as sibling donors. My stomach twists in panic the more I think about it. Ignoring his demand to settle down, I slap my hands to the glass and scream.

A loud thud sounds against metal and the car shakes. "Release her! You're of no association to the Alibur Hotel," Sawyer shouts, blocking the car. "Her name on the contract is Ruby Vixen. That is the only alias anyone knows."

Glass shatters, and glittering pebbles spill across my lap. Monroe grabs my arm, trying to drag me out of the vehicle. I screech, clutching onto him. Nails dig into my leg as Lawrence pins me to the seat. Gunshots pop, ringing in my ears, and Knox shoots a gun through the back window. One grazes Lawrence's ear, and he growls and revs the engine, but the car only smokes as Sawyer uses his strength to keep it from barreling over him.

"Five fucking seconds, fucker. She is ours. You're stupid if you think you're getting out of here with her." Monroe throws a knife, stabbing it into the vampire's chest.

Lawrence flashes his fangs. "It was against the leadership law for her to even go to auction. She belongs to me and no one else. My sister assured it. Now, move. I will kill you otherwise."

What the fuck? Fuck! Twisting in my seat, I slap my hands and scratch my nails, trying to do anything I can to hurt this guy. He's trying to kidnap me. He wants to steal me away. He thinks I belong to him. It was one thing to know that I'd be rotated around the Strip, but this guy? I don't know him or what he wants. It's the fear of the unknown that pushes me to resist.

"Hayley!" Monroe shouts again. "Hayley!"

Lawrence snarls and hits a button, sending a shock through me. I jerk and shudder with the pain, and my vision blurs.

"We'll fucking kill you!" Sawyer shouts! "You're dead!"

Extending his fangs, Lawrence grabs my hair and drags me onto his lap, squishing me between his body and the steering wheel. "She's dead if you don't back up now!"

Sinking his fangs into my neck, he bites me hard and in such a way that I scream in agony. Fire blazes over my skin, and I gasp, unable to do anything. Sawyer roars and jumps on the hood, stomping his boot into the windshield.

"Hayley! Fuck!" Knox yells.

Monroe leans into the car, grabbing my ankle. "That's not a kill bite."

The pressure of Lawrence's bite eases away, but the pain refuses to fade. "Like I said, she doesn't belong to you. She's my heir. Now if you don't move, I assure you that you'll regret it. She's not your personal blood donor. There is nothing that you can do. Leave."

"Fuck you!" Sawyer snaps. "She's our girl!"

Stomping the gas pedal, Lawrence sends the vehicle

barreling forward. Sawyer clutches onto the hood as the vampire speeds away from the Bella. I clutch my neck, trying to see through my darkening vision. But I can't. I can't even think.

My body screams in agony.

My heart shatters.

Sawyer's figure suddenly disappears from the hood of the vehicle.

I try to stay conscious, but it's too much. I'm not sure if I'll even survive.

A cool hand pets my shoulder. "Settle now, my dear. The pain is only fleeting. It'll be over soon."

Sawyer, Knox, and Monroe's images swirl through my mind. I cling onto the thought, praying to the universe that this isn't the end for me or the beginning of something worse. But I know in my heart that the universe is against me.

I fall into immobilizing, burning, all-consuming darkness and despair.

THE CAR IDLES outside a strange fenced in compound. Lights sparkle and illuminate the dark world around us. I have no idea how long I've been out, but it has been long enough that I missed seeing Lawrence leave La Vega. He had to have. While this compound looks like it has casinos and hotels like the ones in La Vega, it doesn't look to have more than a handful.

The chain-link gate comes to life, the soft hum trickling in through the broken windows. I gasp a few breaths, my anxiety tearing my insides apart. Hundreds of figures blur around the strange new city in front of me, and Lawrence barrels forward, not trying to avoid the vampires. There aren't as many as I've seen on the Strip of La Vega, but all it takes is one asshole to kill me.

"Welcome to the Whiskey and Falo Ills, Hayley," Lawrence says, keeping his gaze on the road ahead. "I want you to know how happy I am to have you here. It was about time that I could take you from that idiotic asshole. Alex has no idea what he even managed to create all those years ago when he bit your mom while she was pregnant with you."

I frown and turn in my seat. I know better than to look him in the eyes, but his words pique my curiosity. "What? Drinking from pregnant donors is illegal."

A smirk stretches his smile. "Don't be naïve. He didn't drink from her. He bit her with his venom and managed to start a dhampir line—half-human, half-vampire, and one of the most incredible beings in all of history. You're a rare breed."

I laugh in exasperation. "I think you have me confused with someone else. There is no way."

He growls and snatches my wrist, squeezing my arm tightly. "Do not disregard things you can't possibly understand or know. If I tell you something, I expect you to accept it. You are to understand your place. You are mine, and I will not tolerate any disobedience. It could be both of our downfalls otherwise."

I wince and shrink away from him. Fuck. Why did I even think for a second that I could speak freely? My day with the Bella Crew messed with my head. "I'm sorry."

Sighing, Lawrence parks outside of a brightly lit hotel. I clench my jaw, keeping my eyes averted from his. "Apology accepted. Now, before we go in, I want you to understand your place. You are in fact a dhampir. My venom bite proved it because you neither transformed into a vampire nor died. Had you been a purebred blood donor, that wouldn't have been the case."

What does any of this even mean? How did he know? He makes it sound like Opal and Alexander knew. I rack my brain, thinking about my life as best as I can. Opal did mention that I was special and that the Bella Crew didn't know how to care for me. Alexander did also mention that he made me. I thought he meant that he turned me into the most popular headliner in all of La Vega.

"There are some rules you also need to understand," Lawrence continues, keeping his voice low. "Not many vampires know or understand what a dhampir is and what they are capable of. Many fear them for their craving for vampire blood and would consider them a threat." He chuckles at his statement. "Which is so far from the truth. You, my dear Hayley, were bred to be stronger than a donor, but you're still one. Forever. Your blood can satiate many and for longer. You're going to be my most prized possession. Stronger and faster with my venom, but I can easily let it all fade away. I could let you starve. I could end your life. I will end your life the second you try to disobey me. But, if you keep mind of your place, I will ensure you thrive and have a content eternity."

My heartbeat pounds in my ears. I still can't comprehend anything he's saying. I want to ask questions, but the second I dare to look at him, he scowls. Jerking my attention to my hands, I tighten my mouth and remain silent.

"You will understand more soon enough." Flinging his door open, Lawrence exits the vehicle and strides around the hood to my side. He doesn't give me a chance to get to my feet and drags me out. "You will adjust. I promise."

I run beside him in silence, trying to keep his pace, but the ache in my neck throbs worse than ever. If he didn't rush me inside and through the casino, I'd have taken a second to touch my throat. Shoving a door open, he drags me into a strange room like it could've been a part of the casino long ago but has since been cleared of all of the slots and tables.

My whole body turns cold, my stomach flipping at the sight before me.

Oh, God.

No.

Dozens and dozens of stacked beds create aisles in the giant room. It takes my eyes a moment to adjust to the darkness, but now I see that the beds are full. Long lines dangle from the placated donors' arms, the darkness of the tubes surely blood as they're drained into some sort of strange machine. Attached to their mouths are wider tubes, looking like they pump something into their throats.

It's now that I realize that they're not all donors. The top bunks are vampires—bound and being bled the same way but into the donors. I don't know how or can see much else, but I nearly throw up at the sight. I thought La Vega was brutal, but it's nothing compared to this place.

"Lovely, isn't it?" Lawrence asks me, his eyes boring into the side of my face in my peripheral vision.

I don't react. I can't. If I open my mouth, I'll scream.

"Don't be too afraid, my dear. You'll only be required to join the herd during the days and you'll recover fast.

You have a show to perform." He hums under his breath like the idea satisfies his monstrous nature. "We must test your capabilities first."

Numbness crashes over me as my brain processes everything. This can't be happening. This can't be my life. I'd rather die.

Lawrence comes to a halt outside of another door. Goosebumps prickle over my skin, my fear instincts screaming in terror. I yank away from him, my need to run outweighing my need to protect myself.

I don't make it far.

Pain explodes in my shoulder as he digs his fingernails into the bite on my throat as he lifts me off my feet by my neck. He flashes his fangs in my face, his eyes glowing silver. I pray for my death to be quick. Maybe disobedience is the only way to end this.

"What did I fucking say?" he shouts, sending my short hair flying from my face. "Learn your place!"

Kicking open the door, Lawrence tosses me inside the dimly lit room, and I land on my hands and knees on something dark and sticky. The strange fragrance wafts through the air, and I squint, trying to figure shit out. The door slams, cutting me off from the draining room and Lawrence, and I gasp, sobbing uncontrollably.

A low, rumbly noise stills my whole body.

I whip my head up at the sight of the filthy, silver-eyed vampire in the corner of the small room.

Flying toward me, he rips me off the ground and throws me toward the wall. The air escapes my lungs, and all I can do is open my mouth in a silent scream.

He bites my throat, latching on and pinning me to the wall.

I slacken in his arms as he sucks my neck. If only he didn't stop and drop me. If only he would give me my final donation.

To be continued...

Thank you so much for reading Vampire Nights! Don't forget to check out the next book in the series Bloody Nights. You don't want to miss the bloodiest show around!

THE VAMPIRE HEIRS WORLD

La Vega Vampire Showstoppers
Vampire Nights
Bloody Nights

The Divine Vampire Heirs
Blood Match
Blood Rebel
Blood Debt
Blood Feud
Blood Loss
Blood Vows

The Royale Vampire Heirs Series:
Rebel Vampires
Rebel Dhampir
Rebel Match
Rebel Heir
Rebel Fight

Academy of Vampire Heirs Series:
Dhampirs 101
Blood Sources 102
Coven Bonds 103
Personal Donors 104
Blood Wars 105

THE MATES OF MAGAELORUM WORLD

The Pack Mates of Lunar Crest:
The She-Wolf Games
The Wolf-Mate Trials
The Omega Hunt
The Witch Chase
Winter Wolf Games

Fated Mate of the Dragon Clans
Caged by Her Dragons
Freed by Her Dragons
Saved by Her Dragons

SEVEN SINNERS WORLD

The Seven Sinners of Hell's Kingdom
Her Personal Demons
Her Deadly Angels
Her Darkest Devils
Her Sinful Saints

ABOUT GINNA MORAN

GINNA MORAN IS the author of over seventy novels including the popular La Vega Vampire Showstoppers, The Pack Mates of Lunar Crest, The Seven Sinners of Hell's Kingdom Academy of Vampire Heirs, The Divine Vampire Heirs, and The Royale Vampire Heirs Why-Choose novels.

She always carried a fascination for all things paranormal and wrote her first unpublished manuscript at age eighteen. Her love of the supernatural grew stronger through her adult life, and she now spends her days with different creatures of the night. Whether it's vampires, werewolves, dragons, fae, angels, demons, or mermaids, Ginna loves creating and living in worlds from her dreams.

Aside from Ginna's professional life, she enjoys binge watching TV, crafting and design, playing pretend with her daughter, and cuddling with her dogs. Some of her favorite things include chocolate, mermaids, anything that glitters, learning new things, cheesy jokes, and organizing her bookshelf.

Ginna is currently hard at work on her next novel and the one after, and the one after that.

www.ingramcontent.com/pod-product-compliance
Lightning Source LLC
Chambersburg PA
CBHW051157190726
48288CB00006B/1694